Studies in Forensic Psychiatry

Bernard Glueck

Contents

STUDIES IN FORENSIC PSYCHIATRY

BY

Bernard Glueck

EDITORIAL ANNOUNCEMENT

This volume is one of a series of Monograph Supplements to the Journal of Criminal Law and Criminology. The publication of the Monographs is authorized by the American Institute of Criminal Law and Criminology. Such a series has become necessary in America by reason of the rapid development of criminological research in this country since the organization of the Institute. Criminology draws upon many independent branches of science, such as Psychology, Anthropology, Neurology, Medicine, Education, Sociology, and Law. These sciences contribute to our understanding of the nature of the delinquent and to our knowledge of those conditions in home, occupation, school, prison, etc., which are best adapted to elicit the behavior that the race has learned to approve and cherish.

This series of Monographs, therefore, will include researches in each of these departments of knowledge insofar as they meet our special interest.

It is confidently anticipated that the series will stimulate the study of the problems of delinquency, the State control of which commands as great expenditure of human toil and treasure as does the control of constructive public education.

PREFACE

When, in 1810, Franz Joseph Gall said: "The measure of culpability and the measure of punishment can not be determined by a study of the illegal act, but only by a study of the individual committing it," he expressed an idea which has, in late years, come to be regarded as a trite truism. This called forth as an unavoidable consequence a more lively interest on the part of various social agencies in the personality of the criminal, with the resultant gradually increasing conviction that the suppression of crime is not primarily a legal question, but is rather a problem for the physician, sociologist, and economist. Whatever light has been thrown in recent years upon this most important social problem, criminality, did not issue from a contemplation of the abstract and more or less sterile theses on crime and punishment as reflected in current works on criminal law and procedure, but was the result of research carried on at the hands of the physician, especially the psychopathologist, sociologist, and economist. The slogan of the modern criminologist is, "intensive study of the individual delinquent from all angles and points of view", rather than mere insistence upon the precise application of a definite kind of punishment to a definite crime as outlined by statute. Indeed, the whole idea of punishment is giving way to the idea of correction and reformation. This radical change of tendency cannot be looked upon as a mere misdirected sentimentality on the part of modern society, but is the inevitable result of the final conviction that the solely punitive criminology upon which society has been relying in its efforts to eradicate criminal behavior from its midst has proved a total failure.

The idea of punishment as a deterrent of crime is, as a consequence, gradually losing its hold upon modern criminologists, and in its stead we have been experimenting for some time past with such measures as probation, suspended or indeterminate sentence, and parole. Now it can not be too strongly emphasized that in giving these measures a fair trial we ought to guard against those very same grave errors which were chiefly responsible for the failure of the old, solely punitive methods, namely, the dealing with the criminal act rather than with the individual committing it. If these new measures of probation, suspended sentence, and parole, which are perfectly adequate in theory, are to justify their existence in the practical everyday handling of the problem of criminology, we must not fail to take into full account the very obvious natural phenomenon that human beings vary within very wide limits in their susceptibility to correction or reformation, that some individuals because of their psychological make-up, either qualitative or quantitative, are absolutely and permanently incorrigible and present a problem which can be dealt with in only one effective way--namely, permanent segregation and isolation from society. It is on this very important account that the psychopathologist's place in criminology is fully justified. In endeavoring to aid in the solution of the problem of criminology, the psychopathologist need not seek new methods of procedure but may safely rely upon those which have aided him in elucidating in a very large measure the problem of mental disease. For criminology is an integral part of psychopathology, crime is a type of abnormal conduct which expresses a failure of proper adjustment at the psychological level.

It was not until the advent of the Kraepelinian School of psychiatry, with its intensive search for facts and the resultant more accurate delineation and classification of types of mental disorder, that we began to acquire real insight into psychopathology and were enabled to render more accurate prognoses. This more or less purely descriptive method of study is at present being followed by an intensive analysis of the facts thus gained as exemplified in the present psychoanalytic movement. It is conceded by all thoughtful observers that criminology will have to follow the same route on its way to final solution. The series of studies here presented reflect an effort in this direction. It is aimed to present a series of well-rounded-out case histories of criminal types as studied from the psychopathologist's viewpoint, and in one instance, at least, an attempt is made at an accurate and intensive psychological analysis of the biological forces which were at the bottom of a career of habitual stealing. No attempt is made at hard and fast formulations. Our knowledge concerning the criminal is still too meager to justify one in drawing dependable conclusions. But it is felt that this clinical material emphasizes sufficiently the necessity of the psychopathological mode of approach to the problem of criminology. For that matter, the excellent work being carried on by Dr. William Healy in connection with the Chicago Juvenile Court and by psychopathologists in a number of other cities attests that this need is being gradually recognized by society. One desires only to express the hope that the time is not far distant when our penal and reformatory institutions will likewise serve the purpose of clinics for the study of the delinquent, and that such clinical instruction will form part of the curriculum of at least every public prosecutor.

I desire to express my indebtedness to Messrs. Lea and Febiger, the J. B. Lippincott Co., and to the editors of the American Journal of Insanity, and the Journal of the American Institute of Criminal Law and Criminology, for their kind permission to reprint some of the material herein presented.

Before concluding this preface I desire to avail myself of this opportunity of expressing my sincere gratitude to Dr. William A. White, Superintendent of the Government Hospital for the Insane, for his kind and very stimulating advice and encouragement which made these studies possible.

GOVERNMENT HOSPITAL FOR THE INSANE,
    January, 1916.

CHAPTER I
PSYCHOGENESIS IN THE PSYCHOSES
OF PRISONERS

That mental disorder may be due to causes purely psychic in nature is acknowledged by everyone. The older psychiatrists laid much stress on this point, a revival of which may be seen in the present-day widespread psychoanalytic movement. The reaction to the all too-embracing materialistic tendencies which have dominated psychiatric thought in recent decades was bound to come. It was especially the clinician who gave the impetus to this movement, because in pursuing the materialistic bent he found himself totally helpless as a therapeutist in the great majority of mental cases, and was therefore eventually forced to seek more promising paths.

Bleuler's attitude towards this question, because of the prominent position he occupies in the world of psychiatry, is interesting.

"Bleuler, who succeeded Forel as Professor of Psychiatry and Medical Director of the Cantonal Insane Asylum (BurghÃ¶lzi) at Zurich, having become convinced that no solution could be arrived at along this anatomical path for the many riddles offered by the disturbed mental life, had for years chosen the psychological path. He was led to take this course because he knew that of the chronic inmates of the asylum, only about one-fifth showed anatomical changes of the central nervous system sufficient to explain the mental deviations exhibited."[1]

The results already achieved by this change of attitude in psychiatry are sufficient justification for its existence.

One became especially convinced of the potency of mental factors in the production of mental disease from the observation and study of the psychoses of criminals. Here the conflicts which lead an individual to seek in mental disorder a satisfactory compromise are so concrete as to leave no doubt concerning cause and effect.

Kraepelin[2] asserts that mental disorders occur ten times as frequently in prison as in freedom. The criminal, who in most instances is already burdened with a more or less strong predisposition to mental disorder, upon being placed in prison finds himself at once in a most favorable environment for a mental breakdown. It is true, imprisonment acts more deleteriously upon the psyche of the criminal by passion, the accidental criminal, but even the recidivist who would be expected to feel less keenly the painful loss of freedom, falls a prey to the deleterious effects of prison life. The unfavorable hygienic surroundings which are found in most prisons, the scarcity of air and exercise, readily prepare the way for a breakdown, even in an habitual criminal. Above all, however, it is the emotional shock and depression which invariably accompany the painful loss of freedom, the loneliness and seclusion, which force the prisoner to a raking occupation with his own mind, to a persistent introspection, making him feel so much more keenly the anxiety and apprehension for the future, the remorse for his deed, that play an important rÃ´le in the production of mental disorders. This is especially true when it concerns an accidental criminal, one who still possesses a high degree of self-respect and honor. Imprisonment furnishes us with a great variety of mental disorders, the origin of which can be traced in a more or less direct manner to the emotional shock and influence upon the psyche which it brings about.

The psychogenetic origin of the psychoses of criminals can be established far more clearly in prisoners awaiting trial. Here the deleterious effect of confinement upon the physical health can be ruled out almost entirely, and the etiologic factor must be sought for exclusively in the emotional shock which the commission of the crime and its attending consequences provoke. The strong effect upon the psyche produced by the detection and confinement, the raking hearings and cross-examinations, and the uncertainty and apprehension of the outcome of it all are the factors that are at play here.

Reich,[3] in 1871, was the first one to call attention to the mental disorders of prisoners awaiting trial. He could observe the development of mental symptoms even during the first hours of confinement, and the relation between the psychosis and the emotional shock of the situation at hand could not be doubted. He describes this acute mental disturbance as follows:--"Already in the first hours or days after imprisonment, or soon after a severe emotional shock, a sort of psychic tension sets in. The prisoner becomes silent, chary of words, lost in brooding. He observes little that goes on about him and remains motionless in one spot. His face takes on an astonished expression, the gaze is vacant and indefinite. If he makes any movements at all they are hesitating, uncertain, as those of a drunken man. Vertigo and aura-like sensations appear; severe anxiety overpowers the patient, which with the entire force of a powerful affect crowds out all other concepts and sensations and dominates the entire personality. Consciousness becomes more and more clouded, soon illusions, hallucinations, and delusions appear, and the prisoner becomes especially taken up with ideas of unknown evil powers, of demons and spirits, and of being persecuted and possessed by the devil. Simultaneously they complain about all sorts of bodily sensations. In isolated cases one may observe convulsive twitchings of the voluntary and involuntary musculature. Finally severe motor excitements set in. The patient becomes noisy, screams, runs aimlessly about, destroys and ruins everything that comes his way. With this the disease has reached its height. At this stage consciousness is entirely in abeyance and the disorder is followed by complete amnesia." Reich supposes that this acute prison psychosis may be included in that large group of abnormal psychic processes, developing from affect and affect-like situations.

Reich's important work remained the only one on the subject until 1888, when Moeli again called attention to it. Moeli[4] spoke of patients in whom an apparent total blocking of all thought processes took place. They would exhibit complete ignorance of the most commonplace facts, would forget such well-known things as their own name, place of birth, or age; were unable to recognize the denominations of coins, etc. He noted, however, that although the answers these patients gave were false, they had a certain relation to the question. For instance, coins of a lower denomination would be mistaken for higher ones, postage stamps were called paper, etc. They also showed a marked tendency to elaborate all sorts of false reminiscences about their past life. Along with this failure of the simplest thought and memory activity, these individuals were otherwise well-ordered and behaved.

The reader will at once recognize in the above description the well-known Ganser symptom-complex, the several variations of which have been so frequently discussed of late years. Ganser[5] further showed that these cases frequently evidenced vivid auditory and visual hallucinations. At the same time there existed a more or less distinct clouding of consciousness, with the simultaneous presence of hysterical stigmata, especially total analgesia. After a short time recovery took place, the patients suddenly awoke as if from a dream and evidenced a more or less complete amnesia of the events which had transpired.

Numerous discussions concerning this disease-picture have appeared of late years in literature. The Ganser syndrome, or twilight state, has been enlarged upon, and several variations of this condition have been isolated. The chief contention, however, of the various authors on this subject seems to be whether this symptom-complex should be considered as hysterical or whether it should be placed among the large group of degenerative states. Both views are ably defended by prominent psychiatrists. I have recently observed the Ganser syndrome in an undoubted case of toxic-exhaustion psychosis.

Raecke[6] designated this disease-picture described by Moeli and Ganser as an hysterical twilight state in psychopathic individuals. These conditions were developed in them as the result of emotional excitement in imprisonment. The constant hearings, the confusing cross-questioning, the fear of punishment, finally the injurious effect of solitary confinement, shock and weaken the slight mental tension of the prisoner to a marked extent. As a result of this, we have on the one hand a condition of apathy, of inability to concentrate the mind, of incapacity to think and of a sort of feeling of being wholly at sea, accompanied by vertigo and other nervous manifestations, while on the other hand the physical despair, the obstinacy of the prisoner, now increase to pathological maniacal attacks, now again are changed to stubbornness, mutism, with refusal of food. At the same time the more or less constant wish to be considered sick, and in consequence to be freed from imprisonment (and in this we see perhaps the hysterical component), may influence deleteriously and in a peculiarly modifying way the disease-picture. The various questions put to the patient by the examiner may act as so many suggestions. Raecke further calls attention to the manifold similarities which these conditions may show with catatonic processes. In these hysterical twilight states, quite aside from mutism, negativism, and catalepsy, peculiar mannerisms were noted, a sort of affected, childish way of speaking, motor stereotypies, swaying of the head, running in a circle, queer actions, and sudden expressions of senseless word combinations. In a later work Raecke[7] describes a symptom-complex, which he designated as "hysterical stupor in prisoners", and in which the catatonic symptoms exist in a still more pronounced manner. The severe forms of this disorder, which may extend over weeks and months, are liable to be confused with progressive deteriorating processes, especially so because those symptoms which were wont to be considered by many as positively unfavorable prognostically, may be found here in very deceptive imitations. Thus the affected, silly behavior, impulsive actions, temporary verbigeration, senseless word salad, grimacing, stereotypy, attitudinizing, etc., which these patients exhibit, may easily be mistaken for the typical catatonic picture of dementia prÃ|cox. According to Raecke's view the hysterical stupor is closely related to the Ganser twilight syndrome. Stuporous conditions may introduce the latter, and, vice versa, Ganser complexes may creep into the stupor. Raecke's stupor, like Ganser's twilight syndrome, frequently develops in criminals immediately after arrest or as a result of great physical or psychic exertion. Sometimes the stupor is preceded by convulsions, at other times by a prodromal stage of general nervousness. In still other cases, unpleasant delusions and elementary hallucinations precede the stupor, which may follow immediately after this prodromal state or may be again preceded by a short attack of mania with clouded consciousness. In contrast to the genuine catatonia, Raecke's stupor as well as Ganser's twilight state, are characterized by a high grade of impressionability to things in the environment, which may at any time suddenly cause a complete transition from an apparently deep stupor to normal manner and behavior. Headaches, vertigo, and various hysterical stigmata are common to both the hysterical stupor and the Ganser twilight state. At times recovery takes place suddenly, but as a rule it is gradual and remittent in character. The duration of the disorder differs. It may last for hours or months, and there generally remains a more or less pronounced amnesia for the entire period of stupor.

Kutner,[8] in a work on the catatonic states in degenerates, describes this condition at length. Although recognizing a good many hysterical features in these patients, he prefers to place these catatonic conditions under the general group of the psychoses of degeneracy. He does not add anything worthy of note to what Raecke had to say concerning this mental disorder, but the differentiating points which he advances between it and the genuine catatonia are of interest and should be mentioned here. Among these he mentions, first, the development of the disorder upon a grave degenerative basis; second, the sudden development of the psychosis as the immediate result of a situation strongly affective in nature, such as a threatening or beginning prolonged imprisonment; third, the more or less sudden disappearance of the entire symptom-complex upon a change of environment; and lastly, the lack of secondary dementia. This absence of dementia cannot be explained by mere assertions that these cases have perhaps not been followed out long enough. Bonhoeffer kept account of some of these cases for as long as ten years, and in none of them could he observe any sign of a deteriorating process.

It may, perhaps, be of interest to finally mention here Raecke's fantastic form of degenerative psychosis, which is nothing more nor less than another attempt at describing the original Ganser twilight state in a modified form.

It will be seen from the preceding that the disease-pictures described by Reich, Moeli, Kutner, Ganser, Rish, and others, are so closely related that any attempt at separation must of necessity be more or less of an artificiality. The question whether this condition, because of certain isolated hysterical components, deserves to be considered as hysterical in nature, is by no means solved. The mere presence of physical, so-called hysterical, stigmata, is not sufficient to call a disorder hysterical. Bonhoeffer, who, in opposition to such authors as Wilmanns, Birnbaum, Siefert, and others, insists that this so-called prison-psychotic-complex in its narrower sense is of hysterical nature, does so because he claims to be able to see in these patients the dominance of a wish factor, namely, the wish to be considered insane, and consequently to be transferred to an institution for the insane.

He explains the recovery of these patients upon being transferred to such an institution on the basis of the fulfillment of this wish. My experience has been that it is very difficult in most instances to differentiate these acute psychogenetic states from certain hysterical conditions. Some of them show a good many hysterical symptoms, while in others such symptoms are absolutely wanting. One of the cases herein reported illustrates this point especially well. This patient was admitted to our hospital on two occasions, the first time while awaiting trial on a charge of murder, and the second time soon after conviction and sentence to life imprisonment. His first attack showed very little, if anything, of a hysterical nature, while his second attack had so many features of hysteria that it could hardly be considered anything but a psychosis of an hysterical nature.

CASE I.--E. E., Negro, aged 32 years. One sister insane, a brother is said to be subject to convulsions. Patient's birth and childhood normal; attended school for three or four years, where he made normal progress. He entered upon the life of a common laborer when quite young, and always managed to earn a substantial livelihood for himself and family. With the exception of typhoid fever at six or seven years, he was never ill before. He used alcoholics in moderation, and denies venereal history. Criminal history is uncertain; according to his statements he was arrested but once before, for fighting. It appears that he was working as usual until August 19th, when he was arrested on a charge of assault and robbery. The patient has a hazy recollection of this; he cannot say how long ago it was, but thinks it was sometime in August; he was arrested at night; cannot state at just what time, but is certain that it was after sunset; does not know who arrested him; says there were several of them; does not know whether they were policemen or detectives. The police records show that he was arrested on the night of August 19th, after a desperate fight. The

following day he suddenly became insane in his cell at the fourth
precinct station house. He became very excited; commenced to shout
that he had been shot in the abdomen by an enemy. When offered food he
threw it at the policeman through the bars of his cell door, and then
began beating his head against the walls of his cell. He was
transferred to the observation ward at the Washington Asylum Hospital.
The records of that institution show the following: On admission he
was yelling, cursing, and very much excited; completely disoriented;
repeated the same sentence over and over again in a singing fashion.
He talked to the Lord, and answered imaginary questions; had auditory
and visual hallucinations, and various delusional ideas; thought
someone was talking to him constantly; that he was being shot at every
few minutes, and yelled with anguish at every supposed shot. He cried
and sang alternately. Owing to his marked excitement he had to be
kept in constant restraint.

On admission to the Government Hospital for the Insane, on August 23d,
three days after the onset of the disorder, he was in a semi-stupor;
no replies could be gotten to questions, and his attention to the
extent of looking at the examiner could be engaged only after vigorous
shaking. General hypalgesia was present; he responded but very feebly
to pin pricks. He was absolutely passive to the admission routine, and
offered no resistance whatever to what was being done to him. His body
did not show any resistance to passive movement, on the contrary, it
was rather limp. He was lying in bed staring in a fixed manner
straight ahead of him and would emit an occasional grunt, and a few
unintelligible words. He refused nourishment, was untidy in habits,
and appeared to be wholly oblivious to his environment. Respiratory
and cardiac action somewhat accelerated, pulse rapid and feeble.

August 25th:--Continues in the same stuporous state; absolutely
oblivious to his surroundings; refuses food; untidy in habits. Aside
from an unintelligible word or two, has not spoken any since

admission. There are several beginning pustules on his back.

August 28th:--Some improvement noted; asks for water spontaneously; when spoken to says his back aches, and that they are pouring water on him. "I read the book, I went to church." Unable to feed himself or dress without assistance; totally disoriented.

August 30th:--Came out in the hall today, and spent the time sitting quietly on a settee; does not take any interest in his surroundings; has not spoken any spontaneously. Answers are given in a brief and retarded manner, preferably in monosyllables, and not to the point. On being questioned concerning orientation, says: "My back, church, the book", "they are burning me up." Appearance indicates marked confusion.

September 3d:--The patient suddenly became clear mentally this morning; seems to have completely recovered from his stupor; attends to his wants, and answers questions in a clear, coherent manner. Approached the physician this morning and asked for a laxative; says that he remembers nothing that transpired during the period since his arrest, and a day or two ago, when he began to see things more clearly; complains of pain in back; does not know where he is, and thinks he came here yesterday.

"What is your name?"

"E. E."

"Age?"

"I will be 33 the 16th of this coming April."

"When were you born?"

"In 1879."

"What is your occupation?"

"I am supposed to be a huckster."

"Where were you born?"

"At Columbus, South Carolina."

"What day is this?"

"Sunday." (correct)

"Date, month and year?"

"It's the 9th month, 1911, I don't know the date; I have not seen an almanac."

"What is the time?"

"I don't know, sir; I think it is pretty near one o'clock." (correct)

"Where did you come from?"

"I don't know where I came from; they hit me over the head."

"When did you come here?"

"I don't know; I look out of that building that looks like the House of Rep." (After studying the surrounding country a while, says:) "Let's see, this must be Anacostia, ain't it; I never was out here before." (correct)

"How long did it take you to get here?"

"I don't know, sir."

"Name of this place?"

"You've got me now."

"Where is it located?"

"It seems to be in Anacostia, the way I can figure it out." (correct)

"What sort of a place is it?"

"Well, to my judgment, it looks as though it's all right."

"Who are these people about you?"

"I don't know, sir."

"Is there anything wrong with them?"

"Well, I don't know, I am afraid to say; I don't know the nature of anybody but myself."

"Why do you suppose you are being asked these questions?"

"Well, I think it is to sound my knowledge."

"Why were you sent here?"

"I don't know, sir."

"How do you feel?"

"I feel all right, with the exception of my back."

"Are you happy or sad?"

"Well, I am neither one."

"Are you worried about anything?"

"No, sir."

"Did anything strange happen to you for which you can't give yourself an account?"

"I can't understand what happened to me, or why I am here."

"Do you hear voices talking to you?"

"No, sir."

"Do you see any strange things?"

"No, sir, I don't see anything strange, only my surroundings."

"Do you ever have fits or convulsions?"

"No, sir."

"Did you ever try to commit suicide?"

"No, sir, and ain't never going to try it."

"Is anybody trying to harm you in any way?"

"Yes, I really believed somebody tried to do something to me."

The foregoing questions were answered without any hesitation and in a prompt manner.

September 6th:--Today, patient gave in a coherent and relevant manner his past history. He talked freely, and all evidence of suspiciousness or evasiveness was absent. Upon examination he was found to be perfectly oriented in all spheres; free from delusions and hallucinations, and possessing quite a degree of insight into his recent mental disorder. While reluctant to admit that he had been insane, he fully realized that something was wrong with him. He showed a normal emotional reaction to the situation at hand; felt satisfied with his surroundings, and was very much concerned and anxious about his release. Special intelligence tests failed to reveal any intellectual defect. He was found, however, to be a rather ignorant negro. Memory and attention were unimpaired. Apperception good; physical examination showed him to be a well-developed man of medium size, height five feet, three inches, weight 150 pounds. Aside from several pustules on the back, he showed no physical disorders. Neurological examination, negative.

September 14th:--Patient was today discharged by a jury, as not insane. He presented a normal appearance upon leaving the Hospital. Insight was good, and there existed a total amnesia for the period between August 19th, when he was arrested, and September 3d, when he recovered from his stupor.

This case illustrates in an excellent manner the development of a mental disorder as an immediate consequence of a situation strongly affective in nature,--in this instance, threatened imprisonment for a grave offense.

The emotional shock of the arrest called forth in this, to all appearance, previously normal individual, a marked excitement accompanied by hallucinations and fleeting delusional formations. This excitement, which required the application of constant restraint, was followed by a stuporous state and total clouding of consciousness. Upon being removed to a hospital, and surrounded by a new environment, patient gave evidence, after a sojourn of only a few days, of the salutary effect of such procedure. On September 3d, ten days after admission, the stupor disappears, and the only residue of the one-time psychosis is a complete amnesia for the entire period. The amnesia and the hypalgesia, which the patient manifested on admission, are the two symptoms which may perhaps be considered as more or less hysterical in nature. Aside from this, it is difficult to see wherein the psychosis resembles an hysterical disorder. Another point which should be mentioned here in passing, and which will be dilated upon later, is the medico-legal importance of this class of cases. This patient was wanted for assault and robbery in an adjoining State. Upon his admission to this institution an inquiry was received from the U. S. Attorney for the District of Columbia as to the probable duration and course of this man's disorder, as they had in possession extradition papers from the authorities of the State in which the crime was committed. It was only by recognizing the nature of this disorder that we were able to furnish the authorities with intelligent information concerning the prognosis of the case, and which the course of the disease corroborated in every detail. By recognizing the fact that these disorders are consequences of the criminal act, the possibility of considering the man insane at the time of the commission of the act is obviated in a large measure.

CASE II.--R. S. C., a white male, age 48 years, who is now serving a life sentence for murder. One brother and one sister died of tuberculosis. Another sister and two maternal aunts were insane.

Father alcoholic. Patient has always been regarded as rather sickly. Had the usual diseases of childhood and has been subject all his lifetime to frequent headaches. His school career was very irregular in character and he never advanced beyond the elementary subjects. Socially, he belonged to a very ordinary stock of frontiersmen and his chief occupation consisted of farming and certain minor speculations. He apparently led an honest and more or less industrious life. Married in 1886, and his conjugal career is uneventful. In March, 1901, he moved to Addington, Indian Territory. This was a newly-established frontier town and he had bought, sometime previously, several lots there, intending to establish himself in the lumber business. Soon after this he got into some financial difficulty with a town-site boomer, and finally, in a fit of passion, shot and killed the latter and wounded a relative of his own. He was admitted to the Government Hospital for the Insane, December 13, 1901, from the Indian Territory. From the medical certificate which accompanied him on admission it appeared that soon after the commission of the crime the patient began to show evidence of insanity by incoherent talk, false ideas, nervousness, and outbursts of vicious excitement. Later, this was followed by mutism, refusal to eat, and stupor. On admission to this hospital he was in a deep stupor, absolutely oblivious to everything about him. Eyes were wide open and staring, pupils dilated, voluntary movements markedly in abeyance. He was mute except for an occasional incoherent mumbling to himself. He evidenced no initiative in feeding himself, but swallowed food when it was placed in his mouth. Habits were very untidy; involuntary evacuation of bladder and bowels were present. His mental content could not be determined at the time, as his replies were indistinct and monosyllabic, and were obtained only after much effort. He appeared to comprehend what was wanted of him, although this was not absolutely certain. His perception was very dull, ideation slow and laborious. His attention could be gained only after considerable difficulty, and he had to be aroused first from a more or less profound stupor. Spontaneous speech was almost wholly absent, but occasionally he would utter a word or two about his wife and children. No delusions or hallucinations could be elicited. Physical examination showed him to be quite thin and emaciated. Gait slow and unsteady. Voluntary movements retarded. Knees trembled and knocked against each other. No paralyses or pareses noted. Marked general tremors were occasionally seen. Musculature well developed but flaccid. All deep reflexes diminished. Cremasteric absent. Other superficial reflexes were noted to be normal. Organic reflexes abolished. Involuntary urination and defecation. There was a systolic murmur present and a slight impairment of the upper lobe of the right lung. Breath very offensive. He remained in this stuporous condition, leading a more or less passive existence, for about a month after admission. For two months following this he was quite agitated, and his outward reactions indicated that he was quite depressed. On April 25th, about four and a half months after admission, when asked how long he had been in the Hospital, he replied three days. From that time on he began to improve. Consciousness became clearer. In June, he talked and acted quite rationally. He had a total amnesia of what had transpired during his stuporous and agitated states and a retrograde amnesia for several days prior to, and including the commission of the murder. He continued clear mentally and in a more or less normal state until the latter part of November, 1902, when he again went into a stupor. From this time until the later part of April, 1903, he had alternating periods of stupor and lucidity, with amnesia for the stuporous states. On June 21, 1903, he was discharged as recovered and returned to the Indian Territory to undergo trial for his offense. Unfortunately, no mention is made in the hospital records of any possible relation between his periodic stuporous states and any environmental condition which may have provoked these; nor does there appear in the hospital records any mention of the degree of insight, if any, the patient possessed at the time of his release from the institution.

He remained in jail at Ardmore, I. T., until April 8, 1904, when he was tried and found guilty of murder in the first degree. He was then returned to jail and after about a year's sojourn there was sentenced to life imprisonment and transferred to the United States Penitentiary at Leavenworth. He was readmitted to the Government Hospital for the Insane on March 25, 1906, from the United States Penitentiary at Leaven worth. No medical certificate accompanied him on admission and it is therefore impossible to set, even an approximate date, for the onset of his present mental disorder; but inasmuch as he had not been in prison even a year before his transfer to our hospital, and as it usually takes several months to carry out the required legal proceedings, his mental disorder must have set in quite soon after his confinement in the penitentiary.

He was again in a stuporous condition on his readmission to our hospital, and absolutely oblivious to his surroundings. For about twenty-four hours he was wholly inaccessible, would not reply when spoken to, and had to be aroused from a sort of lethargic state before his attention could be gained at all. On the following day consciousness cleared up to some extent and he recognized some of the attendants whom he had known on his previous admission. He remained, however, more or less confused for several days, after which his mental horizon became clear, and simultaneously with this, delusions of suspicion and persecution became evident. He did not know how long he had been in this confused state and had a complete amnesia for the entire period. Stated that he had been poisoned and that attempts to kill him had been made at the Penitentiary. He knew he had been doped any number of times. Aside from this paranoid complex he had a complete left-sided functional hemiplegia with all the concomitant signs. Left visual field considerably contracted. From May, 1906, to February, 1907, he passed through a number of stuporous periods, during which he was confined to bed from a few days to a week at a time. At these times he would lie with a vacant and staring expression, and questioning would often fail to elicit any reply. At times he would partake only of liquid nourishment, then again would have to be spoon-fed. During his lucid intervals he would be up and about and more or less cheerful. Occasionally played games with his fellow patients. He continued to be very suspicious; frequently spoke of being doped and poisoned. Refused to take medicine, and at times refused to take nourishment because he believed it to be doped. A stenogram of February 10, 1907, shows him to have acquired some grandiose ideas and to be still disoriented to a large extent. Some of his replies were absolutely unreliable. For instance, when asked how long he had been here he replied: "If I came on March 25th, I have been here for three hundred and sixty-five thousand days. It is reasonable but you wouldn't understand it. When a man is answering for something he should not answer for, every day amounts to a thousand years with the Lord." He stated that he knew that attempts were being constantly made to affect him with chemical substances; these were placed in his food and rubbed on the walls of his room, making him dizzy and giving him a sort of peculiar feeling, etc. He could hear of things occurring in distant places and even in foreign countries just as though he were there. He could tell what was going to happen; had no trouble at all to look into the future. He attributed this ability to some superhuman power, but which was natural to him. This power was bestowed upon him by the superhuman power itself. In prison every possible means to kill him were used but without success. They even tried to chloroform him for a day and a night, but could not kill him.

May, 1907:--Still delusional, hypochondriacal; paralysis very much improved. Complains at times of quiverings in the right extremities and a numbness of the left side.

August, 1907:--Has been again in a stuporous state for four days. Still entertains paranoid ideas, hypochondriacal. This was followed by a lucid period which lasted until November 25th, when he again went into a profound stupor and became totally oblivious to everything about him.

April, 1909:--Very much disturbed for about a week. Complained that the physicians and attendants were torturing him in order to drive him insane. Called them brutes and threatened to starve himself to death.

December, 1909:--Neurological Examination--Hemiplegia almost entirely disappeared, but numerous physical stigmata still persist. Has been uninterruptedly clear mentally since his last stuporous state, in November, 1908.

January, 1911:--Clear mentally. Answers questions coherently and readily. Attention easily gained and held without difficulty. Memory, for both recent and remote events, fair, with complete amnestic gaps for the stuporous periods. He shows the characteristic hysterical make-up. He is morbidly suggestible and suspicious. He is markedly egotistical; becomes easily irritated at the least provocation. Is extremely hypochondriacal and shows a marked tendency to exaggeration of actual ills. Constantly laments his fate of being compelled to stay in a place of this sort, which is a thousand times worse than a prison. Is certain that his trial was crooked and irregular and that he had not been given a fair chance. His sentence is inhuman and unjust, as he was not responsible for the crime he committed; he remembers nothing of the occurrence and consequently must have been insane at the time. He is inclined to a great deal of fantastical day-dreaming, writes poetry and religious dissertations. He is constantly bewailing his unfortunate lot in letters to people of high station, imploring their compassion on the poor, down-trodden martyr. Is clear mentally throughout and no definite delusions nor hallucinations can be elicited. His morbid suspiciousness, however, leads him to interpret various occurrences in his environment in a more or less delusional manner.

August, 1911:--No change from the above note except that the physical stigmata have almost completely disappeared. Patient has an adequate amount of insight into his stuporous state, but does not realize that his entire make-up is more or less pathological in character.

The patient had finally sufficiently recovered to be able to be returned to the Penitentiary, and as he was very desirous of the change, he was, accordingly, discharged from further treatment, March 25th, 1912, to be returned to the United States Penitentiary, Leavenworth, Kansas. At this date, November, 1915, I am informed that the patient gets along very well at the Penitentiary, working in the hospital of that institution.

We are dealing here with an individual who, to start with, comes from a badly tainted family. He leads an honest, more or less industrious life, until one day, in a fit of passion, he shoots and kills a man with whom he has some financial differences. Being uncorrupted and of a non-criminal make-up, the enormity of his crime suddenly dawns upon him with its full force. He is unable to withstand the emotional shock which the realization of his deed provokes, breaks down under the stress, and develops a mental disorder. He is removed to a hospital and under the salutary influence of new environment gradually recovers his normal mental health. Simultaneously with this he begins to nourish the hope that he may escape punishment for his deed. The amnesia for the period during which the crime was committed lends support to his optimistic views concerning the outcome of the case, and his mind becomes, in consequence, wholly taken up with the idea of being acquitted of the murder charge. He remembers nothing of the deed, and therefore must have been absolutely unaware of what he was doing at the time. His hopes are shattered when he is found guilty and sentenced to life imprisonment. His nervous system is unable to withstand this blow and it yields a second time, only in a more pronounced manner.

One need not enter into a lengthy discussion in order to show that we have here a mental disorder, the origin of which can be definitely traced to psychic causes, the emotional shock accompanying the crime and conviction. Cause and effect are clearly in evidence here. We have before us a well-defined psychogenetic psychosis. In addition to this the course of this man's mental disturbance was influenced to such an extent by his immediate environment that one could practically shape the symptomatology thereof at will. Once, after a prolonged period of a state which might be considered almost normal to the individual, he induced the attending physician to bring his case for consideration before the staff conference with a view to being returned to prison. At this conference it was decided that in view of the very deleterious influence which prison life has had in the past upon this patient it would not be advisable at this date to send him to the penitentiary. Upon being told that he would have to remain at the hospital, patient again became morose, hypochondriacal, refused nourishment, and commenced to hold himself aloof from the other patients. His suspiciousness and vague persecutory ideas with reference to the personnel of the hospital became more pronounced, and he could see no other reason for being kept here than that the officials are continuing in their persecutions of him. I am convinced, without a doubt, that should this man be pardoned, all the manifestation which he now possesses, and which may be considered as pathologic in character, would at once disappear. The difference in the symptomatology of the two attacks serves to illustrate how difficult it is to positively state what relation these disorders have to hysteria. Here we have an individual whose past life fails to indicate anything which may be taken as of an hysterical character. He develops a psychogenetic disorder in consequence of his crime, the symptomatology of which shows little, if anything, of an hysterical nature. In due course of time he gets well, and after having thrust upon him a life sentence, again returns to us with a mental disorder, the chief feature of which is a functional hemiplegia. There is very little doubt that by studying a cross-section of his second attack we could easily place it under the group of hysteria. Considering, however, the history of the case in toto, we would have to proceed rather cautiously in judging of the hysterical element thereof.

CASE III.--G. W. W., white, male, aged 26 years, whose hereditary history cannot be definitely determined. It appears that mother was a janitress in Boston, and had several children by various fathers. Patient grew up in an orphanage, and worked on farm until age of 18, when he drifted to Denver, Colorado, and enlisted in the U. S. Navy. He served one enlistment with a good record, was a good sailor, and got along well in every respect. He reÃ«nlisted the second time about the middle of 1909, when at the instigation of a fellow sailor he deserted from the Navy in company with the latter. On August 20, 1910, they held up the captain of a ship with the intention of obtaining some money which was stored on board the vessel. In the encounter the captain was killed by the patient's companion, who made his escape, while the patient was apprehended and held on a charge of murder. On August 24th, he was placed in jail at Oakland, California. From the beginning he was regarded by the jail officials as rather silly and defective. He did not appear to be very much interested in his case, and never spoke of his own initiative to his attorney about it. On May 8, 1911, he was seen for the first time by a psychiatrist. He was then found to be very distractible and inattentive, seemed suspicious and excited and assumed stiff attitudes. He was well oriented, and recognized that he was on trial for murder. It might be mentioned here that although the jail officials apparently noted from the first that the patient was not right, the legal proceedings were continued, and it was only on the 4th or 5th day of his trial that his conduct became such as to strongly suggest that he was insane. A psychiatrist was then called in and he pronounced the patient insane, whereupon the proceedings were stopped at this juncture. Examination at that time revealed the following:--General sensation markedly reduced; hypalgesia, he allowed needles to be stuck into his tongue without flinching; walked in a stiff and stooping fashion; no Romberg; moderate vaso-motor stasis, with bluish, cold hands. Gait uncharacteristic. Eyes reacted to light, directly and consensually, and to accommodation. Patellar, Achilles and arm reflexes markedly exaggerated and equal. No foot clonus, no Babinski; abdominal reflexes present, cremasteric not elicited; catalepsy not always present.

Mental Examination:--Attitude was variable, but was distinctly that of one in a stupor. Arms, hands and legs, placed in uncomfortable positions, would remain fixed indefinitely, *i.e.*, so observed from 20 to 30 minutes. Did not resent liberties taken with him; smiled in a silly fashion at each person. Orientation perfect; no insight; hallucinations and delusions could not be elicited. Attention could only be gained with great difficulty, and held for a very short time. Retardation was present; movements were slow and stiff. When stimulated, however, he responded promptly and had no retardation. Speech and writing showed nothing characteristic.

May 11:--Flexibilitas cerea more marked; mutism; retention of saliva; eats food voluntarily; bowels require frequent attention.

May 20:--Requires spoon-feeding; sleeps well; remains always in bed in stiff attitudes.

June 1:--For three or four days refused food, except for one or two meals daily. At times suddenly surprises attendants by sensible remarks, as: Another patient said, "That is G. W. W.," and patient promptly replied, "No, it is Rip Van Winkle." Negativistic signs more marked. Knows physician when eyes are pushed open. At times tries to whistle.

June 13:--For past week has been noisy and excited. When he hears dishes rattle, yells "Chow-chow" for a long time. Continued hot bath for one hour always relieves this excitement. Physical signs negative; Wassermann negative; blood and urinary analysis negative.

June 18:--Admitted to the Government Hospital for the Insane. The Marshal who accompanied the patient from California to this institution states that the patient was resistive and negativistic; that he assumed various constrained attitudes; was untidy, mute, and refused food. All these tendencies were markedly influenced, however, by positive requests of the Marshal. When told that he would be chastised if he did not give up his untidy habits, these disappeared, etc. On admission to the Government Hospital for the Insane the patient had to be carried into the ward, as he refused to walk. He was mute, negativistic, and assumed various uncomfortable and constrained attitudes. Every now and then he would snap at those who handled him, and this would be accompanied by a growl. He was very resistive to the taking of a bath, and suddenly snapped at the attendants who cared for him. When reprimanded, however, by the Supervisor, and told that he would have to take the bath, he quietly underwent the procedure.

Physical Examination:--Pupils widely dilated. Face somewhat distorted. Pupillary reflexes normal; although limbs would remain in a fixed attitude when so placed, he did not evidence the typical flexibilitas cerea. It seems as though he anticipated the passive movements, and there was present a certain amount of voluntary intent. All superficial reflexes active; winced when pricked with a pin but there was a decided hypalgesia present. He refused food; was mute, and apparently oblivious of everything about him. This, however, was only apparently so, as he showed by various acts that he was more or less aware of his surroundings. For instance, during the examination he suddenly snapped at the examiner, and upon the latter's discomfiture he emitted a momentary giggle. When feeding-tube was placed in his nose, preparatory to feeding, he jumped up and said, "I'll drink it," and drank the entire contents of the pitcher. While some parts of his body remained absolutely fixed, restrained and immovable, his face was constantly undergoing various grimacing motions, accompanied now and then by the snapping of his jaws and a growl. During the following several nights he was very noisy, excitable, singing and shouting throughout the night. Mental content could not be determined at this date.

June 28, 1911:--He remains in same apparent stuporous and catatonic attitude. For past few days has exhibited various childish and silly acts of a meaningless and monotonous nature. Still mute except for an occasional growl. Became very untidy today, but when reprimanded and told he must use the toilet he did so.

July 1, 1911:--Patient has been very noisy on several occasions in the past few days, but always becomes quiet when requested to do so. Continues negativistic, stuporous and attitudinizing. Today he was overheard saying: "I am a monkey; want to go out in the yard and sit on the benches; there was no plea of insanity; who are those boys? Come in, boys; water, won't drink it because there is poison in it, it looks good, so try it. Don't believe there is anything in it." He persevered in repeating these phrases.

July 2:--Sang all morning in an undertone. Would stop singing and recommence his facial grimaces when anyone entered his room.

July 3:--For the first time since admission patient answered examiner to questions.

Q. "What is your name?"

A. "George Washington."

Q. "How old are you."

A. "36."

Q. "When born?"

A. "1884."

Q. "Occupation?"

A. "Farmer."

Q. "Where born?"

A. "Around Boston."

Q. "What day is this?"

A. "Someone says Tuesday."

Q. "What date?"

A. "June 17, 1911."

Q. "How long have you been here?"

A. "I cannot tell you."

Q. "What is the name of this place?"

A. "U. S. Hospital."

Q. "Who brought you here?"

A. "Can't tell you, he looks like a monkey."

Q. "How long did it take you to get here?"

A. "One night and twenty-four hours."

Q. "When did you come here?"

A. "I cannot tell you when I did come here."

Q. "Don't you really know the name of this place?"

A. "Well, sailors in the Navy call it the 'Red House.'"

Q. "Where is it located?"

A. "Washington, D.C."

Q. "What sort of a place is it?"

A. "Why, it's as good as any place else."

Q. "Who are these people about you?"

A. "They might be soldiers; what are they out there for?"

Q. "Is there anything wrong with them?"

A. "How should I know?"

Q. "Are any of them insane?"

A. "Darn'd if I know."

Q. "How do you feel?"

A. "How did I get cured of my headache? I'll stick a pitchfork through you, and if a pitchfork goes through you, it will go through me too."

Q. "Are you sick?"

A. "I was sick; had a pain in the head."

Q. "How do you feel now?"

A. "Oh, pretty good."

Q. "Is there anything wrong with your mind?"

A. "I don't know, I can't tell you."

Q. "Do you hear any strange noises or voices?"

A. "Can you go over to that tree? Sounds like a baby squealing; it's the man that choked the baby."

Q. "Do you ever see strange things?"

A. "Did I ever see strange things? I might read about them in the magazine."

Q. "Do you ever hear voices?"

A. "I hear voices say to you; 'You are not guilty.'"

Q. "How much money are you worth?"

A. "$100; I'll give it you for my life."

As will be seen from the foregoing stenogram, the patient is only partially oriented, perhaps more so than he shows, because of his tendency to answer questions in a sort of careless manner. There is a slight suggestion of "by speaking" (Vorbeireden). The stenogram also suggests the possibility of the existence of fallacious sense perceptions. Of the utmost importance, however, for our consideration, is the fact that the occurrence which brought about the mental breakdown plays an important rÃ´le in the consciousness of the patient. Amid what may be considered an almost total oblivion to his immediate environment, he hears the voices tell the examiner that he is not guilty, he would give the $100 which he possesses for his life. These are unmistakable signs of the psychogenetic nature of the disorder.

July 31:--Patient is well oriented, talks in a retarded manner; questions are answered for the most part correctly; occasionally, only nearly correct. His memory is good for remote events, but very much clouded for events which have transpired since the commission of the crime. Partial insight is present. He realizes that there must have been something wrong with him. Emotionally not deteriorated. Refuses to discuss his crime, saying it makes him feel bad; talks in a childish, affected tone of voice, and undergoes various grimacing movements; gives frequent evidence of being fully aware of occurrences in his environment; talks and eats voluntarily and is tidy in habits. Occasionally laughs in a silly, affected manner. Flexibilitas cerea and catalepsy entirely disappeared; gained considerably in weight; continues to show marked tendency to be influenced by occurrences in his environment. In general, shows a decided improvement in his condition.

We are dealing here with an individual whose past career is uneventful, as far as is known. He is charged with murder, and upon being tried for this develops a mental disorder. The symptomatology of his psychosis could easily be mistaken for that of catatonic prÃlcox, and, as a matter of fact, had been so diagnosed by the first observer. In studying the case more thoroughly, however, it becomes unmistakably evident that we are not dealing here with a case of catatonia. In the first place, the immediate relation between the emotional shock of the crime of murder and the probable punishment for it, and the development of the mental disorder must be taken into consideration. This is not a mere accidental relationship. But even if we grant that this point cannot be definitely decided, the psychogenetic character of this case cannot be doubted when we remember how the entire symptomatology is absolutely dependent upon and influenced by occurrences in the patient's environment. He refuses to eat, a symptom very common in catatonia, but it is indeed a rare occurrence for a catatonic in the midst of a negativistic stupor and mutism to say, "I'll drink it," and actually drink voluntarily the entire contents of the pitcher in order to avoid tube-feeding. He is untidy in his habits, another common catatonic characteristic, but is it to be expected that a catatonic, in the height of his disorder, will abstain from his filthy habits when threatened to be punished for these? Many more instances of similar nature could be cited in this case.

Another feature which removes all doubt of the psychogenetic nature of this disorder is the important part which the mental experience which was active in the production of the disorder played in the fashioning of its symptomatology. I alluded before to the patient's answer to the question of whether he heard voices.

The disorder itself, as far as the symptomatology is concerned, is not absolutely typical of any one of the acute psychogenetic states. It

partakes of Kutner's "catatonic states in degenerates" as well as
Raecke's confusional hallucinatory disturbances in these individuals.
That the patient can be classed as one having a degenerative soil is not
at all certain in this case.

I have considered briefly the importance of a proper recognition of
these cases from the viewpoint of rendering a proper prognosis. There
is another important question which must be discussed in connection with
these cases and that is the question of malingering. Picture to yourself
an individual, who, to all appearances, has led a normal existence, and
never showed anything mentally which might be considered pathologic. He
commits a crime, and upon being arrested or upon being placed on trial
for his offense, suddenly lapses into a condition of apparently complete
dementia. The man, who formerly showed nothing in his conduct and
behavior indicative of a mental disorder, suddenly changes into a state
where he does not know his name, age, or his whereabout. His answers to
questions are irrelevant and of a remarkedly silly coloring. He begins
to act in a childish, affected manner, executing many silly, meaningless
acts, or he may break out in a wild furious excitement, loudly
proclaiming his innocence, and threatening those who arrested him. In
addition to this, it is noted that this apparently pathologic condition
can be definitely influenced by using strict and positive measures. The
untidy habits of the patient may be corrected by urging or threats. The
man who has been mute and refuses to eat can be made to talk and eat
voluntarily by threatening him with tube-feeding. Furthermore, in the
midst of this apparently total dementia, total blocking of all thought
processes, the patient frequently surprises those about him by very
sensible remarks of a very clever and pertinent nature, indicating that
although apparently oblivious of his environment, he knows what is going
on about him.

A picture like this may readily arouse the suspicion that we are dealing
with a malingerer, and, indeed, some very prominent German psychiatrists

have reported as malingerers cases similar to this. The trained
psychiatrist, if unfamiliar with this class of cases, will find himself
at a loss to know under what known group of mental disorders to place
this condition, as it will at once become apparent to him that it does
not fit into any of the well-known psychoses.

In defense of the genuineness of the psychotic manifestations of these
patients, I would recall again the transitory mental disturbances of
students undergoing examinations. The genuine loss of all knowledge of
well-known facts which the old-time strict and severe schoolmasters
frequently provoked in school children, differs very little from the
pseudo-dementia with which we are dealing here. It concerns a similar
total blocking and inhibition of all thought processes, and, like all
psychogenetic disorders, has a tendency to disappear upon the removal of
the causative factor.

Still, nobody would think for one moment that the child malingers when
it is unable to answer questions, though these might concern well-known
facts. The consequences of failure to recognize this acute
prison-psychotic-complex as a genuine mental disorder may prove to be
very disastrous when we remember to what extent the symptomatology of
these psychoses is dependent upon environmental conditions.

THE DEGENERATIVE PSYCHOSES

I have considered thus far those psychogenetic mental disorders, the
etiologic factor of which consisted of a single, more or less isolated
emotional occurrence. We have seen that the majority of these patients
showed very little, if anything, in their past life which was in any way
incompatible with leading a more or less successful existence in the
community in which they lived. These patients, we might say, would never
have been brought to the attention of the psychiatrist had it not been

for the occurrence in their life of an experience which provoked a mental breakdown.

I will now consider a group of cases, in whom the degenerative soil is so prominent that they have been properly called "Psychoses of Degeneracy." They should, however, be considered here, because the various psychotic manifestations of these individuals are purely psychogenetic in nature, and evoked by a certain milieu in which the individual was placed. As my material is derived from the criminal department of the Government Hospital for the Insane, the causative factor in these cases will again be found to be imprisonment. These cases differ from the so-called acute prison-psychotic-complex in that the etiologic factor does not consist in a single emotional experience. We are not dealing here with patients in whom the commission of a crime is an accidental occurrence in their life, that is, still uncorrupted individuals upon whom the criminal act in itself might act in a deleterious manner. The patients belonging to this group are, as a rule, old offenders, who have long been hardened to crime, and whose entire life is an uninterrupted chain of conflicts with the law. To this group also belong those high-strung individuals with early antisocial tendencies, who from childhood show a marked degree of egotism and self-love; who are very vindictive and revengeful in their reaction to frictions in social life. Upon falling into the hands of the law, they are incapable of adjustment to the new situation, react in an insane and wild manner to the prison routine, and, in consequence, frequently commit grave offenses during imprisonment.

We owe our present knowledge of the psychopathology of these individuals to the excellent work of the followers of the great Magnan, who contributed so richly to the study of degeneracy.

Siefert[9] was the first to clearly differentiate the purely endogenetic disorders from those dependent upon a degenerative soil, and evoked exclusively by outside influences. He divided the eighty-seven cases of psychoses in criminals studied by him into two distinct groups, namely, the real psychoses and the degenerative psychoses. Under the former thirty-three cases he places the well-known forms of dementia prÃ¦cox, epilepsy, paresis, etc. These, according to him, are not in the least influenced by the milieu in which they occur (in this instance, prison environment). His fifty-four cases of degenerative psychoses, on the other hand, were characterized above all by the fact that they stood in the most intimate relation with the environment in which they occurred, and were wholly influenced by the same. The pathologic, degenerative soil which permitted of the development of the psychosis in these individuals consisted of irritability, lability, autochthonous fluctuations of mood, fantastic day-dreaming, a heightened subjectivity to the environment, inability to form correct critical judgment concerning unpleasant occurrences about them and a strong tendency to suggestibility. On the physical side these patients were subject to headaches, migraine, restlessness and anxiety, often associated with disturbances of heart-action, hypochondriacal complaints, and a tendency to become easily tired upon physical or psychic exertion. They also showed, as a rule, intolerance for alcohol, and were wont to react to alcoholism in a strongly pathologic manner.

Siefert divides his fifty-four cases of degenerative prison psychoses into the following groups:--

First:--Hysterical degenerative state. These consist of undoubted cases of grave hysteria, with convulsions, physical stigmata, endogenous states of ill-temper, confusional states, Ganser twilight syndromes, etc.

Second:--Simple degenerative states. These differ from the preceding group in that hysterical stigmata are wanting. These patients are subject to severe maniacal outbreaks, motor excitements, mutism, attacks of anxious, delirious states, with confusion, etc.

Third:--Fantastic degenerative forms. This group concerns markedly degenerated individuals with a pathologically exaggerated imaginative faculty, a strong auto-suggestibility, a tendency to deceit and lying, to inherent fluctuations of mood and hysterical stigmata. On this basis there develop conditions of pseudologia-phantastica, systematized delusional formations of all sorts, delirious psychoses, etc.

Fourth:--Paranoid degenerative forms. This group he again subdivides into the querulent and hallucinatory paranoid forms. The former may resemble the typical "Querulantenwahn", a psychosis artificially built up out of extraneous circumstances, and one which rarely develops in freedom, but is of very frequent occurrence in prison. The hallucinatory paranoid form consists of fallacious sense perceptions and delusions of a persecutory nature, often substantiated by a strongly hypochondriacal element; in short, a picture which simulates very closely the real paranoid state.

Fifth:--Prison psychotic states with simulated symptoms.

Sixth:--Dementia-like processes. The individuals belonging to this group are habitual criminals in whom the criminal tendencies become evident at a very early period in life, and who, without giving distinct evidence in their past history of a mental disturbance, develop after prolonged confinement a progressive change of character which eventually leads to frequent rebellious outbreaks against the prison management. They become absolutely unmanageable, neglect their work and duties, and finally have to be transferred to an insane asylum. Here they show nothing characteristic of the well-known dementing processes, as hebephrenia, for example; but very frequently, although quite young, their entire manner and behavior suggest a certain dilapidation and deterioration.

Siefert considers the above-mentioned disease processes as entirely dependent upon and provoked by prison life, in individuals with a tendency to mental deterioration. He comes to the conclusion that the prison psychoses are reactions of pathologic nervous organizations to definite deleterious conditions of life. They are nothing more than irradiations, distortions, and new creations, on the same degenerative soil which also conditioned the crime.

The importance of Siefert's momentous work cannot be doubted, but whether he was justified in his many subdivisions of the degenerative states is questionable. His own description of the various forms immediately suggests the difficulty of clearly differentiating one from the other.

Bonhoeffer,[10] in a monograph devoted to the subject, endeavors to establish the existence, on the basis of degeneracy, of acute psychotic processes which do not belong to either the manic-depressive, hysterical, or epileptic temperaments, which cannot be placed under any of the known forms of dementia prÃ¡cox, and which develop as wholly independent psychotic manifestations in particularly predisposed individuals. The material which served for his thesis was gathered from the Berlin Observation Ward for Criminals, among the inmates of which institution he found a great number of degenerative psychoses. In a recent work on the subject of psychogenesis he upholds his former views, and believes he has been able to separate his cases into three distinct groups. The first group comprises certain unstable individuals who show a tendency to the development of simple paranoid psychoses. It concerns patients of a very labile make-up with increased affective reactions, with marked tendencies to impulsions and antisocial acts. These cases are characterized by the fact that they do not concern psychogenetic psychotic exaggerations of a certain temperamental predisposition, but psychically evoked disease states which appear to be irreconcilably opposed to the original personality.

He calls attention to the epileptic seizures of these individuals, which have been so ably described by Bratz.[11] In contradistinction to the genuine endogenetic epilepsy, these patients manifest epileptic seizures as reactions to situations purely psychic in nature. In them, without ever resulting in epileptic dementia, there occur along with the epileptic seizures attacks of unconsciousness, of excitement, dream states, and porio-maniacal outbreaks. They differ from the genuine epilepsy by the absence of the characteristic dementia, of attacks of petit mal, and by the fact that the seizures are never purely endogenous in origin. They are always due to extraneous causes, eminently such of a psychic nature. He believes that more frequently even than actual epileptic seizures are the dream states, excitements, and maniacal outbreaks brought about in these individuals by emotional experiences, and as a result of certain ideas and concepts. He places in this group the proverbial "wild man", the man who goes into a frenzy upon seeing a policeman, etc. Although alcohol may in these individuals prepare the way, the immediate causative factor, however, is the emotional experience, or the recollection of such an experience.

These psychogenetic excitements of degenerates often simulate symptomatologically genuine epilepsy so far as the ferocity of the excitement and the state of consciousness are concerned. In some cases the retention of suggestibility during the attacks shows clearly the psychogenetic character of the disorder, while in others the tendency toward the theatrical and exaggeration is so marked that we are forced to think of an hysterical component. Certain slight symptomatologic features of these psychogenetic states of excitement in degenerates appear to furnish a differentiating point between them and the true epileptic condition. Bonhoeffer refers to the strong tendency to disgust-evoking manifestations, to copro-practice which manifest themselves in the soiling of the walls and face with excrements, the drinking of urine, etc. Another characteristic is the frequent total misunderstanding of the situation by these individuals in that they consider themselves to be threatened with impending grave physical danger. In consequence of this they manifest a certain over-aggressiveness, which goes far beyond mere protective reactions, and manifests itself in a senseless breaking and demolishing of furniture. These individuals can be easily distinguished by their superficial intellectual endowment, by a tendency to change of occupation, and early criminality. During imprisonment and under the influence of the stress incident thereto, they develop an acute paranoid symptom-complex, a delirium of reference, accompanied by ideas of prejudice, isolated elementary hallucinations, and irresistible desire to a depressive recapitulation of their past, and a nervous, irritable temper. Consciousness is not clouded, and they remain perfectly oriented in all spheres. The duration of the disorder may vary from a few months to two years, with occasional intermissions. The delusional formation continues only for a short period, and in no instance leads to a retrospective change of the content of consciousness. Very frequently the process subsides upon the removal of the patient into a new environment without leaving any change in the personality of the individual. Insight is not always perfect. The delirium of reference and prejudicial ideas concerning the prison personnel may remain unconnected.

The cases belonging to his second group are those well-known pestilent individuals who from childhood show an abnormally affective reaction to frictions in social life, in so far as their highly exaggerated, egocentric self-consciousness permits them to endow every unpleasant experience with a personal note of prejudice. They are the poor martyrs, who somehow never seem to get what is coming to them in this world, who are ever ready to assert their rights and leave no stone unturned until they receive what they consider full justice. Such individuals may pass through life, if fortunate enough, without developing a real psychosis. They are then merely burdensome and uncheering elements within their narrow social sphere. Should they, however, meet with an experience, which to them appears as an injustice, they may at once develop typical paranoid pictures, the characteristic feature of which is that the psychic experience which forms the origin of the trouble remains always in the foreground. Bonhoeffer identifies these conditions with Wernicke's psychoses of hyperquantivalent ideas. He very justly says: "The narrower the sphere of activity in which these individuals live, the more frequent the opportunities for conflict are offered by law, discipline, and subordination, the easier it is to develop a psychotic exacerbation of the abnormal temperament even on a lesser pathological basis. This is the reason why officialdom and especially the narrow limits of prison life bring out so forcibly these psychogenetic disorders. In prisoners the psychogenetic character of the disorder becomes especially apparent. One sees how in many cases the transfer from one prison to another, to an observation station, to an insane asylum, puts an end to the process. In certain instances the process seems to revive itself again when the individual is placed in a similar environment."

Of Bonhoeffer's three subdivisions of degenerative states the preceding one would as a whole appear to me to be especially deserving of a separate classification. Anyone who has had any experience with insane criminals will recall that group of cases in whom the entire psychosis seems to be more or less centered about a certain idea; in most instances, about the idea of not having received a just trial. These individuals, without showing any intellectual impairment, in fact without showing any characteristic which would fit their mental disturbance into any of the known psychoses, constantly evidence a sort of paranoid habitus, a paranoid trend which is exclusively directed against those who had anything to do with their conviction and safe-keeping. The most trivial occurrences in their environment are endowed by them with a personal note of prejudice. The delay of a letter, the refusal to grant some of their unusual requests, an attendant's accidental failure to sweeten their coffee sufficiently, the slightest deviation from the routine greeting of the visiting physician; in short, any such trivial, insignificant occurrence is at once endowed with a special meaning, and explained in a more or less delusional manner. Yet these individuals can reason in a perfectly rational manner on any subject which is not concerned with their conviction or confinement. They are as a rule intellectually bright and keen, and fail to show any evidence of emotional deterioration. On the contrary, their emotions are of such fine and sensitive nature that incidents which an ordinary individual would overlook entirely, offend them to a marked degree, and are reacted to by them in a very decisive manner. Indeed, one frequently asks himself whether their persecutory ideas deserve to be endowed with the value of actual delusions. I fully agree with Sturrock[12] when he says: "If I refuse to allow a prisoner full scope because he has lifted a knife from the table with which to attack the charge warder, I do not call it a delusion of persecution if he spends the night threatening to murder me because I do not give him justice." One must remember that this is in a measure the normal attitude of the captive towards the captor, and can be seen in a more or less pronounced degree among criminals enjoying a short respite from the law. The essential point here is not the so-called psychosis, but the soil which made the development possible. Not all prisoners, by far, react in this manner to the prison environment. It is only those degenerative individuals who have shown this well-marked paranoic trend all their lifetime, who furnish these cases. As a general rule these conditions are seen in habitual offenders whose entire life has been a round of conflicts with everything they come in contact, and who, outside of prison, figure chiefly in the saloon and gambling house brawls.

That these conditions deserve a more definite classification than the nondescript paranoid state cannot be doubted. These paranoid manifestations are distinct reactions to a definite situation, in this instance, conviction and imprisonment, of individuals whose peculiarly degenerative make-up makes such reactions possible. The question of the particular coloring which these disorders may assume can only take a secondary position to that of the character or make-up with which we are dealing.

Bonhoeffer further speaks of a certain hysterical element in these cases, but does not believe that on this account these paranoid manifestations should be considered as hysterical. He rather believes that they are more closely allied to the epileptoid temperament. The hysterical component manifests itself in either hysterical stigmata, or, as has often appeared to him, in the fact that the falsifications of memory which these individuals frequently manifest concern themselves solely with the simple overvalued paranoid ideas, and lead to a complete blocking out of unpleasant recollections of the individual's past career. Thus, previous sentences, imprisonments, etc., are totally forgotten. In this, perhaps, we might see the well-known wish factor of hysteria.

The cases which comprise his third group show such a varying symptomatology that it is difficult to form an exact idea of just what characterizes them.

After perusing the work of Bonhoeffer, one feels that the author's endeavors to subdivide his material into this or that group are somewhat artificial. Granted that we are dealing with mental disorders, whose existence can be possible only by a certain degenerative predisposition, the question arises, "Of how much practical value is this constant endeavor at classification and subdivision of the psychotic manifestations which these individuals show?" One must acknowledge that the salient feature here is not the particular coloring which these psychoses assume, but, as we have stated before, the soil upon which they develop. At most, we might say that the symptomatology of these psychoses would depend on the question whether it is the ideational sphere which is mostly concerned, or the affective sphere. Turning to Wilmanns' excellent contribution to this subject one again meets with the same endeavors at subdivision and classification. Lack of space will not permit us to enter into an extensive discussion of this author's work. We have already indicated here and there in passing, some of the essential points in the views of this author.

One turns with quite a degree of relief to the momentous work of Birnbaum[13] on the Psychoses of Degeneracy. As far as can be ascertained the author does not endeavor to subdivide his degenerative states into so many types and forms. According to him, the essential characteristics of the degenerative psychoses--namely, the extraordinary determinability and influence which outside impressions have upon the disorder, the mode of genesis and the psychological evolution of the delusions, etc.,--may be attributed to the essential ear-marks of the degenerative character; that is, to the exaggerated auto-suggestibility, the great instability of the existing conditions and mental pictures, the disharmony between the perceptive and imaginative capacities and the preponderance of a lively fantastic coloring to the dry thinking of these individuals. They do not form disease processes of a definite characteristic form, but episodic psychotic manifestations on a degenerative soil, and the manifold phases of the collective forms are to be considered as repeated fluctuations about the psychic equilibrium of these individuals. He further noted that the symptomatology of these disorders remained limited to a relatively well systematized delusional fabric, which, however, in contradistinction to paranoia, does not persist for any length of time, but disappears for certain definite reasons. They do not form any typical symptom-complex. The delusional ideas may take on any character; hallucinations may occur in all fields of the sensorium; consciousness may or may not be clouded, but is usually so in the beginning of the disorder. Recoveries are as a rule gradual, but may set in quite suddenly. Insight may or may not be present. The course of the disorder, like its symptomatology, offers nothing of a definite, characteristic nature.

Thus we see that the distinguishing feature of Birnbaum's degenerative psychoses does not lie in their mode of appearance, in their symptomatology, but in the mechanism of their evolution, and, above all, in their total dependence upon extraneous influences. They are typical psychogenetic disorders, the psychic etiology of which is potent not only in the incitation of the processes, but in the modeling and fashioning of them. Although Birnbaum notices the close relation that exists between these psychoses and the hysterical psychotic manifestations, he would separate them distinctly from hysteria.

CASE IV.--A. C., colored female, age 32 on admission to the Government Hospital for the Insane, on June 18, 1909. Father died of dropsy; one brother was killed in a railroad accident; one sister suffered from St. Vitus' dance; another died of tuberculosis. Patient was born in Jamestown, Virginia, was healthy as a child. Does not remember having had the usual diseases of childhood; had a severe attack of typhoid fever when quite young. Attended school until fourteen years of age, having reached the third grade. Upon leaving school she went to work as chambermaid and soon became addicted to the excessive use of alcohol, as a result of which she got into numerous fights and quarrels. In 1895, while intoxicated, she stabbed a man in the back and was sent to Albany Penitentiary for five years and eleven months. During her sojourn there she was sent to the Matteawan Hospital for Criminal Insane, where she remained forty-five days. Upon being discharged she returned to her home and lived with her mother, assisting her with washing and ironing, following which she led the life of a prostitute for about two years. In 1901 she was sentenced to thirty months imprisonment at Moundsville, Virginia, for theft. Previous to this she had been confined in the Government Hospital for the Insane for about a month with an attack of delirium tremens. After the expiration of her sentence at Moundsville, she returned to

Washington and soon after was again arrested for housebreaking and robbery and sentenced on two counts to twenty years imprisonment at Moundsville. While there she had more or less trouble all the time; had numerous fights with other colored women, in several of which she sustained injuries. On February 12, 1907, while working in the sewing room, she became implicated in a quarrel with another inmate, whom she stabbed in the left side of the neck with a pair of scissors. In describing the incident she says: "I pushed them in as far as they would go, twisted them around, opened them and then pulled them out." The woman lived about five minutes after this. The quarrel presumably originated because her antagonist called her some name and accused her of having to serve a "young life sentence." She then told this woman to go back to Anacostia and get the baby she threw over the Anacostia Bridge, at which the latter became quite angry and attacked her with a pair of scissors which culminated in the murder. A. C. was placed in a cell after this and the next day transferred to a dungeon, where she remained until her transfer to this Hospital. While in the dungeon she suffered a great deal with headaches and nervousness; she was absolutely isolated, no one came to her cell, ate her meals through the bars. In this condition she remained about three months. She says she prayed a good deal during this period, because she was told that she might have to stand trial for murder, in which event they would surely hang her. She was admitted to this institution the first time on May 8, 1907, on a medical certificate which stated that one sister died of pulmonary tuberculosis, and that another is now afflicted with chorea. The patient was addicted to the excessive use of alcohol and cocaine and is considered to be a sexual pervert. Ever since she was admitted to the penitentiary she has exhibited signs and symptoms of insanity; her present symptoms are described as ungovernable temper, attacks of extreme nervousness, attacks of fits resembling those of acute mania, with loss of judgment and complete disregard for the consequences of any of her acts. Delusions of persecution were also noted. Her mother stated that the patient throughout her lifetime would frequently have outbursts of temper, and her brother would tie her down during these attacks to prevent her from injuring members of the family. Physical examination on the first admission was negative. Mentally she complained of being nervous and easily awakened at night; consciousness was clear; she was well oriented; no hallucinations or delusions could be elicited. Intellectually she appeared to be above the average negro in intelligence; she read and wrote, spelled correctly and used good English. Her memory was good for both past and recent events. Throughout her entire sojourn here she was oriented to time, place and person; except for having stated at one time in a sort of careless and apparently indifferent way that she had heard someone calling her by name, and upon looking for the person could find no one, she manifested no hallucinatory disturbances. No delusional ideas were elaborated at any time. Her conduct here was characterized throughout by marked irritability; she frequently threatened to get even with the ward physician, saying she did not propose to fight open-handed any more and would not enter into a fight without a weapon. She frequently broke window lights without any apparent reason; often was very surly in manner; then again was pleasant and agreeable and assisted with the work on the ward. She assaulted several of the nurses when an attempt was made to restrain her, in order to prevent her breaking window lights. When spoken to about these outbursts of temper she would deny all knowledge of them, saying that she never threatened nor assaulted anyone. She was discharged as recovered on January 12, 1909, and returned to Moundsville Penitentiary. She was again admitted to the Government Hospital for the Insane on June 18, 1909, on a medical certificate which stated that she was very irritable and had a mania for breaking windows; that she was suffering from delusions. No further evidence of insanity was given. On admission she was sullen and disagreeable, had a frown on her face, sat on a chair looking out of the window and was exacting in her demands. She requested to be removed to another ward, where she thought it would be livelier; asked for various medicines, etc. When told that her requests could not be granted, she became very cross and abusive, making threats of things she would do. In the afternoon scratched her arm with a pin and quite a flow of blood was produced, which necessitated restraint. At this she became very excited and endeavored to break the wristlets and get out of the room, proclaiming loudly that if she was going to have wristlets on she would rather be back at Moundsville. She was not very communicative concerning her return to the Hospital; told one of the nurses that she had "carried on high" to get back, and that Moundsville was "a hell of a place." The following day she begged continuously for hypodermics, complained of headache and tried to produce emesis by putting her finger down the Å"sophagus. When questioned, she answered promptly and intelligently, but in a sullen manner; stated that on her return to the penitentiary she was placed in a cell formerly occupied by the woman whom she had killed, and that this made her nervous, and frightened her. She would not sleep on the bed provided but used for sleeping purposes a box intended for a table. She said she cried and prayed a great deal until finally, after three weeks, was transferred to another ward. She said that she behaved well and caused no trouble after having been removed from the first cell and does not know why they transferred her over here. Her entire sojourn here on this occasion was characterized by irritability, impulsiveness and destructiveness to property. She was fault-finding to a great extent and threatened the life of some of those about her. She was surly, selfish, and showed a marked tendency to lying. She was shrewd in her endeavors to get herself into the good graces of those in charge of her and on one occasion stated that she was pregnant in order to receive more considerate treatment. This, like many other of her assertions, was false. She was oriented throughout; memory good; no hallucinations or delusions could be elicited; she was very unstable emotionally; reasoning and judgment were defective. Her entire symptomatology was controlled and fashioned almost wholly by her immediate environment. When refused a privilege she would become surly, abusive and threatening to those about her, would destroy everything she could lay hands on, and attack the nurses when the opportunity was favorable. The granting of a privilege again would serve to keep her in a rather tranquil mood. She remained this time until June 21, 1910, when she was again returned to the penitentiary at Moundsville. From information obtained from some officials of that penitentiary, it appears that she is continuing to have her old-time outbursts of temper, during which she becomes absolutely unmanageable, and the only way to deal with her seems to be to isolate her and leave her absolutely alone until she is over her disturbed state. Between these attacks she behaves quite well, but such behavior has to be encouraged by the granting of various privileges.

CASE V.--J. J. M., aged 24 years, white male, is a well-built young man, whose family history is unknown owing to his refusal to give it. He was born at Chester, South Carolina, in 1885. Childhood and school life uneventful as far as is known. He was a bright scholar of ordinary intellectual attainments. His industrial career, which began early in life, was, according to his statements, normal. He admits, however, losing several positions on account of outbreaks of temper during which he had fights with other employees. He had several gonorrhÅ"al infections, the first one at the age of fifteen; was infected with lues at a very early age. He used alcoholics to a certain extent, and admits having been intoxicated on numerous occasions. In 1906 he was struck on the head with a club by a policeman. Later in the same year he received an injury to the head during a street riot. Neither of these injuries was accompanied by any untoward symptoms. In 1907 or 1908 he was struck on the head by an overhead pump while riding on top of a car. Was unconscious for some time afterwards, later got up and walked unassisted to a nearby station, where he took a train to Cincinnati. There he was confined to a hospital for ten days, undergoing treatment for this injury. He left the hospital one day without being properly discharged; had no ill after effects from this injury. In the summer of 1909 he was arrested in Washington, in company with another fellow, for robbery. They were both released on bond. The patient, however, left the jurisdiction, and when the police went to a nearby city to arrest him he met them with a loaded pistol. After considerable effort he was finally subdued and arrested. His companion received a short term sentence, while the patient was committed to five years in the Leavenworth Penitentiary. At that time he was living on the earnings of a professional prostitute, to whom he claims he had been married for several years. From correspondence between him and this woman it appears that he fully sanctions her mode of life. Soon after his arrival at the prison the physician noted his excitable and irritable disposition, which became progressively aggravated, finally necessitating his transfer to the observation ward, on December 9, 1910, a little over a month after his imprisonment. The records of the observation ward of the Leavenworth Hospital show the following:--

December 12, 1910:--Patient says he is frightened and asks to go to bed; put to bed at 4 P.M.

December 22, 1910:--While nurse Miller was taking the afternoon temperatures of the several patients at the guard's desk, he was suddenly attacked by M., who began to beat Miller about the head and face, drawing blood. It was noted that M. and another prisoner had resolved themselves into a select coterie for the purpose of being loud and boisterous and disobeying the hospital rules generally. Not a day passes that some gross breach of prison discipline is not committed by them.

December 23, 1910:--M. told the nurse: "If my wife don't write pretty soon, I am going to jump off the landing and kill myself." He complained that the attendant and nurses were talking about him, and that he feels sometimes like going over and smashing some of them, adding: "I know I am a damn fool for thinking that they are fixing up against me, but I can't help it. I know I am going crazy; I wish I could kill myself, cut my throat or something." This patient is decidedly worse, easily excited, suspicious, hypersensitive, imagines persons are plotting against him. When in conversation, gesticulates with both hands, wags his head and looks wildly out of the eyes. A particular instance of his excitable temper is a startled wild look upon being awakened to have his temperature taken in the morning.

December 24, 1910:--Says he is scared of something, doesn't know what, and wants to go to bed. Continues to receive epilepsy tablets.

January 2, 1911:--Complains of pains through the head and acts as if frightened. His eyes have a glassy appearance and pupils are dilated. At times a suicidal mania attacks him, seemingly using all his strength to overcome it.

His further sojourn there was characterized by maniacal outbursts, during which he would attack those about him. He showed an utter disregard for prison rules, absolutely refused to obey orders, and when an attempt was made to enforce these, his condition became noticeably aggravated, and the maniacal attacks more frequent. He frequently spoke of being frightened at something, of the attendants plotting against him, and persecuting him. During one of his depressions he made a superficial cut on his neck with a piece of glass which necessitated the application of physical restraint. One day two physicians who examined him spoke in his presence of the advisability of operating on his head. Following this he constantly spoke of his fear of being cut up by the physicians, whom he designated as a bunch of anarchists, and the elaboration of this fear remained the dominant feature of his mental disorder. He continued, however, to be profane, vicious and unruly in his behavior. His periodic outbursts of rage were as furious as formerly, he tore up his bed-clothing and personal attire during these fits of anger, which continued to be more or less reactive in character. He is noted as having had several attacks of convulsive seizures closely resembling epilepsy. Patient was admitted to the Government Hospital for the Insane on April 7, 1911. On admission he was very nervous and apprehensive, would jump and become startled when touched or approached by anyone and when spoken to became highly wrought up emotionally. His body fairly shook with excitement, pupils dilated, face became flushed and he could hardly speak on account of the emotional upset. He spoke of having come from a hell, from a dungeon where a bunch of anarchists were persecuting him, and were going to cut him up and operate on him, that he had heard them talk about it. He was imperfectly oriented, somewhat confused, and to all appearances lacked full appreciation of his new environment. He quieted down, however, at the close of the day and slept well during the night. Physically he was slightly emaciated. No neurological disturbances were noted except that he complained of headaches. When an attempt was made the following morning by a physician to examine him, he flew into a rage, became highly emotional, profane and threatening, showed marked apprehensiveness and expressed the fear of being cut up. He reiterated the persecution of him by the officials at the penitentiary, that he did not care what happened to him, whether he went to hell or heaven, etc. He spoke of killing himself before he would submit to an operation. He refused to eat, saying that the food was not fit to eat, and that he would refrain from taking nourishment until he was given better food. A visit from his wife served to appease him. When given a Hospital night-gown to wear he threw it away, saying he could not sleep in coarse clothing, and this had to be finally substituted by a silk one which his wife brought him. For two weeks following this he was allowed the freedom of the courtyard, where he was quiet and well-behaved, except when spoken to by the physician. At times he would turn with lightning suddenness into a maniacal state, and his paranoid ideas would come to the front, among which his fear of being operated upon was always predominant. At this time he had not completely transferred his paranoid ideas to the officials here. His clouded consciousness cleared up completely. He read the newspapers daily, took an active part in his immediate environment, and except for the periodic outbreaks of rage when talking to the physician, he showed no outward conduct disorder. He was taking nourishment regularly after a special diet was ordered for him. After a sojourn of about a month, the attention of the officials was called to the fact that the patient was planning an escape by overpowering the attendants, in which plot his wife, who was at that time an inmate of a disreputable house, was to assist him by furnishing him a gun. It was thought advisable to take special precautions with the man, and consequently his freedom of the courtyard had to be curtailed, and he was confined to his room. This was immediately followed by a marked exacerbation of his psychotic manifestations. He became very unruly, abusive and threatening. His outbursts of fury assumed the character of an excited epileptic. They differed, however, from this, in being accompanied by clear consciousness, and in not being endogenetic in their occurrence, but distinctive reactive manifestations to definite situations. Every refusal of a request was followed by one of those outbreaks, during which he would be profane, abusive, destructive and violent, threatening to kill the officials who had anything to do with his safe-keeping, and would elaborate an ill-defined general paranoid trend towards them. He was simply persecuted by a bunch of unchristian anarchists who were running this place; that they would see him in hell first before they would make him behave himself; that he is not here to please anybody except himself; that he recognizes no superiority other than Jesus Christ, etc. Conversely, the granting of a privilege served to bring him to a perfect calm, when he would talk in a rational and coherent manner, and be free from psychotic manifestations. The granting of the privilege of seeing his wife served to get him to submit himself to a thorough examination, which could not be attempted before. The objective examination revealed no intelligence defect. His reasoning and judgment were unimpaired, memory good, and aside from his paranoid ideas, which consisted in his belief that the officials were persecuting him, and that they were trying to operate on his head, no psychotic manifestations could be determined. Hallucinations had not been evidenced at any time and he possessed no insight. Recently he requested the physician to administer him a dose of 606, for which he was very grateful. He also entered of late into an active correspondence with some attorneys in town with a view to having something done for his case. On July 15, 1911, he appeared before the staff conference of the medical officers of the Hospital for the purpose of determining whether his condition was such as to warrant his transfer back to the penitentiary. Although having been tranquil and normal for several weeks prior to this, upon entering the examining room he at once became highly emotional, abusive and threatening, and everyone who saw him at that time was impressed with the great affective lability which the patient possessed. For a day or so following this experience he continued to be very emotional, irritable and boisterous. Later on his privileges were again returned to him and he resumed a tranquil state of mind, which existed until the time of his transfer to the prison on August 10, 1911. He told the supervisor who accompanied him to the depot that he intended to behave himself when he returned to prison, so that he might enjoy the benefit of his good term allowance and thus have his sentence shortened. Upon his return to the penitentiary he was immediately placed under observation on account of his peculiar behavior.

The records of that institution show the following:--

August 16:--Became very profane during the afternoon and evening, declaring that the prison authorities were holding up his mail from

his wife, and was very profane and vindictive in speaking of the
officials.

August 17:--Cursing the prisoners of parole room I as they were coming
in from exercise, stating that they were a lot of G.d d....d s..s
of b.....s and that they were holding up his mail.

August 18:--Shouting and cursing through his window during the
evening. Got out of bed at 2 A.M., and began to swear and fight an
imaginary foe, keeping it up for two hours.

August 19:--Continues to use the most profane language he can towards
the prisoners or anyone whom he chances to see.

August 20:--Was very excitable and irritable during the day and
evening. Attempted to throw his food in the guard's face, cursing the
officials for keeping his wife away from him; claims that he can hear
her calling him outside of his cell at night.

August 21:--Cursed the guard because he would not allow him to go out
of isolation; sang and whistled during the evening.

August 22:--Very profane and vindictive in his accusations towards the
prison officials.

August 23:--Denounced the guard as a black-hander, and said that the
guard is bribing the prison officials to hold him in isolation, but
that he will not give the guard a damned nickel.

August 29:--Actions and language continue along the same line except
that they are growing progressively worse; cursing the officials,
prisoners, etc.; claims they are keeping his wife away from him, and
that his mail is being held up; is afraid of being murdered, and says

that he is being kept here while his wife is starving; constantly uses
loud and profane language.

August 30:--Prisoner whistled and sang during the evening,
interspersed with very vile language.

August 31:--Became very violent today, cursing officials, claiming
that he was being kept away from his wife and child who were starving.
Kept shouting, singing and cursing at intervals all day and far into
the night.

September 7:--Continues to have periods of violence almost daily; has
hallucinations that he is being haunted by some imaginary foe, whom he
sees sitting on his bed when he wakes up at night--a red-headed fellow
by the name of Smith. Says that he can hear his wife and child crying
outside of his cell, and repeatedly requests that he be allowed to go
home to them. Says that his wife and children are starving, and that
the prison officials are trying to starve him. Complains of pains in
his head, and that his eyes hurt him and that he is going blind. He is
inclined to be destructive of late, breaking his electric globes,
smashing stool, throwing magazines against window and cell bars.

September 14, 1911:--Says he knows that red-haired Smith is trying to
steal his wife, and that he is following him all over the country;
that he was about to kill him in Jacksonville, Florida, but that he
jumped out of a window. His violent attacks are becoming more severe
and pronounced, and he requires constant watching to prevent him from
doing himself bodily harm. He was also noted to have occasional mild
attacks of *petit mal*.

On his way to Washington from the penitentiary at Leavenworth, upon
his second transfer to this institution, the patient had been
shackled to another prisoner who was supposed to be suffering from

pulmonary tuberculosis. M. kept on begging the guards to be separated from this prisoner, and this request was finally granted. While going through the State of Iowa he jumped out through the window of the moving train. He was handcuffed at the time. After having gone about thirty miles he was recaptured. He had removed handcuffs soon after his escape from the train.

September 27:--On admission the patient limped and complained of great pain in both knees. Knees were swollen, bruised and discolored, and there was marked tenderness on touching. Patient entered the ward quietly, recognized those about him, and answered questions rationally. Said that aside from having been hurt in the knees, his left shoulder pained him a great deal. Upon being placed in bed he was asked by the examiner why he was sent here, to which he replied: "To get killed, I suppose." Further questions failed to elicit any answers, and the interview had to be discontinued.

September 28:--Patient answered the following questions to the attendant on the ward:--

Q. "What is your name (full Christian name and surname)?"

A. "J. J. M."

Q. "How old are you?"

A. "25."

Q. "When were you born?"

A. "1885."

Q. "What is your occupation?"

A. "Railroad man."

Q. "Where were you born?"

A. "Charleston, South Carolina."

Q. "What day is this?"

A. "Don't know."

Q. "What month, date and year is it?"

A. "August, 1911. Don't know date of month."

Q. "What time is it?"

A. "Don't know."

Q. "Where did you come from?"

A. "Leavenworth."

Q. "Who brought you here?"

A. "Bunch of cut-throats, Sons of ---- tried to starve me to death all the way down."

Q. "How long were you in coming?"

A. "Don't know."

Q. "When did you come?"

A. "Don't know what time it was."

Q. "What is the name of this place?"

A. "Don't know."

Q. "Where is it?"

A. "On an island, I guess, some damn thing across the river."

Q. "What sort of a place is this?"

A. "Mad-house."

Q. "Who are these people about you?"

A. "Here to murder me."

Q. "Is there anything wrong with them?"

A. "Nothing but black-hands anarchists."

Q. "Who am I?"

A. "J. S." (correct)

Q. "Why do you suppose I am asking you all these questions?"

A. "Don't know."

Q. "Why were you sent here?"

A. "To be dumped off, I guess."

Q. "How do you feel?"

A. "Pretty bad this morning, my head hurts me."

Q. "Are you sad or happy?"

A. "Neither one."

Q. "Are you worried about something?"

A. "Why, sure I am."

Q. "Did anything strange happen to you for which you can't give yourself an account?"

A. "No."

Q. "Do you hear voices talking to you?"

A. "Yes, hear you talking to me now."

Q. "Do you see any strange things?"

A. "No."

Q. "Do you ever have fits or convulsions?"

A. "No."

Q. "Did you ever try to commit suicide?"

A. "No."

Q. "Is there anybody trying to harm you in any way?"

A. "Yes, those black-hands anarchists."

Q. "How much money are you worth?"

A. "Nothing."

The foregoing two cases are representative of a group which unquestionably forms the most difficult part in the problem of caring for the insane criminals. Here we have a couple of individuals whose entire psychotic manifestations, if such they may be considered, consist of a most wild and vicious rebellion against imprisonment. They are individuals who cannot be kept under any prescribed mode of living, and when this is insisted upon, they react to it in an insane manner.

Bonhoeffer justly termed them "wild men", for wild indeed they are when in one of their tantrums. The question arises, "Wherein lies the cause of this rebellion against discipline?" It certainly cannot be wholly attributed to the environment, for these individuals behave in a similar manner even when removed to the far more lenient régime of a hospital. We must seek an explanation for the behavior of these individuals in the individual himself, in his make-up.

Looking at the life history of the two foregoing patients we find them both to be of the most depraved class of society. The one is a professional prostitute; the other subsisting upon the earnings of a prostitute. Their relation with man has always been characterized by a sort of vicious vindictiveness. Their high-strung emotional make-up brought them into serious conflict with those about them on many occasions before. Being finally taken hold of by the law and made to submit to a certain well-regulated mode of existence, their inherent characteristics assert themselves in a most decisive way and they react to the situation in the manner of a trapped tiger, stopping at no means to gain their point. The one commits a homicide during one of her outbreaks of passion; the other risks his life to obtain his purpose, by jumping out of a moving train with his hands shackled. Their life seems to be one long series of impulsions, fostered and sustained by the extreme lability of their emotions. Intellectually they show no defect. They are keen and alert to every opportunity which presents itself to them and are very shrewd in the execution of their criminal acts. Finding themselves under a rÃ©gime which exacts from them a certain submission to rules, to regulations, they begin to misinterpret ordinary occurrences in their environment in a sort of delusional manner: They are persecuted by the warden because the latter insists upon making them behave themselves; the keepers are a bunch of anarchists, whose entire occupation seems to be to persecute them and down them. This for no other reason than because they are made to work and to behave themselves. J. J. M. tells me that he will not behave himself, that he is not here to please anyone but himself and recognizes no authority other than that of Christ. The other says she raised so much hell at the prison that they had to send her back to the hospital. The distinguishing feature of their psychotic manifestations is that they are provoked essentially by definite situations. They are not a mere wild, misdirected, meaningless series of insane acts, such as one would expect from a demented person, but distinct reactions to situations. Refuse them a request and they at once become wild, abusive and vicious, smashing up everything that they can lay hands on; conversely, when granted some of their unreasonable requests, it serves at once to appease them for the time being at least. Their conduct, however, is very detrimental to the prison rÃ©gime, as discipline cannot be maintained with such disturbing elements about. Their interpretations of discipline are considered as delusions of persecution, their outbursts of temper as typical maniacal outbreaks, and consequently they are shipped off to an insane asylum. Now the question arises whether we are doing our duty by society in declaring these individuals as irresponsible for their acts. In other words, should these individuals with marked and incorrectible criminalistic tendencies, be, so to speak, licensed to ignore the law in its entirety by giving them the protection of an insane asylum? Of course, from a broad, humane point of view, we must realize and appreciate that there is something distinctly wrong with these individuals, that their mental endowments are the essential factors which determine their behavior. On the other hand, we must not forget that these individuals fully realize that once they have been sent to an insane asylum, they are protected from punishment by law for all future time and they are ever ready to utilize this knowledge, as has been my experience with quite a number of recidivists, who somehow never get into an insane asylum until they are in the hands of the law. The scope of this paper will not permit me to enter into an extensive discussion on the treatment of these cases. I will say this, however,--that we are very far from having solved satisfactorily the question of the care of this particular class of insane criminals. As this paper is not primarily a discussion of the degenerative psychoses, I will refrain from reporting further cases. I believe I have shown by the preceding two cases that the mental disturbances of the degenerative individuals are essentially psychogenetic in origin.

NOTES

[1] VAN RENTERGHEM, A. W.: *Journal of Abnormal Psychology*, Jan.-Feb., 1915.

[2] KRAEPELIN, E.: "Psychiatrie." Achte Auflage. Leipzig, 1910. Bd. 1.

[3] REICH: "Ueber Akute SeelenstÃ¶rungen in der Gefangenschaft."
Allgem. Zeitschr. f. Psych., 1871, Bd. 27, p. 405.

[4] MOELI: Ueber irre Verbrecher, 1888.

[5] GANSER: "Ueber einen eigenartigen hysterischen DÃ¤mmerzustand."
Archiv f. Psych., 30, 1889.

[6] RAECKE: "Hysterischer Stupor bei Gefangenen." *Allgem. Zeitschr. f.
Psych.*, 18. 409, 1901.

[7] RAECKE: "Beitrag zur Kenntniss des hysterischen DÃ¤mmerzustandes."
Allgem. Zeitschr. f. Psych., 18. 115, 1901.

[8] KUTNER: "Ueber Katatonische Zustandsbilder bei Degenerierten."
Allgem. Zeitschr. f. Psych., 67, p. 363.

[9] SIEFERT: "Ueber die GeistesstÃ¶rungen der Strafhaft." Halle a. S.
1907.

[10] BONHOEFFER: "Klinische BeitrÃ¤ge zur Lehre von den
Degenerationspsychosen." Halle a. S. 1907.

[11] BRATZ: "Dass Krankheitsbild der Affect-Epilepsie." *Aerzt.
Sachverst.* Berlin, 1907. XIII. 112-116.

[12] STURROCK: "Certain Insane Conditions in Criminal Classes." *Journal
of Mental Science*, 56. 1910, p. 653.

[13] BIRNBAUM: "Psychosen mit Wahnbildungen und wahnhafte Einbildun-
gen
bei Degenerierten." Halle a. S. 1908.

CHAPTER II
THE NATURE AND TREATMENT OF
THE PSYCHOSES OF PRISONERS

Those who still believe in an exclusively materialistic theory of mental disorder must find it extremely difficult to maintain their doctrine in the face of the many incontrovertible facts brought to light through modern research in the field of psychopathology.

The modern trend in psychiatry is distinctly in the opposite direction. We no longer today insist upon material changes in cells and tissues for every psychotic phenomenon, but rather endeavor to investigate mental life, be it normal or abnormal, from the biologic point of view. We are being constantly confronted with the undeniable fact that whatever may be the physical substratum of mental disorder, it does not aid us in understanding the peculiar expression which a given psychosis chooses to assume. Why it is that one paretic greets us with the exalted mien of his grandiose delirium, while another spreads about him the gloom of a depressive delirium--the changes in the pyramidal cells do not explain. There must be, then, factors other than material ones which determine this.

Mental life, after all, expresses itself in a series of reactions destined to result in a proper adaptation to environmental conditions, and the causes which determine a given reaction may be psychic as well

as physical in nature. Indeed, in the realm of psychopathology we see
indubitable evidence of the predominance of psychic causes of mental
disorder over physical ones, and the subject under discussion here
further emphasizes this.

The problem of the prison psychoses, although extensively discussed in
psychiatric literature in the last half century, is far from being
solved, and for this and many other reasons deserves further attention.
The psychotic manifestations of prison life are of sufficient frequency
to deserve some definite place in our nosological tables; they develop
in a milieu artificially created by society, and if this milieu is
responsible for the production of mental disorder, it is of the utmost
importance, both from a preventative and curative standpoint, to
investigate the causes operative here, and lastly, these psychoses
concern individuals who form one of the most important problems society
has to deal with, and any light which the study of psychotic conditions
in these individuals may throw upon the general problem of crime and the
criminal, should be very much welcomed.

I fully believe that in time the study of the psychotic phenomena
developing in criminals will give us a correct insight into the nature
of the criminal personality and thus aid in the solution of that problem
which baffles criminologists today.

We know that while pure experimental psychology and psychopathology have
aided us in understanding the human mind both in health and disease, we
owe the bulk of our knowledge in this field to the investigations of
Nature's phenomena and experiments. The human mind, the most complex
and intricate organ, lends itself but very feebly to analysis when all its
component parts work in unison, and it is only when through disease it
has become, so to speak, disintegrated into its various units, that a
more ready access to it becomes possible. This is being fully
appreciated both by psychologists and psychopathologists. Mental

medicine, however, if it is viewed from the present-day broad conception of the term, must not confine itself exclusively to psychotic manifestations in the strictest sense of the word, but should embrace within its realm that great mass of unfortunates who populate our prisons, poorhouses and reformatories. It is now being universally recognized that the pauper, the prostitute, and the criminal classes are primarily products of mental defect and degeneracy and as such must come within the purview of mental medicine. This being the case, the same truisms which apply to the insane in general must likewise apply to the above-mentioned types.

We are here especially concerned with criminals who, because of a mental breakdown, have come under the observation of a psychiatrist, and if we agree with many eminent criminologists that the present juvenile state of this science and the ineffective methods of dealing with crime are due to a lack of proper scientific understanding of that anomalous species which is grouped under the term "criminal man", why not endeavor to solve this problem by approaching it from the psychiatric point of view. If the study of psychopathology has given us such valuable data concerning the normal mind, why not expect that a similar study applied to the insane criminal will bring to light some important facts concerning crime and the criminal in general. It is for this reason that that large group of mental disorders developing in criminals during imprisonment which has been included under the term "prison psychoses" is of special importance to the psychiatrist.

The older extensive literature on this subject, although very interesting from an historical standpoint, offers very little that is of scientific value, and it is only within recent years that a more rational approach to this problem has been attempted. It is easily conceivable that this branch of mental medicine must have shared the fortunes of psychiatry in general in its various phases of evolution, so that in the history of the prison psychoses are reflected the various views which in their day have dominated psychiatry. At present it is the school of degeneracy of Magnan and Moebius which is especially concerned with this problem.

Briefly stated, the exponents of this subject belong in a general way to either of the following two schools. The one maintains that the mental disorders occurring in prison differ in no way from those met with in freedom and that imprisonment at most but lends to them a peculiar common coloring which in itself, however, is not of essential importance. The other school takes a directly opposite view. The followers of the latter maintain that the mental disorders which they are wont to term "prison psychoses" are products of predisposition plus external factors. They differ from the true endogenous psychoses in that they are purely psychogenetic in character, and that their highly colored and extremely variable symptomatology is nothing more than a reactive manifestation of a particularly predisposed psyche to definite environmental conditions. According to them we are not dealing here with mental disorders whose origin, course, and termination are independent of the crime and imprisonment, as is the case in the ordinary well-known forms of functional and organic disorders developing in prison, but with psychotic manifestations which bear the most intimate relation to some definite situation, and which are characteristically colored and shaped by the prison milieu.

As a matter of fact, the population of institutions for insane criminals divides itself into two distinct and unmistakable groups. On the one hand we meet with the well-known functional and organic psychotic entities such as occur in individuals in freedom; we see patients who in the course of their careers as insane people have come in conflict with the law either accidentally or because of their insane ideas. In them the psychosis develops and takes its definitely determined course independently of the milieu in which the individual happens to be placed. In the majority of instances they suffer from the various forms

of dementia prÃ¦cox and progress toward demential end-results in the same
proportion as the general run of dementia prÃ¦cox cases do, whether or
not they have come in conflict with the law. Occasionally we also see a
case of organic brain disease or manic-depressive psychosis, and in more
frequent instances a case of epilepsy. The other, and according to many
authorities, by far the most predominant group of mental disorders met
with in imprisonment, belongs to the so-called "prison psychoses", and
bears definite, unmistakable ear-marks which differentiate it from the
former group. These are, as we have stated, products of a particularly
degenerative soil plus definite environmental conditions, and are of the
utmost importance both from a purely clinical and an administrative
point of view.

The term "reactive manifestation", as applied here, is a happy one, and
inasmuch as the accidental criminal differs from the habitual criminal
as day differs from night, we will expect a different sort of reaction
to a more or less similar situation in the two instances. To
illustrate:--An apparently healthy and in most instances law-abiding and
non-corrupt individual, as a result of a series of overwhelming and
uncontrollable circumstances, commits murder in a fit of passion. Upon
being arrested and upon the sudden realization of the enormity of his
deed the entire constitution experiences a tremendous shock and reacts
to it accordingly. He falls into a stupor, into utter oblivion of the
world about him, becomes in turn excited and confused, his senses begin
to functionate in a fallacious manner, and he thus succeeds in shutting
out from consciousness, for the time being at least, the entire
unbearable situation. Upon emerging from his stupor he has a more or
less complete amnesia for the deed and its attending circumstances, and
finding himself confronted with accusations, cross-examinations, and
lastly, conviction, he at once sets about, so to speak, to square
himself with the situation. What does he do? He develops a quite
limited, well-organized delusional system in which he finds himself
absolutely innocent, his accusers are the guilty ones, and the entire

situation is nothing more nor less than a well-planned plot to destroy him. His supposed victim has not been murdered at all, but is living and secretly active in plotting and scheming against him, the accused.

In this artificially created world he lives with comparative ease, and has thus succeeded in reaching a proper adjustment to the situation.

The most interesting part of it all is that this so well-organized and apparently fixed delusional system may disappear at once and the various false ideas may become entirely corrected as soon as the provocative agent which is at the bottom of it all is removed. This is a fair example of what has been termed an acute prison psychosis, and occurs with considerable frequency among prisoners awaiting trial. Naturally, these psychoses, being, as they are, psychologically motived, are extremely variable in their manifestations, but at the root they are all alike and impress the observer as something entirely different from the pure endogenous mental disorders. They are all psychically evoked reactive manifestations of a particularly predisposed constitution to definite deleterious environmental conditions. Some of the cases reported in the first paper of this series are good examples of this type of mental disorder.

We owe our knowledge of these disorders to the contributions of Reich, Moeli, Kutner, Ganser, Rish and others, authors who, although describing a more or less identical symptom-complex, have given to it different names, such as hysterical stupor, Ganser symptom-complex, catatonia of degenerates, etc. The distinguishing features of this disorder are its psychic origin, that is, its development in consequence of some strongly affective experience, and its high grade of impressionability to things in the environment which may at any time suddenly cause a complete transition from deep stupor to normal manner and behavior.

The symptomatology consists of an acute delirioid, hallucinatory episode, usually followed by a more or less complete amnesia which may go back far enough to include the experience which provoked the disorder. Such delusional formation as takes place after the disappearance of the fulminant symptoms may well be considered as part of the repair process, a mechanism which in most instances reflects the individual's endeavor to adjust himself to an unpleasant, unbearable situation, and must not be looked upon necessarily as an indication of the progressiveness of the disorder.

As we have stated before, complete correction of all delusional ideas may suddenly take place upon the removal of the causative factor at the bottom of the entire situation.

As to the treatment of this acute prison psychotic complex theoretically, we should have no difficulty in deciding this question. We are dealing with the sequelÃ¦ of some definite situation, and the removal of that situation may be, and actually is, in most instances, sufficient to bring about recovery. When we come, however, to deal with concrete instances in daily practice, the problem does not lend itself so easily to solution.

What of the man who upon being arrested following the commission of murder, develops a psychosis while awaiting trial, or who having been found guilty of murder develops a psychosis while awaiting execution? The first question which the psychiatrist is called upon to decide in many instances is that of malingering. To the lay mind and to the minds of many of our eminent--but psychiatrically uninformed--jurists the question of malingering suggests itself at once. To them it is perfectly evident that this development of a mental disorder, in the wake of a criminal act, is nothing but a timely preparation for the "insanity dodge." The clinical pictures presented by the acute prison psychosis are especially apt to awaken suspicions of malingering in the minds of the untrained. We see individuals who apparently never before showed any evidence of mental disorder, and who immediately following the commission of a criminal act manifest pictures of grave alienation. Many of them don't know how much twice two is, are absolutely ignorant of the most elementary subjects, remember nothing of the deed, and most important of all fashion their deliria in such a way as to entirely negate the deed, or at any rate justify it.

But why cannot all these manifestations be genuine? Many of us no doubt recall the effect which examinations have upon certain students. The emotional accompaniment of the examination, especially the emotion of fright, causes many a student to forget facts which he knew as well as his own name, and which he is able readily and fully to recollect as soon as the examination is over. Are we to assume that these students are malingering? Decidedly not. Why then should we question at all the genuineness of a mental disorder developing in an individual who faces the gallows or a life-long imprisonment? As a matter of fact cases of pure malingering are among the rarest things which the psychiatrist observes. Wilmanns,[1] in his study of 277 cases of insanity of prisoners, found but two cases of simulation, and in a later review of the diagnoses of the same series of cases, the two cases of malingering do not appear at all. Bonhoeffer[2] in a study of 221 cases of insane criminals found 0.5 per cent of malingerers. This is the experience of everyone who comes in contact with these cases, and there are others who go so far as to maintain that every malingerer of mental symptoms is mentally defective.

But let us assume that we have succeeded in convincing those concerned of the genuineness of the disease at hand; what line of treatment should be recommended? In the first place, we must remember that the mental disorder, if it belongs to the group we are discussing here, is the result of a criminal act, and following in its wake, and that therefore the plea of insanity as an excuse for the deed must manifestly be excluded. But may not this type of reaction furnish us an index to the original personality of the culprit? In other words, should we consider an individual absolutely normal, if, in reaction to some stressful situation, he breaks down mentally and develops a psychosis? The majority of authorities maintain that these individuals are decidedly abnormal, and that it is only a poorly-knit organism which permits of that sort of reaction. Birnbaum,[3] for instance, insists that the possibility of a psychic incitation of a mental disorder is the criterion of a degenerative soil. This is undoubtedly too extreme a view, but the more one observes these cases, the more one is inclined to hesitate in calling these individuals normal in the accepted sense of the term. Let us assume for the moment that these psychotic reactions are indices of an abnormal personality. Is this defect of sufficient import to render the individual irresponsible in the eyes of the law? This question, I fear, cannot be answered very readily. Looking at it from a purely juridical standpoint, we must say no; because an individual is so loosely organized as to break down mentally under a given stress, does not at all imply that a knowledge of the difference between right and wrong is excluded. The jurist is willing to concede to the proposition of a poorly-organized nervous system, a degenerative make-up, a psychopathic constitution; but if these defects are such as to manifest themselves in crime, society must be given the inalienable right to protect itself from such defectives. The result is that either no extenuating circumstances are considered at all, and the individual is dealt with in the ordinary way, or he is adjudged insane and committed to a hospital for the criminal insane, whether or no insanity exists at the time of trial. Thus we have on the one hand a prison population which more properly belongs under the régime of a hospital, while on the other hand, we insist on keeping individuals locked up in hospitals for the insane, whether or no they show actual psychotic symptoms. If one of the latter class endeavors to obtain his release by habeas corpus, a tremendous howl is immediately raised by the public about the "insanity dodge", the worthlessness of expert testimony and the unpardonable offense of letting loose upon society a dangerous criminal. If we stop to consider for a moment, we must admit that in the great majority of instances, we are not dealing here with dangerous criminals. The man who as a result of a series of overwhelming circumstances over which he had little or no control, kills another in a fit of passion, is not necessarily a dangerous criminal. In the majority of cases it is fair to assume that such an individual will never again in his life have to cope with a similar set of circumstances. The great majority of these people have led, up to that single crime of their life, an honest, peaceful existence, and the instances of an accidental criminal turning recidivist are extremely rare.

Society looks on complacently at the repeated sentencing of the habitual criminal and watches without alarm the never failing phenomenon of how each successive imprisonment only serves to deprave him more profoundly; it never considers the danger of letting this type of criminal loose to prey upon it; just so he has served his just and legally prescribed sentence. But let the victim of the "insanity dodge" prejudice endeavor to gain his freedom, and society is at once up in arms.

Thus the matter stands, and until the public learns to know its criminals as they actually are, this problem will remain unsolved. The prognosis of the acute prison psychotic complex is good in the majority of instances. The removal to a hospital rÃ©gime usually serves to put a stop to the process and it is important for the expert witness to bear this in mind for obvious reasons.

We have thus far discussed the psychoses developing in prisoners awaiting trial, and we shall now turn to that group of cases which are sent to us from penal institutions which serve for the confinement of the convicted criminal.

At the outset we shall endeavor to draw a distinction between the class of individuals we have just discussed, and that which we are about to consider now. We have seen that the former is made up of individuals who in most instances have come in conflict with the law for the first time, and that the mental disorder which they develop stands in the closest relation with some definite experience in their life. The patients who come to us from prisons and penitentiaries on account of some mental disorder which developed while they were undergoing sentence are in most instances habitual criminals with a marked criminal career back of them. They differ so essentially from the preceding group, that what has been said about the former can hardly apply here.

The first really worthy contribution to this subject was made by Siefert,[4] the physician in charge of the psychiatric department of the penitentiary at Halle. He published, in 1907, the results of a study of eighty-three prisoners who became insane while serving sentences. He divided his patients into two sharply differentiated groups, the true psychoses, *i.e.*, the well-known forms of functional and organic mental disorders, and the degenerative psychoses, *i.e.*, psychotic episodes developing upon a soil of degeneracy and which according to him form the typical prison psychoses. Before we go any further it must be mentioned that Siefert did not take into consideration the mental disorders developing in prisoners awaiting trial.

"The true psychoses develop out of endogenous causes, attack and manifest themselves in the prisoner in the same way as in any law-abiding individual in freedom. They are not essentially influenced by changes of environment and there exists no intimate relation between the coloring of the symptomatology and the influence of the imprisonment. The degenerative psychoses, on the other hand, develop upon the well-characterized degenerative soil of the habitual criminal, and are products of predisposition plus environmental influence. They stand in the most intimate relation to the deleteriousness of prison life, and are therefore influenced to the greatest extent by change of environment."

On studying critically Siefert's work one gains the conviction that the author not only undertakes to solve certain clinical questions, but endeavors to investigate the problem of the relation between crime and mental disorder. Although he paid the strictest attention to the individual symptoms and described in an excellent manner the manifold and varying symptomatology of these psychoses, he did not succeed in isolating a symptom-complex which might be considered as typical of the degenerative psychoses, and thus deserve the independence of a distinct clinical entity. Above all he occupied himself with the investigation and delineation of the various anomalous individualities, the degenerative constitutions upon which these psychotic manifestations engraft themselves. Thus he divided his prison psychoses into groups like the "simple degenerative", "hysterical degenerative", "phantastic degenerative", etc. Siefert undoubtedly overshot the mark in his clear-cut differentiation between the various types, but he unquestionably contributed a most important work on this subject.

Let us now endeavor to illustrate what he means by this degenerative soil giving rise to these psychoses. As we have stated, the great majority of them are full-fledged habitual criminals and can be easily recognized by their "degenerative habitus." They are that indolent, obstinate, querulent, unapproachable, and irritable class of prisoners who form the bane of prison officials. Constantly in trouble of some sort, they are subject to frequent disciplinary measures, which, however, serve not in the least to improve their conduct. Their extremely fluctuating mood and emotional instability calls forth a quite unfounded wild rebellion against the prison régime. They are constantly after the physician with numerous hypochondriacal complaints, such as a nervous heart, digestive disturbances, insomnia, etc. In short, they impress one as something abnormal, something entirely different from the ordinary prisoner. On this basis, now and then more marked, definite psychotic manifestations engraft themselves. Here and there one of them starts to speak of nightly visions, complains about a feeling of anxiety, speaks of suspicious noises and voices in the vicinity, and finally makes a superficial, ineffectual attempt at suicide. Others become suddenly more antagonistic, vehemently assert their innocence, speak of being the victims of false accusations, etc. Still others suddenly develop a wild, maniacal state, destroy everything within reach, become markedly hallucinated, elaborate various persecutory ideas, and finally have to be transferred to an insane asylum. Here they soon quiet down, the active symptoms subside without leaving any trace behind them, insight may or may not be complete. The characterological anomaly which is at the bottom of the disorder, however, remains, and any necessity for the application of more stringent administrative measures may serve to set the entire process aflame again.

Another group of psychopaths who are prone to develop prison psychoses are those primitive, superficially endowed individuals with a high degree of auto-suggestibility, a marked tendency to phantastic lying, and instability of mood, individuals who have always led a sort of humdrum existence without aim or goal of any kind in view. They drift very early into a life of crime and vagabondage, become addicted to all of the vices which cross their path, are markedly egotistical, have no conception of social life, frequently desert their wives and families, and a great many of them finally end their days in jails or poorhouses.

Upon being imprisoned they are unable to adjust themselves to the strict rÃ©gime, find difficulty in acquainting themselves with the prison regulations and in consequence have to be frequently disciplined. As a result they begin to misinterpret things in the environment and see in these disciplinary measures nothing but persecution on the part of the prison officials. They become suspicious, seclusive, introspective, spend sleepless nights, until suddenly, in the stillness of night, they perceive isolated phonemes. This strengthens their suspicions. They refuse food, become apprehensive, the hallucinations reach a more definite character, until finally they manifest a well-marked persecutory delirium, or may fall into a semi-delirious stuporous state, show numerous catatonic symptoms, become destructive and untidy, and in general present a picture very similar to true catatonia.

Removal to the hospital ward frequently serves to put a stop to the process at once, and often before reaching the hospital for the insane they show no traces of the acute mental disorder.

The foregoing are types of degenerative psychoses met with in imprisonment, and there can be no question that the prison milieu is the etiologic factor here.

To speak here of a progressive disorder to which imprisonment only gives a characteristic coloring is entirely erroneous. A psychosis which is definitely brought on by a certain environment and which is corrected as soon as the environment is changed, must be looked upon as the product of that environment. That the degenerative soil which permits of the development of these disorders cannot be looked upon as a basic disorder, something like dementia prÃ¦cox, is likewise unquestionable. These individuals have always shown the same traits of character; it is these very same anomalies which brought them in their childhood days in conflict with the school authorities, which later made them inmates of reformatories, and which finally were at the bottom of their habitual criminality. Finally, the total absence of progression to more or less definite end-results excludes the possibility of an organically determined progressive disorder. A psychosis which develops in imprisonment and progresses irrespective of the change of milieu is not a prison psychosis in the sense that this term is here used. The following cases are illustrative of the type under discussion.

  CASE I.--A. F., aged 31 years; admitted to the Government Hospital for the Insane April 7, 1911. Father alcoholic; died of cancer of liver and stomach. Mother died of tuberculosis. One brother has been confined in the Gowanda State Hospital for the Insane for past five or six years; has always been an excessive alcoholic. One sister, aged 42, has tuberculosis. One of her children died of tuberculosis of the bones. Another sister is hyper-religious and eccentric.

Patient was born at Olean, New York, in 1871. He knows of nothing unusual attending his birth or childhood. He entered school at the age of six, and attended irregularly for six or seven years. He was usually older than the other children in his class, and was held back a year in the third and fourth grades. He left school at the age of fourteen, while in the fourth grade. He then worked in a shoe store, commencing at a salary of four dollars per week, and receiving six dollars per week at the time of his separation. As far as is known he did his work well, as he was promoted during his stay there. Soon after commencing to earn money he began to indulge in alcoholics. He became intoxicated one day and set fire to a store, which resulted in the death of a human being. It did not take much at that time to intoxicate him--two or three glasses of whiskey being sufficient. He does not definitely say why he set the place on fire; adding, "Perhaps I was drunk and did not know what I was doing and maybe I just wanted to see the fire. I always did like to see fires. Of course, I did not know that somebody was going to get burned to death." He is not certain whether he felt sorry for the deed, adding: "Why should I care? I did not know the man that was burned. He was no relative or friend of mine; anyway, the people around there said he was no good, and that it served him right." He was sent to the Elmira Reformatory, where he remained three years, when he was transferred to the New York State Hospital for Criminal Insane at Matteawan. He did not like the Reformatory a bit, they were nagging him all the time. He says it was like a deaf and dumb asylum; a fellow could not even talk when he wanted to, and if he did he was paddled for it. The paddling didn't make him behave, because, he adds: "You can't make a fellow behave by beating him all the time." He was later transferred to Dannemora, spending about two years in all, in both these institutions. He did not like it at the hospital either, because they made him work, and he hated to work; so finally he asked to be transferred back to Elmira, which request was granted him. On returning there he was put to work at brick-laying, but could not get along with the fellow in charge, the latter was too much of a bully and worked him too hard, so finally, they shipped him to the new reformatory at Napanoch, New York. Here he was given employment by the physician in charge of the hospital, and after ten months of good conduct, was paroled. He says he behaved well these ten months because he was treated well by the doctor. Upon being paroled, he returned to Olean and obtained a position in a tannery where he worked for six months, receiving two dollars per night. He was drinking heavily all this time, and one night, failing to return to work, owing to his intoxicated condition, was discharged. He states that the above is the longest he ever worked at any occupation since. Shortly after being discharged, he was arrested in company with several others for robbing a post office. He was about twenty-three years of age then. He claims that he had nothing to do with this robbery, and it was just an unfortunate accident that he got mixed up in it. He was placed in the jail, and while there the warden tried to poison him. He developed various ideas that poison was placed in his food, that his stomach was all dried up, and because he would not eat, he adds: "They sent him over to this Hospital,--the Government Hospital for the Insane."

He was admitted here the first time on May 29, 1904, on a medical certificate which stated: "About April 19, 1904, he refused to take food and claimed to be kidnapped. He had delusions of persecution--said his head was full of nails and requested that his brain be cut up. Said the President was his friend."

On August 1st, he eloped while at work in company with another patient. The record of his mental disturbance at that time is very meagre, and nothing of a definite nature can be obtained from it.

From here he beat part of his way, and walked part of the way to Cincinnati, where he had a sister living. One night he heard her talking to her husband about sending him back to the hospital, so he robbed them of what money they had in the house, bought a revolver and returned to Olean. He says he bought the revolver to protect himself from a certain police captain at Olean. He frequently refers to this man in a vindictive and abusive manner. States that this police captain was after him all the time; that whenever any crime was committed in the city, he was immediately suspected. He was "tired of this" and bought the gun, intending to kill the police officer if he should bother him any more. Here he adds: "Anyhow, the cur was killed afterwards, I am glad of it." After a series of crimes, tramping and debauchery, during which he suffered from an attack of delirium tremens, and served a sentence of nine months in a Pennsylvania jail, he was again arrested for a post office robbery and sentenced to five years at Leavenworth, whence he was transferred to this institution April 7, 1911.

As has been stated, he commenced to indulge in alcoholics at a very early age and has continued this habit during his lifetime. He states that he had an attack of delirium tremens, during which he received a severe burn on his left arm by jumping out of a window into a bonfire, while trying to escape imaginary persecutors. During the years 1903-04, he was addicted to the steady use of morphine and cocaine. He has led a very loose sexual life; has been infected with gonorrhÅ"a on numerous occasions, and contracted syphilis several years ago. He has never married. He intended to marry once, but the girl, he discovered, was not true to him, so he gave her up. He is a Catholic, attends church occasionally when at liberty, and was in the habit of going to confession while at the Penitentiary.

The medical certificate on his present admission stated that on the night of March 20, 1911, the patient was reported for shouting while in his cell, claiming that invisible enemies were shocking him with electricity. There were no symptoms observable before that. Has delusions of persecution in which invisible enemies are continually shocking him with electricity and other means and are planning to do him other bodily harm.

He complained of not being able to sleep and of being tortured. Said they wired his cell and gave him an electric shock; that he spoke to the President of the United States and was told that the latter would visit him.

On March 22d, complained of being choked by supposed workmen. Later he stated that he had been kidnapped at Erie, Pennsylvania, and expected the President of the United States to get him out in a few days. He requested the doctor to send for a priest, complained that they had failed to send for the President as promised. Said that he had received a severe shock the night before from the people upstairs, and stated that they had stored two thousand volts to turn on him. Following this, he was restless at night and was apprehensive of being burned to death. Finally he wrote a letter to the President in which he complained that his life and health were in grave danger; that he was the victim of a conspiracy, and was being detained illegally at the Penitentiary, stating that when he was walking peaceably along the railroad track, he was kidnapped by enemies who had a design upon his life. He was arrested and while in jail these same officers robbed the post office and later accused him of the crime. They bribed a witness to testify at the trial against him and because of this he received an unjust sentence of five years. He believed that the friends of the chief of police of his home town, Olean, New York, were paying large sums of money to the warden of the Leavenworth Penitentiary in an endeavor to have him electrocuted, and that their efforts had nearly proven successful, as he had been tortured night and day for the past month, in fact he was unable to stand it any longer, and if the President did not come to his relief at once, he intended to take the matter in his own hands and make short work of the warden. He thought he was accused of the murder of the police officer who was killed in his home town, but he insisted that at the time of the murder he was locked up in jail, hence could not have done this.

The patient continued in this trend of thought and conduct until his transfer to this institution, April 7, 1911.

On admission here he talked in a coherent manner, was clear mentally and quite well oriented. He reiterated the story given above, namely,--that he was kidnapped in Pennsylvania on a trumped-up charge of post office robbery, was tried by a "phony" court and sentenced to five years at Leavenworth. Soon after arriving there the warden had an electrical apparatus rigged up with which he was tortured constantly. He complained to the doctor about this and begged to be put in a cell so he could get some sleep as he could not sleep in his cell on account of these electric shocks. He heard them saying from above that they were going to torture him. One night they had him paralyzed on one side.

In an endeavor to explain these persecutions he stated that probably the railroad police who arrested him were friends of the police captain at Olean with whom he had had trouble for a long time, and who was later killed by someone; that probably they blamed him for this killing, and that for this reason they framed up the charge of post office robbery against him. He believed that the electrocuting which he was receiving at Leavenworth was a part of this scheme to get rid of him, as he knew that the police captain at Olean was a friend of the warden of the Penitentiary. In giving this recital he was somewhat irritable and nervous, constantly rubbing his head and face in a troubled manner. He kept to himself, making no acquaintances with those about him and was apparently somewhat worried and apprehensive. He slept well the first night, stating that nobody bothered him. He stated that he was not insane, that there was nothing wrong with his mind. When asked why he was sent here, said simply because of a trick, that he was told that he was coming to the President to secure a pardon, and instead of this, was brought to this institution. He was quite unstable emotionally, very surly and irritable, and soon transferred his persecutory ideas to the officials of this institution. He complained of having electricity on him; stated that the warden at Leavenworth rigged up a wireless apparatus whereby he could send wireless messages to him constantly. Stated that he had been chloroformed at night and that his body was lined with electric wires through which electricity was running all the time. He became very abusive to the physician, stating that the latter was in league with the officials at the penitentiary to torture him. This state of affairs continued, with the addition of the delusional idea that the physician was endeavoring to hypnotize him, until the early part of September, 1911, when he acquired full insight into his mental disturbance, realizing fully that the various ideas which he expressed were delusional, and that he must have been suffering from mental disorder at the time.

Mental examination revealed no defect, and his knowledge was quite in accord with his educational advantages. Morally, he was distinctly defective. Physical examination showed various stigmata of degeneration, such as asymmetry of the face; large outstanding and flattened ears; narrow and dome-shaped palate; irregularly placed teeth; prominent parietal bones; two symmetrical depressions on the occiput; congenital flat-footedness; and a sullen facial expression. His arms were covered with tattoo marks. Sense of pain somewhat diminished. Sympathetic reactions could not be elicited. Wassermann reaction with blood serum nearly complete positive.

The patient finally recovered from his mental disorder, and on January 16, 1912, was returned to the penitentiary to serve out the remainder of his sentence. At this writing, November, 1915, nothing further has been heard from him.

We have before us an individual who to start with, is badly tainted hereditarily. His childhood history is indefinite, aside from his statements of having been usually the lowest in his class at school. He launched upon an industrial career at a very early period in life and simultaneously with commencing to earn money he began to indulge in alcoholics. His industrial career was cut short soon after. He gets drunk and sets fire to a store, causing the death of a human being. This, at the age of seventeen. His moral status can readily be surmised when we remember his reply to the question as to whether he was sorry for the deed. "Why should I be sorry? I didn't know the man that was burned." The usual course of the law was taken in the case and he was placed in a reformatory. He spent nearly six years between that institution and hospitals for the criminal insane, when he was released on parole. It is of interest to note here how he reacted to the stress of confinement in the reformatory. We find that on two occasions during this period it became necessary to transfer him to an insane asylum. We shall have occasion to refer to this again later.

If there ever existed in him any chance for reform, the reformatory apparently killed it, for his life since then has been an uninterrupted chain of crime and debauchery. He has been a prey to all the vices of modern civilization; he is a confirmed alcoholic, was addicted to the habitual use of morphine and cocaine; has been infected on numerous occasions with gonorrhÅ"a; has contracted syphilis and received a serious burn during an attack of delirium tremens. In all, he spent eight of the past fourteen years in penitentiaries, jails, and institutions for the criminal insane, and has, now, an indictment for larceny hanging over him. Released from a six years' confinement he finds himself thrown upon his own resources and is confronted for the first time with the problem of providing for himself. The poorly-begotten organism, whose start in life, already deficient in those attributes and forces which are so essential for an effective struggle for existence and which was rendered still more deficient by a six years' sojourn among criminals, finds himself unable to cope with conditions as they exist, and several months after his release from imprisonment we again find him arrested for robbery. Being taken hold of by the law does not mend matters in the least. On the contrary, we see the same tendency to break under the stress of imprisonment, with the overwhelming burden of an enforced routine existence, reassert itself as on the former occasion, and in reaction to the situation he develops a psychosis which necessitates his transfer to an insane asylum. Placed under the less exacting rÃ©gime of a hospital, he soon recovers and avails himself of the first opportunity for an escape which presents itself. Finding himself again at freedom he endeavors to find some explanation for his unfortunate position in life and in the midst of this he discovers that his sister is planning to return him to the hospital. Even his own sister is against him. He begins to assume that paranoid view of life which characterizes his later existence. Now he knows where the trouble lies. The whole world is against him; no wonder he can't get along; his own sister is trying to force him back into the hands of his persecutors. His own deficiencies and incapacities he projects upon the environment. It is the world about that is at fault; not he. They are after him all the time. He buys a gun with which to protect himself, and with renewed antagonism against society in general he defiantly launches upon a career of crime and vice. Again taken hold of by the law, the old story repeats itself. He lands in an insane asylum.

Upon an analysis of the content of his psychosis, we find that he elaborates a story of having been kidnapped in Pennsylvania, upon a trumped up charge of robbery, taken before a "phony" judge and given an unjust sentence of five years. The police officers who arrested him were friends of the murdered police captain at Olean and were hired to do this job, because he (the patient) was suspected of having had something to do with this murder. He dreads being placed in the penitentiary because he knows the warden is likewise against him, being a friend of the murdered police captain and might perhaps be in league with his persecutors and take this opportunity of avenging himself upon the suspected murderer, and sure enough, soon after his arrival at the penitentiary, the warden has an electrical apparatus rigged up with which to torture him, etc. His psychosis takes the usual course, he recovers soon after having been removed from the oppressing environment.

The question arises here, "Are we dealing with a psychosis which engrafts itself upon the individual without any apparent cause, a psychosis possessing a course and termination wholly independent of outside influences, a psychosis having no tangible relation to any definite situation; or have we here a psychogenetic disorder, a pathologic reaction of a degenerative constitution to an unfavorable situation, a paranoid picture developing as an outgrowth of the individual in reaction to a definite experience?" In other words, are we dealing here with a case of dementia prÃ¦cox, or with one of the degenerative psychoses? If we agree with Stransky[5] that dementia prÃ¦cox depends upon an intrapsychic ataxia, that it is the disturbed coÃ¶rdination between the intellectual and affective faculties of the individual which makes the picture of dementia prÃ¦cox what it is; this is not a case of dementia prÃ¦cox. The acute emotional reaction to all situations which this man manifests, the development of the psychosis in consequence of the depth of his feelings concerning the unpleasant experiences and the entire absence of this important incoÃ¶rdination between his feeling and acting, would, in itself be sufficient to separate his psychosis from dementia prÃ¦cox. If we agree with Kraepelin

and others that dementia prÃ¦cox has a more or less definite onset, a
more or less definite course and termination in a dissolution of the
individual's psyche, our case is not one of dementia prÃ¦cox. Our patient
has had the same attributes of character and personality always. There
is no indication in his life history of a definite onset of a retrograde
process, or of any progression towards dissolution. His psychosis, such
as it is, is the outgrowth of his degenerative personality, and if we
assume this to be true, if we consider the psychotic manifestations of
this individual as a pathologic expression of his anomalous personality,
the question arises--to what extent have his criminal acts likewise been
pathologic expressions of the same underlying degenerative basis? I
believe that the relation between the criminality and mental alienation
of this man is analogous to that existing between two branches of the
same tree. The same degenerative soil which makes the development of the
psychosis possible in one case, expresses itself in crime in another
instance. The factors which determine whether the one or the other phase
will manifest itself, depend largely upon environmental conditions, and
are accidental in nature. The stresses which these defective individuals
meet with in freedom need not have such a strong influence upon them as
to produce a psychosis. The want of moral attributes makes it possible
for them readily to surmount many difficulties by means of some criminal
act, difficulties which in a normal person would require extraordinary
effort to remove. When placed, however, under the stress of imprisonment
where they can neither slip away from under the oppressive situation,
nor square themselves with it by some criminal act, the organism becomes
affected to such a degree that the development of a psychosis is greatly
facilitated. The character of the delusional fabric of these individuals
is such that one can easily find a ready and more or less correct
explanation for it. It is chiefly a compensatory reaction in an endeavor
to make a certain unpleasant situation acceptable.

CASE II.--J. H., aged 37. Admitted to the Government Hospital for
the Insane, March 8, 1909. Maternal grandfather died suddenly from

unknown cause. Was a race-track operator. Father alcoholic. Mother
suffered from vertiginous attacks. There were twenty-one children in
the family, fifteen of whom died in infancy. One brother died of brain
tumor. One sister is neurotic; her eight year old son suffers from
congenital heart disease. Patient was born in Manchester, England. He
was the twentieth child; mother was over forty years old at the time
of his birth. He was an unusually small and puny infant and remembers
using crutches when a child. At seven he was bitten by a dog and
dragged about on the ground for a great distance; when finally
rescued was unconscious for a long time. No further ill-effects.
School life was characterized throughout by truancy and disobedience
and finally terminated in expulsion. At that early period of life he
already showed marked egotism, extreme vindictiveness and an utter
disregard for consequences. The immediate cause of his expulsion from
school was a fistic encounter with a teacher. At the age of eleven,
his family immigrated to this country. He states that he was different
from other boys of his age, did not care for the ordinary childhood
sports, and the only friends he had were a young sister and a dog. He
states that he couldn't get along somehow with the other boys, that he
often thought that the whole world was trying to down him and
persecute him. About that time someone stole his dog. He brooded over
this so much that he finally jumped into a creek, intending to commit
suicide, but was rescued by bystanders. He has made several other
attempts at suicide in later life. In describing these he elaborates
them with a lot of fanciful trimming, dilates on the importance of the
various situations attending them, and how much uproar they caused
among those who knew of them. At the age of fourteen he had a quarrel
with another boy. Upon being reprimanded by the latter's father, he
could not rest until he had obtained a gun and fired at the boy's
father while the latter was sitting at the supper table with his
family. In relating this incident he states with great vanity that he
fully intended to kill the boy's father; he wasn't going to be
insulted by anyone and let it go at that. Here was probably the first

well-illustrated instance of his pathologic emotionalism, the tendency to a complete dominance of a certain affect. He was committed to some sort of an industrial school for a year. Upon his release from there he went to work in a machine shop in his native town. One day a couple of gentlemen and a lady walked through the shop and stopped in front of the machine on which he was working. He did not like this, became angered, picked up the dog which followed them and threw it into the oil tank which fed his machine. At sixteen he ran away from home. He gives a history of an industrial career and apparently he had no difficulty in learning a trade, and it is quite likely that he was a skilled workman. His entire industrial career, however, is characterized by an inability to fit harmoniously into the situation at hand, not because of an intellectual deficiency, but because of the disharmony between his various mental faculties. His extreme sensitiveness and emotionalism, his vindictiveness, the total lack of a sense of responsibility, his impulsive existence, all these, were always at play in his relations with man. If to these be added his extreme egotism and vanity, the reasons for his conflicts become clear. "Here, the foreman thought he knew more than I did." "There, I did not like the way they were running the business," etc. Among his occupations, saloon-keeping and professional gambling played an important rôle. He finally gave up all attempts at leading an honest existence and turned to crime. Our record of the man in this regard is rather incomplete, but according to his record at the Secret Service Bureau, he was sentenced in 1890 to a two years' term for highway robbery. In 1902 to three years for counterfeiting; in 1904 to three and a-half, and in 1908 to six years for the same offense. These sentences were incurred under various aliases. He married at a very early age. He says he made up his mind one night to get married and two days later was married. His conjugal life, like everything else he engaged in, proved a failure and was characterized by repeated desertions. He commenced using alcoholics at a very early age and has indulged excessively all his lifetime. He has had several gonorrhœal

infections, and has an active luetic infection at the present time.
On May 5, 1908, he was sentenced to a six years' term of
imprisonment. Soon after it became necessary to perform an operation
for appendicitis, and upon recovering he began to complain of having
been cut open and of having had poison put inside of him. The U. S.
Government sent men down to the prison who were threatening to kill
him. He saw detectives from Washington whom he recognized. He was very
apprehensive and refused to submit himself to an examination, and made
homicidal attacks upon the officers. On March 8, 1909, he was admitted
to this institution. His conduct here was characterized throughout his
entire stay by the same attributes of character which were at play
throughout his entire antisocial existence. He was at all times very
emotional. He was very sensitive, becoming offended on the least
provocation, and when laboring under some imaginary grievance his
antagonism and vindictiveness knew no bounds. He was constantly
plotting and scheming some means of inciting a revolt among the other
inmates and took every opportunity to put himself forth as the
champion of the other patients. He was very egotistical and vain and
showed a marked tendency to interpret most trivial occurrences in his
environment as having some reference to him. He was always ready to
endow every incident with a personal note of prejudice. He showed
throughout marked fluctuations of mood. One never knew what sort of a
reception one would meet. He was a pathological liar, was keenly alert
to everything that transpired about him and was always ready to
utilize every incident to his own advantage. He was depraved to a very
marked degree morally. He gave his past history without the least sign
of regret and when questioned concerning the reason of his criminal
life, he objected strenuously to being called a criminal, insisting
that what he did was right. At times he impressed one by his mode of
reaction to various daily occurrences as being as naÃ¯ve as a child
and suggestible to a very marked degree. He frequently threatened to
commit suicide if refused some of his impossible requests and showed a
marked tendency to hypochondriasis and exaggeration of actual ills. On

this basis he developed various persecutory ideas, exclusively against those who had anything to do with his care and safe-keeping. The warden at the jail before he came here tried to poison him and took the opportunity of accomplishing this while he (the patient) was undergoing an operation. The Government sent Secret Service men down to watch him and persecute him. Here the physicians are doing the same thing. They are trying to down him, to make his life miserable for him, etc. Throughout his sojourn here he was clearly oriented, knew everything that was going on and failed to show the least indication of the existence of a deteriorating process. He showed also a marked tendency to write a good deal of poetry and fiction in which he spoke of himself as a martyr who had been persecuted and downed all his lifetime. His stories were of a fantastic, adventurous kind, in which gambling, shooting, and similar highly melodramatic situations were enacted. On July 17, 1911, he was returned to prison as recovered. Another point of interest in this case and one to which I have briefly alluded before, was his tendency to the exaggeration of symptoms and to malingering, but the malingering which he manifested was of the kind that the child manifests in an endeavor to attract attention to itself and to arouse the sympathy of those about him.

Here again we have before us a kaleidoscopic picture of the life of a human being who from childhood showed tendencies so antisocial, so criminalistic, that it is hard to get away from the belief that most of the attributes which went to make him just what he is, must have been inherited. Let us take this poorly-begotten organism and follow it through life. We shall see how its existence has been a continuous round of conflicts with everything it came in contact. He entered school and meets with the first obligation, with the first necessity for a well-regulated, purposive existence. What is the result? Truancy, disobedience, and finally expulsion--not because of intellectual deficiency, but because of those same attributes which later served to put him in the penitentiary. It was the first evidence of his pathologic emotionalism and vindictiveness. We next see him in an effort to lead an industrial life, but here, too, everything he does proves a failure, and likewise not because of intellectual deficiency, but because of a disharmony, a disproportion, between his various mental faculties. He could not, somehow, submit himself to any well-regulated existence. His egotism and absolute lack of the sense of responsibility made it impossible for him to adjust himself effectively to the world about him. He next tries matrimony, and the same story reasserts itself. His conjugal life is characterized by repeated desertions; and thus he becomes steadily more debased, more depraved, sinks to the level of the professional gambler and finally even this becomes too strenuous for him, and he turns to a life of crime. At the age of forty we find him with a record of numerous arrests, and as far as known, one-fourth of his lifetime has thus far been spent in jails and penitentiaries. The characterological anomalies at the bottom of his career came to the front already in his childhood days. Before completing his fourteenth year we find him deliberately planning the murder of a human being because of an insult. His idea concerning that situation has not changed in the least since then. He now speaks of it without the least sign of remorse or regret. As a matter of fact, he is inclined to impress one as being rather proud of that deed, and he cannot see the criminality of it. The atavistic nature of his act in throwing the dog into the oil tank is quite evident. Then his attempts at suicide throughout his lifetime, evidence of a pathologic emotionalism, must also be remembered. These are a few examples of his mode of reaction to everyday occurrences in life. Is it at all strange that he has developed finally into the habitual criminal? On the contrary, it would be rather strange that an individual with such attributes should turn out to be an honest, peaceful citizen. He likewise was a prey to all the vices of modern civilization, and these, as in the preceding case, unquestionably added to the dissolution of the originally defective organism. We finally meet with an illustration of the other phase of his mode of reaction. Following imprisonment on a charge of robbery, he develops a psychosis which necessitates his transfer to an insane asylum. Brief as the description of his psychosis has been, it is sufficient to illustrate that here we are likewise dealing with a psychogenetic disorder manifesting itself as a reactive expression of a degenerative constitution to an unpleasant situation. Shortly after his arrest he is being operated upon for appendicitis and upon recovery elaborates the idea that the warden of the jail, one of the members of that large class against whom he has been warring all his lifetime, takes this opportunity of placing poison in his body. He sees and hears people around his cell whom he recognizes as Secret Service men sent down from Washington to torture him. On his transfer to our Hospital he readily carries over his delusional ideas to the officials here. He is simply being persecuted by a bunch of anarchists, who are trying to down him and make life miserable for him.

It has long ago been questioned by psychiatrists whether these so-called delusional ideas of this class of patients deserve to be endowed with the value of delusions. Let us not forget that a similar attitude toward officialdom exists in the minds of criminals enjoying a respite from the law. It is the officers of the law, society's institution for the prevention and punishment of crime, that these people have to fear, and when they speak of being persecuted by those who have their care and safe-keeping in hand, it is not, necessarily, a pathological manifestation. The only difference between such paranoid ideas in the criminal at freedom and the one in confinement is that in the latter case, coupled with the stress of confinement, the stress of a forced routine existence, these ideas assume enormous proportions and in some instances become supported by fallacious sense perceptions. Their exaggerated self-consciousness, their great tendency to introspection, a tendency which is very much enhanced by confinement and plenty of leisure time for such indulgence, and their paranoid attitude toward law and its officers, makes it possible for them to endow the least significant occurrence in their environment with a personal note of prejudice. The least deviation from the normal routine has a meaning to them, a meaning which is readily interpreted as some evidence of persecution, of prejudice, etc. The course of their disorder shows so much evidence of this psychogenetic character that it is impossible to think that we are dealing with a psychosis which apparently has no relation to the situation at hand. Every symptom which they manifest can be traced to some definite cause and can be clearly explained as being of the nature of a reaction, of a motivated expression to a definite experience. It is, I believe, unnecessary to enter into a lengthy discussion to show that we are not dealing here with a case of dementia prÃ¦cox, but with one of the degenerative psychoses and we will consider the criminal tendencies of this individual likewise as expressions of that same degenerative soil which permitted of the development of the psychosis. On July 17, 1911, the patient was returned to the penitentiary to serve out the remainder of his sentence.

CASE III.--P. F., alias H., white male, aged 42. Admitted to the Government Hospital for the Insane, March 11, 1910.

Father is a chronic alcoholic; one brother a wanderer, has not been heard from for twenty years; one sister a suicide; one sister left home at the age of eighteen and has not been heard from since.

Patient was born in England in 1868. Was a healthy child as far as he knows; no history of spasms or convulsions. Talked and walked at the usual age. Of the diseases of childhood he had whooping cough, measles and scarlet fever, from which he apparently made good recoveries. Entered school at the age of seven; attended irregularly until he was twelve years old. After leaving school he made an attempt at learning a trade and worked as apprentice for some time. At fifteen he endeavored to enlist in the British Navy, but was rejected on account of palpitation of the heart. In 1884, at the age of sixteen, he joined the Royal Marines; soon found this to be disagreeable to his tastes, and wanting to secure his discharge, he stole a suit of clothes off a dummy with the avowed purpose of being discharged for the offense. Was arrested, plead guilty, and served a sentence of one month. In 1886, at the age of eighteen, he enlisted in the Royal Fusileers and deserted therefrom about a month later. He then reÃ«nlisted in the eighteenth Royal Irish Fusileers, shortly after deserted, and then gave himself up; was court-martialed, dishonorably discharged, and given a sentence of six months which he served in Brixton's Military Prison, London. In 1887, at the age of nineteen, under the name of Henry Sayers, he joined the Welsh Division of the Royal Artillery, whence he deserted two months later and sold a kit and coat belonging to another recruit; was apprehended, tried and given a sentence of six months. In all, he was dishonorably discharged from the service seven times. In 1892, at the age of twenty-four, he immigrated to this country. On arriving here he worked about a month at railroading and then enlisted in the Army, deserted after serving three months, and crossed the Canadian Border. He subsequently returned and gave himself up to a sheriff, was court-martialed, dishonorably discharged, and given a sentence of one year and a half. After being released he resumed his nomadic existence but in a more pronounced manner. Since 1895, he has had no definite occupation, subsisting on begging, stealing, and peddling minor articles, chiefly on the two former. He has spent most of his life since then in penitentiaries and workhouses, and when at liberty, in cheap boarding-houses and missions. As far as he can recall he has been arrested twenty-two times for vagrancy since 1895, served four years at Moundsville and Atlanta for robbery, and six months for theft. He commenced to indulge in alcoholics at a very early age and has been an excessive drinker all his life. Has been intoxicated on numerous occasions and has had delirium tremens twice. In 1897 he indulged in opium smoking for thirteen days and in 1904 sniffed cocaine for a similar period. On three or four occasions in his life he has had sexual experiences with men and there is a definite history of inversion. He has been married twice. His conjugal life with his first wife was a very unhappy one. He attributes this entirely to his own fault. There were three children from this union, all of whom died in infancy. He left his first wife without obtaining a divorce from her and subsequently, in 1898, married again. This union was happier than the former one. His second wife, however, died in 1905. There were no children from this union. He acquired gonorrhÅ"a and syphilis in 1899. In 1907 he prepared an elaborate attempt at suicide, purchased a dagger for this purpose, and set June 13th for the date. He was, however, arrested shortly before this and thus his plan was frustrated. He stated that it was not disgust of life that drove him to do this. He simply had a desire to see whether he had the nerve to execute such an act. On February 2, 1910, was arrested for vagrancy and begging, and given a sentence of 180 days in the workhouse. While in his cell he attempted suicide by inflicting superficial cuts over the prÅｃcordium, wrists and calves of his legs with a piece of broken table knife. These were very insignificant in nature. While confined in the workhouse he developed various fallacious sense perceptions, saw visions of weird and fantastic nature, and frequently these would take on a religious and sexual coloring--he would see nuns' heads. He also developed auditory hallucinations and would hear voices of a disagreeable nature. He was subject to peculiar sensations as though there was a wire framework inside him which made him squirm. This necessitated his transfer to this institution.

On admission he was well-nourished, but prematurely gray. He had numerous tattoo marks on his body; on the right forearm a woman in tights and the head of another; on the left forearm initials U. S., flag, ship and cross; over the dorsum of left hand a star, and a band across the wrist. His vision was impaired to some extent; otherwise negative. Aside from a futile attempt at suicide which he made shortly after admission, his conduct has been excellent. He has never been known to become involved in altercations or quarrels with his fellow patients and has obeyed fully the rules and regulations of the Hospital. He was somewhat circumstantial during a lengthy conversation, but in a superficial interview he made quite a natural impression. He was clearly oriented and showed no memory defect. His answers to the intelligence tests failed to show any intellectual impairment. His emotional tone was unvaried. He was always very polite, courteous and optimistic, and very popular with the attendants. He willingly assisted with the ward work at all times, was keen and alert, fully cognizant of everything that transpired about him. He spent his time reading and rarely associated with his fellow patients, whom he considered below him intellectually. He believed in reincarnation, and thought himself to have been in a former being Pharaoh of Egypt and the Earl of Warwick. He had tactile, auditory and visual hallucinations of a religious and sexual coloring. These were, however, transitory in type and perhaps better called pseudo-hallucinations, as he was able to bring them on and cause their disappearance at will. He was frank in his statements and discussed the various ideas without hesitation. He was inclined to write a great deal, especially poetry of the waste-basket variety, and considered himself quite proficient in this respect. On February 2, 1911, he appeared before the Staff conference where the advisability of granting him parole of the grounds was considered. Upon being refused this privilege he again attempted suicide by making several superficial cuts across the wrists. These were quite insignificant in nature. At the present writing the patient, I am told, if anything, had improved somewhat. At any rate he shows no intellectual impairment nor evidence of any progressive mental disorder. Patient was eventually discharged on April 7, 1915, as unimproved and went to work in a steel-plant in the District of Columbia. He soon, however, reverted to his old alcoholic habits, came in conflict with the law and was sentenced to the workhouse. While his strictly psychotic symptoms subsided it is quite evident that the original defective constitution which has been responsible for all of his past difficulties has not improved.

Here is another individual who started out in life with a heavy hereditary burden. His early childhood, as far as can be determined, was normal. He entered school and here met the first obligation. He wavered, showed a tendency, that early, to be unable to lead a well-regulated life and in consequence his school attendance was irregular. The next difficulty he met was in attempting to learn a trade. He soon found this too strenuous and sought an environment less exacting in nature, and at fifteen we see him endeavoring to enlist in the Navy. This is probably the first indication of his "wanderlust." He was rejected, and after another year's effort to get along in his immediate environment, finally succeeded in entering the Navy. Soon, however, he found out that Navy life was not what he had pictured it to be. It, likewise, was too exacting. He had to live up to prescribed rules, obey orders--things to which he could not reconcile himself, and in consequence failed of a proper adjustment. He knew he could not stand it, he must get out. He must seek something more suitable, something less exacting. In looking for a way out of the situation he availed himself of the first opportunity, stole a suit of clothes with the avowed purpose of being discharged for the offense. Here is the starting point of his criminal career. He did not reflect upon the consequences. He knew he must gratify his desire to get out of the Navy, must do it at any cost, and yielded to temptation. This yielding to temptation, this lack of power of resistance, characterized his entire life. He yielded to every vice that crossed his path; he stole, he drank, he became a morphine habituÃ©, he sniffed cocaine, acquired gonorrhÅ"a and syphilis in his promiscuous sexual trends, and lastly yielded to sexual perversion. After having served his first sentence he was released and again found himself thrown upon his own resources. He had not, as yet, reached the stage of the habitual criminal with the utter disregard for property rights, nor had he reached that nonchalance of the hobo, whose philosophy rests upon the dogma that the world owes him a living, that tomorrow will provide for itself somehow. He began to yearn for the service again. There, at least, he was provided with shelter and food. There, at least, he did not have to worry for the tomorrow. He entered the Army, deserted, re-entered, deserted again, and kept this up until he was dishonorably discharged seven times. He could stand it just so long. His lack of stability, his inability for any continuous purposive effort, made him slip from under the stress. He has less dread for the future now. He was beginning to acquire that naÃ¯ve philosophy that somehow the world would provide for him. We next hear of him across the ocean. Here his "wanderlust", his love of adventure, reasserts itself, but somehow he did not fit into existing conditions, and unable, because of his particular organization, because of his disequilibrated mentality, to create for himself a suitable environment, his existence continued to be an unbroken chain of conflicts, of contradictions, and of failure. He finally tried matrimony, but here, too, he soon felt the overwhelming burden of duties and obligations. He was not assisted in sustaining these by any moral sense, by any paternal feelings--and after a more or less continuous struggle to cope with the situation, left wife, situation and all. He realized subjectively that he and his wife were not congenial. As a matter of fact, his entire life has been a continual round of uncongenialities, of inability for a proper concourse with men and things in the world. Throughout his life his ego occupied the center of the stage. It is he that has to be satisfied first. After leaving his wife he resumed his nomadic existence and sometime later married again. But by this time he was a full recidivist, as well as an accomplished hobo. The nomad was no longer able to adjust himself to a communal existence. Besides, it required effort. He was expected to provide and he could not be expected to do anything. Fate was in his favor--his wife died. It must not be forgotten that by this time he had made full use of the kind oversight of the law. He had been arrested innumerable times, he had breathed the atmosphere of the workhouse and partaken of the penitentiary menu. The once unfinished product had been shaped and polished by the machinery of the law and order of our modern civilization so that all dread and fear of punishment had lost its value with him. At last the organism which was originally begotten from decayed stock, which had been tossed and knocked about through its entire existence, and preyed upon by all the vices that modern civilization affords, began to falter and shake. He developed a psychosis. I shall not enter here into an extensive discussion as to the diagnosis of the disorder. The total absence of any indication of progression in this man's mental disorder, the pliability of the various delusional ideas and hallucinatory experiences, his perfect control over them in the matter of bringing them on and causing their disappearance at will, speaks sufficiently against dementia prÃ|cox.

CASE IV.--A. W., colored, aged 28. Mother suffers from neuralgia and headaches; one sister died of pulmonary tuberculosis. One brother is now serving a sentence at Moundsville Penitentiary for assault and battery. Another brother has been frequently arrested for various offenses.

Birth and childhood of patient apparently uneventful. During childhood fell from a fence following which he was unconscious for some time. Entered school between the ages of seven and eight, and attended regularly for about two years, when he became unruly and ungovernable--would play truant on frequent occasions, and finally left school before finishing the fourth grade. He worked around home for a little while, and was arrested the first time when eleven or twelve years old, for assault. At fourteen he was again arrested for some minor offense, and shortly afterwards was sentenced to one year in jail. On August 20, 1902, at the age of eighteen was arrested for carrying concealed weapons and discharging them in the street, for which offense he served five months in jail. March 3, 1903, sentenced to serve thirty days for larceny, and on the same date was further charged with disorderly conduct, for which he was given fifteen days in the workhouse. May 1, 1903, he was sentenced to sixty days in jail for petty larceny; July 18, 1903, charged with fornication, but charge was withdrawn. August 31, 1903, sentenced to thirty days in jail for being drunk and disorderly, and committing assault. November 1, 1903, sentenced to fifteen days in the workhouse on a charge of disorderly conduct. November 17, 1903, sentenced to twelve years for assault and highway robbery. He commenced using alcoholics at a very early age, and has indulged heavily since then. He was admitted to the Moundsville Penitentiary, December 13, 1903, where he remained until July 4, 1908, when he was transferred to Leavenworth. His record at the penitentiary is a very bad one, he was frequently punished for various offenses and showed a constant tendency to disobey rules and get into altercations with fellow prisoners. He was in solitary confinement several times, and forfeited almost all of his good time. Frequently became mildly excited, singing, shouting, praying and cursing in the most irrational manner. This state of excitement persisted unremittingly for seventy-two hours on one occasion. He declared that his lungs were rotting with tuberculosis or some other foul disease, and that he was suffocating. He persisted in exposing himself in a nude condition and refused nourishment.

He was admitted to the Government Hospital for the Insane, December 24, 1909.

Physical examination showed him to be a well-developed, healthy negro. Both deep and superficial reflexes exaggerated; ankle clonus both sides; hyperÃ¦sthesia of abdomen and face. He stated that two or three months prior to his admission to this Hospital he became suspicious of his food; had a burning in his stomach after eating; believed that his health was failing him; his breath became short; voice weak and lungs rotting. Early in December, 1909, he believed that he had been chloroformed by the prison officials for five days; he was not certain how this was done but believed that it might have been poured through the keyhole. During this period he sang like a graphophone; voices said "move his head", and his head would move itself. When his eyes were open he saw nothing unusual but when they were shut he could hear them operating a machine on his body; they were pumping his stomach, and he became a skeleton. This was done to him through prejudice; did not know who was prejudiced against him, but at the prison they know all about it. Said he had not slept a wink since his admission to the Hospital; his breath is short; he has pains around his heart, but thinks he is getting better now.

He was a negro of limited mental capacity and possessed very little acquired knowledge. He was clean and tidy in his habits, keenly interested in his environment, and well oriented in all spheres. He lacked insight into the nature of his trouble. Attention could be easily gained and held; he comprehended well and readily, and showed no memory defect. There was a very marked tendency to hypochondriasis and exaggeration of actual ills. Soon after admission the active symptoms of his disorder disappeared, and he gradually acquired an adequate amount of insight, realizing that he had been insane. His conduct, at first orderly, now assumed the same character as that at prison. He frequently became involved in altercations with other patients and on several occasions manifested decidedly vicious tendencies. He was almost absolutely unamenable to the Hospital regulations and on that account had to be frequently reprimanded. He incited the other patients in his ward to all sorts of misdemeanors, and when not having any complaints himself, would fight the other patients' battles. He remained clearly oriented throughout. He was decidedly deficient morally--could not see where his life had been an unsocial one, and did not even promise to lead a better one in the future.

Here, again, we see disease and crime rampant in the family history of a man who himself began to manifest criminal tendencies at a very early age. His school career is characterized by truancy, and he never made an effort at an industrial career. At the age of eleven or twelve, we already find him arrested for an offense against the person, and before having reached his twentieth year he has received a penitentiary sentence of twelve years. His psychosis is unquestionably one belonging to that large group developing on a degenerative basis, the same soil which is at the bottom of his criminal career. What his future life is going to be may readily be surmised; he has not yet reached his thirtieth year--and by turning him loose at the expiration of his present sentence, society adds only another parasitic and infective organism to gnaw at its roots. It would be indeed ridiculous to expect the boy who at the age of nineteen was placed in the environment of a penitentiary--the hot-bed of crime--to be turned out a better man after having spent twelve years there. Something over two years has elapsed since the original publication of this paper and I am able to furnish some additional data concerning this case.

Upon the expiration of his sentence we were obliged to discharge the patient because he showed no symptoms of mental disease, and in consequence we had no authority for holding him in a hospital for the insane. He was discharged in March, 1912. In October of the same year he was again arrested, charged with assault with a dangerous weapon and received a seven-year penitentiary sentence.

There can be very little doubt as to what his future career will be following this second penitentiary sentence.

CASE V.--W. A., white male, aged 36 on admission to the Government Hospital for the Insane, January 18, 1911. Father was an alcoholic; mother neurotic, one sister insane, one uncle suicide. Mother enjoyed good health during her pregnancy with the patient, but birth was an extremely difficult one.

Patient learned to talk and walk at the age of five, when he was severely scalded which necessitated his confinement to bed for a long time. Entered school at the age of seven and attended for about eight years, reaching the 6th grade. He experienced no difficulty in learning but played truant on frequent occasions. His industrial career constitutes an uninterrupted chain of failures. He was frequently discharged for various offenses and quarrels with his associates. He commenced to indulge in alcoholics at a very early age and has been an excessive drinker all his life. Married in his twentieth year and managed to live with his wife for six years, when she left him on account of infidelity, non-support and drunkenness. One miscarriage and one apparently healthy child were the results of this union.

He came in conflict with the law for the first time at the age of twelve or thirteen for some offense against the person. We have an incomplete record of his criminal career, but this can easily be surmised when we take into consideration that part of it which we do possess. Between March, 1903, and December, 1910, he was arrested thirteen times for assault, twenty-eight times for disorderly, and drunk and disorderly, twice for housebreaking, once for petty larceny and twice for vagrancy. Habitual drunkenness, destruction of private property, and depredation on house furniture, add to the list of charges against him. During this period he served a penitentiary sentence, was tried for murder, and acquitted on a second trial on a plea of self-defense, and on four different occasions, was ordered to be examined mentally. Following a debauch, during which he was arrested three times for assault, he developed a mental disorder in jail while awaiting trial, which necessitated his transfer to the Government Hospital for the Insane.
He developed the idea that someone was always around him looking for a

chance to kill him. Continually heard strange voices and noises. Was very nervous and irritable.

The records accompanying him stated that for years he had had a particularly bad and dangerous temper. That he had had several previous attacks of mental disorder; had repeatedly committed assaults, and was found not guilty of murder seven years ago--an act of insanity. Had been arrested by the Washington police about seventy-five times.

His mental disturbance soon cleared up, and on admission to the hospital he was absolutely free from any psychotic manifestations.

He was a well-developed man of average intellectual attainments. He was somewhat unstable emotionally, and his promises to lead a better life in the future were usually accompanied by a good deal of crying. He was a monumental liar, and although endeavoring to impress the examiner with the idea of being quite remorseful about his past life, it was clearly evident that his moral status was a very low one and that his promises and resolutions were merely brought forth to aid him in securing his freedom. He was extensively tattooed and showed remains of an old syphilitic lesion.

Upon his release from the Government Hospital for the Insane, he was given a year's sentence in the workhouse, and the Press has been reporting frequent misdemeanors performed by him in the workhouse.

This case is interesting only in so far as it illustrates exceptionally well the rÃ´le of alcoholism in the habitual criminal. It is, however, very difficult to decide whether the alcohol should be considered here the cause of the man's degeneracy or its result. It would appear that whatever injurious effect inebriety had upon this man, and unquestionably it had, he owes his anomalies of character to causes over which he had no control. We find that his father was a chronic alcoholic, his mother a neurotic, a maternal aunt insane, and an uncle a suicide. That these pathological traits in the antecedents left their impressions on him cannot be doubted for one minute. He was abnormal before environment and personal habits had had time to make themselves felt. He, too, oscillated between penal institutions and the Hospital for the Insane all his lifetime. That the same degenerative basis lies at the bottom of both his moral and mental alienation, cannot be doubted. Here, too, we are able at this date to furnish other additional information. The patient was eventually discharged from the Hospital for a similar reason as in the preceding case, and in spite of all his promises and new resolutions was readmitted to the Hospital on October 13, 1913 with an attack of delirium tremens.

Let us endeavor to see now in what respects the above individuals simulate one another, and whether this similarity is of sufficient import to warrant the grouping of them into one category. Commencing with the family history we find disease and crime manifest in the antecedents, either direct or indirect, of all of them, that in all probability because of this, not one of these unfortunates was brought into the world with a sufficient impetus to carry him successfully to his goal. In every instance we find that the characterological anomaly became manifest already during their school career. It was the persistent truancy, disobedience and antagonism to submission to a well-regulated existence and not so much the incapacity to learn, which distinguished them from the other children in school. The same attributes of character which were at the bottom of their conflicts with the school authorities brought them into the hands of the police authorities soon afterwards. The contact with the outside world soon served to bring out other pathological traits of character. We now see them manifest a pathologic emotionalism, an unbounded egotism, a relentless vindictiveness and an apparently total disregard of consequences. Frictions with the surrounding world, which a normal individual meets in an ordinary manner with a view towards an efficient adaptation to existing conditions, were reacted to by them in a distinctly antisocial manner, with methods entirely void of consideration of the rights of others, an attribute so essential for a proper concourse with man. Thrown finally upon their own resources, when they had to rely for their existence upon some industrial pursuit, we find them lacking the most essential prerequisite for the efficient struggle for existence--definiteness of purpose, and continuity and persistence of effort. We find them leading a harum-scarum existence, drifting from place to place, and from occupation to occupation, never able to remain at any one undertaking for any length of time.

The next features which stand out prominently in the lives of these individuals are their recidivism and the fact that every one of them came under the observation of an alienist on one or more occasions in his life. What is at the bottom of all this? We cannot, of course, deny the very evident fact that these individuals differ from normal man and that this difference is due to their inferiority. But what characterizes this inferiority? Is it the lack of something which normal man possesses, or is it rather a disproportion, a disharmony between the various individual mental faculties of these individuals? In other words, is their inferiority a quantitative or qualitative one? Taking pure intelligence into consideration we find that they show no deficiency in this particular sphere. On the contrary, most or all of them show a degree of shrewdness and keenness which absolutely precludes the existence of an intelligence defect per se. Their recidivism is not due to an inability to distinguish between right and wrong. They know very well what is and what is not right, at any rate, as well as the average person, but they feel decidedly different from the average person about this distinction. They are what they are because of a discord, a disproportion between their various psychic attributes. The exaggerated egotism, which is so common to these individuals, serves to establish a pathologic degree of self-consciousness. This in turn makes them feel with an extraordinary keenness the everyday frictions in life, and now the pathologic emotionalism comes into play and being unsupported by any sense of altruism and morality they give way to their feelings in some criminal act. Their pathologic vindictiveness should also be mentioned. A sustained real or imaginary injury can never be forgotten by them.

These, in brief, I believe to be the characterological anomalies which distinguish the individuals herein reported from normal man and which at the same time are sufficiently common to all of them to justify their segregation into one distinct group of criminals.

I shall not enter here into a discussion of what part, if any, environment played in the shaping of the lives of these individuals, for several reasons, chief among which, however, is the fact that I have not had the opportunity of investigating thoroughly the environmental conditions in which they grew up and am therefore unable to evaluate properly this phase of the question. The fact, however, that my cases were culled from various sources and that the anomalous traits manifested by them were already present at an age when environment could hardly have had any lasting influence upon them, leads me to believe that it is heredity that is responsible for the major portion of this anomalous product. However, we shall leave this question to the decision of the practical eugenists. Personally I fully believe that we are dealing here with a type in which heredity plays an important rÃ´le. I fully believe that these individuals were always the same as they are now and that the probabilities are that they will always remain so. Assuming then, for the moment, that we are correct, the question arises:--"Has society dealt with these individuals in a proper manner?"

This question must be answered decidedly in the negative. I will not enter here into an extensive discussion of a system of penology which

might be specifically applicable to this class of individuals. I can
only agree fully with the current opinions of eminent criminologists on
this subject.

At the 1911 Congress of Criminology and Anthropology at Cologne, the
following resolution among others was adopted:--"Hardened and
professional criminals, recidivists, who present a great danger to
society must be deprived of their liberty for as long a time as they are
dangerous to the mass. Their liberty should be as a general rule,
conditional."

Archibald Hopkins, Esq., has been recently quoted by Gault as
follows:--"The Head of Scotland Yard, in London, said not long ago that
nine-tenths of the serious crimes there were committed by men who had
served one or more terms of imprisonment and who might be regarded as
belonging permanently to the criminal class. His judgment was that if
they could be eliminated from such a situation, violation of the law
would be diminished to less than a third of what it has been. Why cannot
this be done? Let the Courts be clothed with power, after two or more
offenses, in its discretion, to pronounce a man incorrigible, who shall
be sentenced for life, to whom no pardon shall issue. By an arrangement
between the general government and the states, a colony could be
established, say in the Island of Guam, where escape would be
impossible, and where, under military guard, convicts could be made to
earn their own living. Surely society has the right to protect itself
from these incorrigibles, who are released only to prey on it again.
They also are the class who rapidly produce their kind, and at present
society puts no obstacle in the way.

"It is exactly as if, instead of forming colonies to which all
lepers are compelled to go and remain, we permitted them, after a brief
term in the hospital, to go where they please and to marry and produce
more lepers. The incorrigible criminal is worse than the leper because

he deliberately and purposely defies society and spreads his contagion. It can hardly be questioned that the permanent segregation of the professional criminal class would very greatly diminish crime, nor can it be questioned that society has the right to adopt such a measure of protection, nor that it would not be entirely practicable." (See Journal of American Institute of Criminal Law and Criminology, April, 1912, pp. 821 f.)

The only argument, and a very weighty one it is, which can be raised against the foregoing proposition, is whether the incorrigible criminal is sufficiently characterized by such unmistakable features as would enable us to recognize him when we see him, and thus justify his permanent isolation from the community. I believe he is, and the cases here reported are fair representatives of that class. Another problem which presents itself is: "Where shall we put the incorrigible criminal?" If we agree that he owes his criminality to causes over which he has no control and that the crime here is the outgrowth of a degenerative personality, a personality which is distinctly abnormal, it would seem that he belongs in a hospital rather than a penal institution, but is this unequivocally so? It is unquestionably true that these individuals are abnormal, that without actually being insane they evidence from their earliest childhood a more or less distinct deviation from the normal; they may therefore be considered as "border-line cases," *i.e.*, cases which deviate from normal man and incline toward the insane through numerous gradations. As soon, however, as their abnormality manifests itself in distinct incorrigible antisocial tendencies, the right of society to protect itself from such an element must be considered. When free from actual psychotic manifestations (which very easily engraft themselves upon this degenerative soil) these individuals do not belong in a hospital for the insane. Here they serve only as a very troublesome and disturbing element, and wield an undesirable influence over many easily impressionable insane patients. They do not belong in a general penal institution because of the very deleterious influence they exert on the accidental but uncorrupted convict with whom they come in close contact in these institutions. It is my opinion that these individuals, forming as they do a distinct species of humanity, should be segregated into colonies especially designed for them, where under proper medical supervision, they should be made to earn their subsistence by means of some useful occupation. It is very obvious that an indeterminate sentence is the only rational way of approach to this problem and this should be supplemented by the vesting of the parole power in the hands of a board composed, not exclusively of members of the legal profession, but largely of physicians, and particularly those trained in psychopathology.

The foregoing cases, while distinctly abnormal mentally, owe their recidivism to a qualitative rather than a quantitative defect.

Since the original publication of this paper, I have had occasion to observe a number of recidivists in whom the defect was essentially a quantitative one, *i.e.*, patients ranging in intelligence all the way from idiocy to moronism.

The following case is a good illustration of this type:--

R. W. (colored) was admitted to this Hospital for the first time from the District of Columbia Reform School on February 8, 1898. He was at that time serving a sentence for housebreaking. He was twenty years of age at that time and examination showed him to possess the intelligence of an imbecile. During his sojourn here he had several maniacal outbreaks, but recovered from these and was discharged into the care of his parents on November 23, 1898. Sometime in 1900 he was again sent to the Reform School and was readmitted to this Hospital on November 17, 1900. He suffered at this time from an acute hallucinatory episode from which he soon recovered and was allowed to go out on a visit on February 20, 1901. He never returned from this visit but on July 23, 1902, was sentenced to twelve months imprisonment for larceny. While serving this sentence he was admitted to the State Hospital for the Insane at Norristown, Pennsylvania, where he suffered from an acute maniacal attack with persecutory delusions. He was discharged from that institution, by order of the Court, on September 29, 1903. On January 1, 1904, he was arrested for housebreaking and sentenced to three years imprisonment at the United States Penitentiary at Moundsville, Virginia. From the above institution he was admitted to this Hospital on May 8, 1905, suffering from an acute maniacal attack. He soon recovered again and was discharged on August 18, 1906, with a diagnosis of imbecility with recurrent mania. He was readmitted here October 3, 1907, and discharged April 1, 1909. On January 23, 1910, he was given a two months workhouse sentence for petty larceny. On September 7, 1912, he was again sentenced to four years in the Penitentiary for grand larceny, from which institution he was readmitted here on January 19, 1915.

I shall not enter into a detailed discussion of this case. It is simply quite illustrative of the absolute necessity for permanent segregation of mental defectives.

When some of this clinical material was first published in 1912 it met with very gratifying recognition at the hands of those who were interested in criminalistics.

I wish to take this opportunity of expressing my particular appreciation of Dr. Healy's kind words of approbation and encouragement.

We all must agree that the first essential step towards a better understanding of criminal types consists in a thorough study of the criminal individual, such as is reflected, for instance, in the very excellent book by Healy on the "Individual Delinquent." Such studies have thus far, however, with but rare exceptions, not been made at the proper source,--that is, in the criminal laboratory, the penal institution.

The work which is being done with the juvenile offender is, of course, very important and very valuable; but in order that this work may be checked up scientifically it must be supplemented by thorough catamnestic studies of the juvenile offenders. This, I believe to be the only rational way of approach to the problem.

This will in time, I believe, furnish us data concerning the criminal which will enable us to evaluate in a correct manner the various traits and characteristics of the juvenile offender and thus enable us to render a correct prognosis in a given case. Once we shall reach a stage in the science of criminology when we shall dare to say of a juvenile offender, as we now unhesitatingly say of the leper, "Here is a human being who will always be a danger to his fellow-man and, therefore, should be permanently isolated from his fellow-man", the problem of recidivism will be solved.

We cannot, however, arrive at a proper conception of the nature of a juvenile offender by merely studying a cross section of him at any given moment of his life. In order to understand man, especially abnormal man, we must study him in a longitudinal section; we must note his mode of reaction to experiences in everyday life, under all manner of conditions and circumstances; we must investigate the motives and desires which prompt his conduct; we must find out how effectually he adapts himself to the environment in which he happens to be placed and in how far he is able to modify the world about him so as to make it subservient to his needs and wants. The same problems which confront criminology today, psychiatry had to face some years ago. In order to be able to rationally and scientifically deal with the insane the psychiatrist found it essential to establish certain criteria which might enable him to tell, with some degree of certainty, what the future life of a given insane person will be. In the last analysis it is this same thing which we are aiming to attain in our dealings with the criminal. The problem which is constantly before us in dealing with juvenile delinquency is what might be expected of the future life of the juvenile under consideration and what must be done towards directing his future into proper channels. So, after all, it should be our aim to establish certain criteria by means of which we should be able to render a proper prognosis. That we possess no such criteria at present can be denied by no one.

As I have already stated, psychiatry had to face the same problems. With the advent, however, of the Kraepelinian school these have in a great measure been solved. Kraepelin, by studying the entire life history of his patients, was able to show that certain disease pictures when studied in cross section may simulate one another very closely clinically and at the same time be of the most diverse significance prognostically. He further showed that certain acute psychotic disturbances are merely the outward expressions of an underlying progressive disorder, and though the acute manifestations may disappear and leave no apparent trace behind them, the great majority of these individuals will spend the rest of their lives in institutions for the insane. By calling attention to certain symptom-complexes, which are especially characteristic of certain mental disorders, he gave us the means by which we are able at the present time to predict with a fair degree of certainty what the future life of a given patient will be. We can now tell without great fear of contradiction which of our patients are going to spend the rest of their lives in institutions.

Now, criminality is generally conceded to be an expression of a diseased personality and there is no reason why the same principles which served to advance our knowledge of psychiatry should not be employed here.

In the foregoing study we aimed to carry out these principles, but we believe that better results still could be obtained at the hands of a trained psychiatrist right at the penitentiary. The reasons for this are quite obvious. The relationship between prisoner and physician would then be quite a different one, the data could be more readily verified with the assistance of the machinery of the law, and the subjects would be in a more accessible mood than when suffering from a mental disorder. As a matter of fact the best work thus far done on the mentality and disorders of mentality of prisoners was done by a prison physician, Dr. Siefert, of Halle.

Thus we see that the question of the degenerative prison psychoses has an important relation to the question of criminology in general.

This becomes at once apparent, if we accept the contention of many authorities that the degenerative soil which makes the development of these psychoses possible, is likewise responsible for the criminality of these individuals; in other words,--if we agree that crime and psychosis are here branches of the same tree. Manifestly any discussion of the treatment of these psychoses must of necessity touch upon the vastly broader problem of the treatment of the habitual criminal, the recidivist, and therefore a slight digression from the subject at hand will be unavoidable.

If we admit that it is the prison environment which serves to bring out the prison psychosis, it is perfectly evident that the first therapeutic indication is the removal of the prisoner from that environment as soon as the disorder is recognized. This problem is at present dealt with in several ways. There are certain penal institutions, especially in Europe, which have within their walls a psychiatric department for the reception of these cases. Others send their insane convicts to the criminal department of some hospital for the insane. In this country there are States in which still a third system is in vogue, namely, the confinement of these cases in special hospitals for insane criminals. Now the points to be kept in mind in the treatment of the insane criminal are, briefly stated, these:--First, they should of course come under the supervision of a trained psychiatrist. Second, the transfer from prison to hospital must take place with as little delay as possible and not be burdened with a lot of red-tape procedures. Third, the hospitals for the housing of these patients must be fully equipped in accordance with the modern ideas of hospital construction, and at the same time afford ample security for the prevention of escapes. Fourth, the interest of the inmates of the general hospital for the insane and the feelings of their friends and relatives must be kept in mind, when we begin to advocate the populating of our hospitals for the insane with criminal characters.

The psychiatric annex in connection with the penal institution meets all these requirements better than any arrangement for the care of the insane criminal. An annex of say fifty beds, in connection with every State Penitentiary would obviate entirely the delay in transferring a patient from prison to hospital and *vice versa*. As soon as a prisoner begins to show signs of mental disorder, and a prison physician trained in psychiatry will be able to recognize these early signs, or as soon as there is the least suspicion of mental disorder, the patient could be transferred without delay to the psychiatric department. Here they should be kept under observation for at least six months. This will be sufficiently long in most instances to enable the physician to determine whether he is dealing with a progressive deteriorating psychosis or with one of those transitory prison psychoses. In the cases of the former, i.e., if it is definitely established that the patient is a dementing prÃ¦cox or a paretic, the fact that he happens likewise to be a criminal is really of little or no importance. A demented individual is never dangerous enough to require confinement in an especially secure hospital, though he is a prisoner, and unless he is criminally insane, i.e., unless he manifests dangerous or criminal tendencies as a result of his mental disorder, really forms no special administrative problem. He could be kept either in the prison annex until the expiration of his sentence, if there be room for him, or could be transferred to the nearest hospital for the insane and treated the same as any other insane patient.

It is the second group, however, *i.e.*, those patients suffering from the transitory prison psychoses, which especially justify the establishment of psychiatric annexes in connection with prisons. We have seen how detrimental to prison discipline these individuals are, even when in a condition which might be considered normal to them, and we can easily surmise what it must mean to care for them in prison during one of their mental upsets. It is therefore of the utmost importance, both for the prison administration and for the individual, that these patients should be transferred to a properly appointed hospital in as short a time as possible, and this can be done most readily when the hospital and prison are within the same walls, and more or less under the same management. On the other hand, we owe it to the prisoner to bring him under proper care as soon as possible. The practice of sending these individuals to criminal departments of general hospitals for the insane has many objections. In the first place, no matter how modern the equipment of such departments, most of them cannot afford the proper kind of treatment to these individuals. The idea that the removal from prison to a criminal department of an insane hospital will have a beneficial effect upon the prisoner because of the more lenient environment into which he is taken is entirely delusional in the case of the degenerated habitual criminal. These individuals, if the public safety is to be kept in mind, can receive but very limited privileges in a hospital for the insane. The modern hospital is not constructed with the idea of caring for dangerous criminals, and in many instances the habitual criminal, who because of his dangerous tendencies and ever readiness to escape, has to be constantly kept under lock and key, would be much better off if he were treated within the enclosure of the prison. There the construction of the place permits of a wider latitude of outdoor exercise. An annex located within the enclosure of a prison could well afford to allow its patients the freedom of the enclosure, while this can manifestly not be done in a general hospital for the insane. Then again, there is the unavoidable delay attendant upon the commitment of a prisoner to an insane hospital. As I have already stated elsewhere, it is not a rare occurrence to receive patients into the hospital who have entirely recovered from their mental disorder before leaving the prison. Furthermore, the expense and danger always connected with the transfer of insane criminals from prison to hospital and back again, if the hospital is any distance from the prison, must be kept in mind.

A word to those who, from a false altruistic standpoint, insist that the insane criminal requires no different treatment from that which the ordinary insane patient does. This is very true in the case of prisoners who develop mental disorders which have no relation to crime or imprisonment. These do not require special measures of treatment. It is likewise true of the psychoses of the accidental criminal, but it is entirely different with the criminal who suffers from a degenerative prison psychosis. Here we are not dealing with individuals who tend to dement, who have little or no conception of whether they are in a prison or in a hospital. In short, we are not dealing here with paretics or senile dements, who, although being at the same time prisoners, remain subject to the same unavoidable lot of the paretic or the senile dement. The habitual criminal who suffers from a degenerative psychosis, unless he is in a stupor, is constantly on the alert for a chance to escape. No matter how delusional or hallucinated he may be, he always manages to keep in mind that the thing which he most desires is to be free from the hands of his captors, and anyone who has had to deal with this class will bear me out in this. The shrewdness with which they carry out their escapes is amazing, and some of the more depraved ones do not hesitate to commit serious assaults in order to gain their freedom. Here, measures other than those used with the ordinary insane patient are required.

Now as to special hospitals for insane criminals which certain States have. Of course the same objections, namely, as to the delay in getting the patient under treatment and the danger of transfer, etc., hold true also here; but these hospitals, it seems to me, have the additional disadvantage that they necessitate the segregation of all insane criminals, irrespective of whether they suffer from a recoverable psychosis or from a dementing process. In other words, here we have an admixture of cases who unfortunately fell into the hands of the law because of some mental disorder and who certainly should be confined as any other patient in an ordinary hospital for the insane, and patients in whom the crime and mental disorder are expressions of the same underlying degenerative defect, and who in a great majority of instances suffer from recoverable transitory mental disorders.

To insist upon keeping a paretic all his lifetime in such an institution is highly irrational, to say the least. The most rational, and the only scientific way, of dealing with the insane criminal is to bring about a state when the psychiatric hospital will be made accessible to him just as easily as the surgical and medical wards are, and this can only be accomplished by having psychiatric annexes in connection with prisons. The only serious objection which can be raised against this plan is that in time the annex will be made up exclusively of a very dangerous and troublesome population, but this objection likewise applies to the special hospital for the insane criminal. Certainly it is far safer to have this class of cases within the prison enclosure than to allow their accumulation in a general hospital for the insane.

Lastly, the psychiatric annex in the penitentiary would form the proper nucleus for the scientific study of the criminal, whence that much needed information concerning this type of man could emanate and be utilized for the rational treatment of the problem of crime.

We have thus far discussed the treatment of prison psychoses in these individuals while undergoing sentence, but what of them after the expiration of their sentences? We are now approaching the problem of recidivism.

Certain it is that society has thus far failed to deal effectually with this problem, and one need not search very deeply for the cause of this. Society has been relying principally upon its punitive methods in dealing with the habitual criminal, and so long as a given offense was punished according to a given statute it felt that it had done its duty. The factor of the personality of the criminal was entirely neglected. In time we have come to realize that our punitive methods not only do not tend to do away with recidivism, but enhance it. It is an undeniable fact that each additional imprisonment only serves to deprave the habitual criminal more deeply, and to release him after the expiration of an arbitrary sentence is to let loose another parasite to prey upon society. Of late years, however, there has been a tendency toward individualization in criminology. "It is the criminal and not the crime that we must deal with," is the modern slogan, and starting from this point of view we have already found out some very interesting facts. We find in looking over the life histories of our habitual criminals that they had shown antisocial and abnormal traits from their earliest youth; that in their early manhood they populated the reformatories and that their recidivism is due to some underlying anomaly which always differentiates them from normal men.

In this chapter we have seen how this underlying anomaly served under certain stressful situations to give rise to mental disorder, and have concluded that crime and psychosis must be, in these individuals, branches of the same tree. If this is true the question arises whether the habitual criminal does not rather belong in a hospital than in a prison. It is a little premature to decide this at the present day, but it is unquestionably certain that it is the psychiatrist who will in time furnish us the most valuable data concerning the "criminal character." It is he who will eventually bring to light unshakable proof that in the habitual criminal we must see an anomalous human being, who stands in the same relation to normal man as disease does to health, and then, the problem of recidivism as well as that of the psychoses of criminals will be easier of solution.

NOTES

[1] WILMANNS: "Ueber GefÃ¤ngnispsychosen." Halle a. S., 1908.

[2] BONHOEFFER: "Klinische BeitrÃ¤ge zur Lehre von den Degenerationspsychosen." Halle a. S., 1907.

[3] BIRNBAUM: "Zur Frage der psychogenen Krankheitsformen." Zeitschr. f. d. ges. Neurolog. u. Psych. 1910.

[4] SIEFERT: "Ueber die GeistesstÃ¶rungen der Strafhaft." Halle a. S., 1907.

[5] STRANSKY: "Ueber die Dementia Praecox, StreifzÃ¼ge durch Klinik und Psychopathologie." Wiesbaden, 1909.

CHAPTER III
THE FORENSIC PHASE OF LITIGIOUS PARANOIA

Maudsley[1] has long ago said: "It would certainly be vastly convenient and would save a world of trouble if it were possible to draw a hard and fast line and to declare that all persons who were on one side of it must be sane and all persons who were on the other side of it must be insane. But a very little consideration will show how vain it is to attempt to make such a division. That nature makes no leaps, but passes from one complexion to its opposite by a gradation so gentle that one shades imperceptibly into another and no one can fix positively the point of transition, is a sufficiently trite observation. Nowhere is this more true than in respect of sanity and insanity; it is unavoidable, therefore, that doubts, disputes and perplexities should arise in dealing with particular cases."

No small amount of the disrepute into which expert medical testimony has fallen is due precisely to a failure on the part of the legal profession to appreciate these truisms. To the legal mind the transition from mental well-being to mental disease is exemplified by that wholly artificial, and to the psychiatrist's mind, subsidiary question of legal certification. The law takes no cognizance of the conditions necessitating this change; it only concerns itself with the delimiting frontier, viz.:--certification. Legally, the insane has become such through the filling out and signing of certain papers and through having submitted himself to a certain prescribed legal procedure. The physician, on the other hand, because of his peculiar relationship to the patient, and as a result of his particular training, looks upon this legal procedure as a necessary evil and merely as typifying the conventional mode by which society settles its accounts with its diseased members. Our legal brethren fail to appreciate, furthermore, the fact that an individual may be very seriously ill mentally and urgently require hospital treatment, without, however, showing those gross disorders of conduct which go to make up the legal evidence and diagnosis of insanity. Neither do they seem to recognize the possibility of a seriously unbalanced individual making quite a normal impression, at any rate before a jury of laymen at the time of his appearance in Court. Nowhere in psychiatry is this so apt to be the case as in that form of mental disease known as paranoia, where we are dealing with a diseased personality which in many respects still approaches and resembles normal man.

The paranoiac, while he may harbor the most intricate and well-organized system of delusions, still remains approachable to us, and intellectually may be not only on a par with the average normal individual, but not infrequently gives the impression of being his superior. Nevertheless, this usually well-endowed human being at a certain point in his career goes off at a tangent and spends the rest of his life in the pursuit of a phantom. The paranoiac, starting out with vague, ill-defined ideas, succeeds in elaborating, step by step, a well-organized system of thought, of ideas which finally assume an all importance in the conduct of his life and remain unshakable.

Kraepelin[2] defines this condition as a mental disorder which is essentially characterized by a gradual and systematic evolution of a well-organized and intricate system of persecutory and grandiose delusions. It is chronic and incurable in its course and does not lead to any appreciable deterioration in the intellectual sphere. The litigious form of this disorder is particularly characterized by a persistent and unyielding tendency toward litigious pursuits. It is for this reason that this form of paranoia is of particular interest forensically. The law is the tool with which these individuals work, and the Courts their battle-grounds. The least provocation suffices to start the stone rolling, launching the unfortunate upon a career of endless litigation. As a rule the disorder originates in connection with some adverse decision or order of the authorities, which the patient considers an unjust one. Whether injustice has actually been suffered by the patient matters not and remains absolutely of no consequence as far as the course of the disease is concerned. The paranoiac litigant is unable to see the law as others see it, and in this respect he does not differ greatly from primitive man, whose conception of legality is that of a collection of concessions for himself and prohibitions for others. To be sure, a tendency to excessive litigation is occasionally met with in what appear to be normal people. Such pursuits, however, become pathological when they are based upon a delusional interpretation of actual occurrences or upon actual delusions, and are not amenable to reason.

According to Tanzi[3] the theme underlying the delusional system of litigious paranoiacs is avarice, and the whole may be looked upon as the slow and permanent triumph of a preconception. "The paranoiacal preconception gradually conquers all evidence to the contrary, and in spite of reality, public opinion and common sense, it becomes organized into a coÃ¶rdinated system of errors which become the tyrants of the intellectual personality and remove it by degrees outside the bounds of normality." The litigant constantly busies himself with his grievances, loses all interest in everything else, and begins to fight for his rights. He stops at no means and is the bane of judges and court officials. Naturally, he has to be refused all aid, either because he is unjust or because the courts find no remedy for his troubles. He refuses to settle actual grievances, carries the case from one court to another and finally develops an insatiable desire to fight to the bitter end.

The statutes appear to him inadequate and even the fundamental principles of law fail him. He cannot abide by the ultimate decision after all the usual means of justice have been exhausted. In his attempts to gain justice he writes to magistrates, legislators and various other people in prominence. It is only after years of persistent misfortune both to himself and the objects of his delusions, which only serve to harden him against his fortunate opponents, his incapable lawyers, the corrupt judges and his ignorant and craven-hearted relatives, that this master of procedure is betrayed into the expression of threats or the commitment of some other offense which conveys him summarily from the civil to the criminal courts, and the unrepentant pursuer becomes the defendant, unless, indeed, the insane asylum has become his refuge. (Tanzi.)

This is precisely what happened with the patients whose histories are here recorded. With all this the paranoiac remains plausible, converses rationally and coherently, shows himself to be exceedingly well-informed on current events, amazes his listeners with his really wonderful memory and his ability to quote *ad infinitum* from law books and statutes. Absence of hallucinations is the rule. Memory and the capacity to acquire new knowledge remain intact, and reasoning and judgment on matters of everyday life which do not touch his more or less circumscribed delusional field may remain quite normal. In short, he shows none of those tangible signs and symptoms upon which we must so frequently rely in our efforts to convince a jury of laymen of the existence of mental disorder. It is only when we take into consideration the entire life history of a paranoiac, which unfortunately is frequently ruled out as hearsay evidence, that the real state of affairs becomes manifest. We then see that where it concerns his delusional field the paranoiac's judgment is formed, not as a result of observation, or logic and reasoning, but as a result of an emotion, a mere feeling that this or that proposition is true. In every adverse decision of the court he sees a deep-laid conspiracy to deprive him of his rights. His lawyers are incompetent and in collusion with his persecutors; the judge is corrupt or ignorant of the law, and the legislators negligent in their duties in not writing into the statutes laws which would take care of his grievance. He constantly harps upon what he calls "the principle of the thing", losing, gradually, all concern in the real issues involved.

Indeed, in watching the amount of attention a paranoiac bestows upon his grievances, the zest with which he takes up every newly discovered flaw in the law, and the dexterity with which he weaves it into the maze of his delusional system, the idea forces itself upon one's mind that what the paranoiac least desires is a settlement of his grievances. One can readily imagine the void in the unfortunate's life were he to be deprived of this all-engrossing, and to him really life-giving, *casus belli*. Thus, not infrequently, when one grievance is actually settled, another soon appears and assumes the center of the stage. The means these individuals use in their efforts to convince the authorities of the righteousness of their cause or of the genuineness of the persecutions to which they are subjected, are really amazing in their ingenuity. They are supported to a considerable extent by retrospective falsifications of memory, and when occasion arises, by a conscious distortion of facts, and prevarication, a point very justly emphasized by Bischoff.[4]

This author relates the case of a paranoiac woman who was in litigation with her father over some trifling inheritance left by her mother, and who accused her father of a murder, and insinuated that she had heard her grandfather call him a fratricide.

The reputation and character of the objects of their delusions are unsparingly attacked by the paranoiac litigant, and this not infrequently results in bringing matters to a head, where as defendant in a criminal suit for libel the paranoiac is recognized in his true light and sent to a hospital for the insane. Before, however, this final scene in the litigious career is enacted, especially where the persecuted has turned persecutor, the objects of his delusions have not infrequently suffered an untold amount of anguish and financial ruin, through having been obliged to play the part of defendants in civil suits based on nothing else but the distorted fancy of a diseased mind.

While one may readily detect the part played by avarice in the pursuits and activities of these individuals, it requires close contact with them, especially in the capacity of one who stands between them and freedom, in order to fully appreciate the degree of malevolence which they frequently exhibit. Indeed, the study of litigious paranoia, more than anything else, illustrates how much method there may really be in madness. Were an alleged lunatic standing as a defendant in a criminal suit to use one-tenth of the amount of ingenuity and conscious direction of his symptoms that the average paranoiac uses, he would furnish the champions of the idea of malingering of mental disease with enough material to convict a dozen lunatics.

The chief aim of this paper is to illustrate by means of two interesting case histories the forensic importance of this form of mental disorder. It is not intended, however, to enter here into an academic discussion of the problem of paranoia. The term "Paranoia" is even pre-Hippocratic, and any attempt to indicate, even in the briefest manner, the changes which this concept has undergone throughout the ages would require considerably more space than we have at our disposal. I shall, therefore, merely mention that in reviewing the history of paranoia one is unmistakably struck by the fact that those view points and ideas concerning this subject which have indelibly impressed themselves upon it occupy themselves with a study of the personality of the paranoiac rather than with the disease picture as such. Some of the investigators have gone so far as to maintain that paranoia is not a disease at all in the sense that typhoid fever is a disease or pneumonia is a disease, but that the paranoiac picture is rather the expression of an anomalous individuality and, as one author puts it, it is the evolution of a crooked stick. Sander[5] recognized this when he so admirably stated that the abnormal condition develops and unfolds itself in the same way that the normal mind unfolds itself in the normal individual.

The cases herein reported have been under my observation now for several years at the Government Hospital for the Insane, and I am indebted for permission to report them to Dr. William A. White, Superintendent of the Hospital.

CASE I is a white man, aged 64 on his first admission to the Government Hospital for the Insane, July 9, 1907. This commitment was the direct outcome of a trial for perjury which took place in May, 1906, in the Supreme Court of the District of Columbia, at which the patient was found guilty. While awaiting sentence he was adjudged insane and sent to this Hospital. The evidence was gathered from the Reports of the Maryland Court of Appeals, dating as far back as 1874, and forms only an incomplete account of the patient's legal activities, inasmuch as many of his law transactions never reached the higher courts and consequently are not reported. In setting aside 1,296 magistrate's judgments obtained by the patient and amounting in the aggregate to $127,836 debt and $2,348 costs, the Court states, among other things, as follows:--

"The gross iniquity of this whole transaction, manifest enough upon its face, is abundantly so by proof. The inference is irresistible that the magistrate who issued these judgments merely wrote them out on his docket without summoning witnesses and without the semblance even of an *ex parte* trial."

It was further brought out at the perjury trial in 1906 that in 1877 the patient had obtained 619 judgments against the A. E. Company,

aggregating approximately $50,000. These were likewise set aside by
the higher Court. We thus see that as far back as 1874 this king of
litigants had already had set aside by the higher Courts as many as
some 1,900 distinct and separate judgments. How many more of those
based on the same flimsy tissue of his distorted imagination he
actually realized on is not known. As far as can be ascertained, the
issue of insanity was never raised, at any rate by the Court, prior to
the perjury trial, and it was only when this master litigant, after
having been active as a complainant for a great number of years, at
last betrayed himself into committing a criminal offense that the
issue of insanity was brought up.

A prominent Maryland Judge, who had known X---- for over forty years,
had the following to say concerning him:--"I have known X---- for
forty years, and he is a general nuisance and menace; he is crazy on
getting money, and for years has been manufacturing bogus judgments
against citizens of this and Montgomery Counties and the
A. E. Company. At one time he held judgments against that Company for
a million dollars for an imaginary wrong, all of which were eventually
gotten rid of on the ground that they were fraudulent. He also, in
some fraudulent way obtained judgments against our County
Commissioners, without their knowledge, for $1,500, which were
impounded by Judge M---- of the United States Court at B----, where as
a then non-resident he brought suit to recover on them. He then went
down to Dickinson County, a remote section of Southwestern Virginia,
and obtained other judgments for some four or five million dollars
against the County and various citizens, which were obtained by
perjury and forgery. They were eventually set aside. His brother died
in 1907, and I became one of the sureties on the executor's bond; last
year a judgment turned up here against the executor and his sureties
for $17,000, which purported to have been given by the Circuit Court
for said D---- County. It was a forgery all the way through; even the
Seal of the Court to the certificate was a forgery. I wrote the Judge

of the Court and he answered very promptly, stating that no such suit had ever been entered and that the judgment was a myth. We succeeded in impounding this judgment. No one up here feels safe when X---- is at large. We have suffered a great deal of trouble and expense in trying to protect ourselves against him, and everybody regards him as being not only insane but also a very dangerous man."

On admission to the Government Hospital for the Insane, July 9, 1907, he was found to be a fairly well-preserved man for his age, entered freely into conversation, comprehending readily what was said to him and exhibiting no difficulty in elaborating his ideas. He talked in a slow, deliberate and rather mysterious manner and a low tone of voice. The family history as given by him was negative. He himself had the usual diseases of childhood, but, aside from chronic indigestion, had had no severe illness. He gave his occupation as that of physician. In 1862 he enlisted in the Union Army as a nurse and was discharged six months later; claims that in 1865 he graduated in medicine from the University of Maryland, which profession he practiced at W---- until 1881. He then moved to Ohio, because, he says, he could endure no longer the persecution of a good many enemies which he had made on account of his service in the Union Army. In Ohio, he states, he engaged in the manufacture of proprietary medicines and claims to have sold out his business sometime later for $50,000.

Some idea of the patient's daily conduct may be had from the statements of his landlady, with whom he lived for a considerable time.

It seems that he occupied a room on the top floor, which he would allow no one to enter. If anyone rapped on the door he would open it very slightly and cautiously, conducting conversation through a crack in the door. He led the life of a hermit, living in absolute seclusion, cooking his own meals in his room. After he was removed to the Hospital this room was entered and newspapers were found piled as high as the ceiling; many of the articles in them were underscored, and numerous clippings were pasted on doors and windows as well as on walls; everything was covered with dirt and dust, and the cooking utensils were strewn all over the room. This lady said that during his stay there he was always very suspicious, kept the blinds drawn, and seemed to be constantly afraid that something was going to happen.

Examination of the patient soon after admission revealed a well-organized and very extensive delusional system, which, according to his story, apparently had its inception during the Civil War. It seems that he had caused the apprehension and execution of a Confederate spy, and ever since then, he states, the relatives and friends of this man have been persecuting him. In 1889 he was granted a pension of $25 per month, but he did not think that this was a fair deal inasmuch as he was not a nurse, but a physician, and should receive at least a hundred dollars per month. He states that he came originally to Washington to have this matter straightened out, but on account of his enemies was unsuccessful. His worst persecutions he believed to have been instigated by the A. E. Company because he had judgment against this Company for about $50,000. He stated that this was obtained in a damage suit which he brought against this Company because they wanted to charge him expressage of something like 40Â¢ on a prepaid package. Following this damage suit, the Express Company's agents, especially members of the R. family, have been spying on him and persecuting him; he finally sued a member of this R. family and obtained judgment against him in the Circuit Court of Virginia for $9,000. When asked to explain how he figures out these exact amounts of damage, he is ready with a thousand plausible reasons why the amounts were as he gives them. He was finally charged with perjury, found guilty, and while awaiting sentence was adjudged by a jury to be of unsound mind and sent to the Government Hospital for the Insane.

He believes that members of this R. family were behind this because they were afraid that the patient would collect on his judgments, which by this time, amounted to something like $20,000, and which, as he put it, "were good, valid and subsisting, not reversed or otherwise vacated."

During his sojourn in the Government Hospital for the Insane, he was always very suspicious and seclusive, keeping to his room practically all the time and aloof from the other patients in the ward. He adhered very tenaciously to his delusional system and believed himself fully justified in all his litigious pursuits. With all this he was clear and coherent in conversation, his memory was quite well-preserved, and he had no difficulty in keeping himself fully informed on current events. Aside from the very evident caution and very profound suspicious attitude which he manifested during a conversation, he made no abnormal impression.

In October, 1908, he was paroled by a Justice of the District of Columbia Supreme Court to his brother's care in Ohio; and patient's reasons for this parole are interesting: He states that he was told by the District Attorney that he would be paroled if he were to go to Ohio and vote for President Taft. This he says he did, believing he had carried out the terms of his parole, promptly returned to Washington and resumed his former activities. The first thing he did upon his return was to have the following two bills introduced in Congress, both of which are wholly based on his delusional ideas:--

"H. R. Bill xxxx, January 11, 1910. Mr. A. introduced the following bill, which was referred to the Committee on Military Affairs and returned to be printed:--A bill to correct the military record of X----. Be it enacted in the Senate and House of Representatives of the United States of America, in Congress Assembled, that the Secretary of War be and is hereby authorized and directed to correct and amend the military record of X----, late assistant surgeon instead of nurse, so as to read: X----, Assistant Surgeon of the United States Army, on the 12th day of April, 1863, and to place the name of X---- upon the retired list of the United States Army as Assistant Surgeon."

The second bill was as follows:--

"Senate Bill xxx. Referred to the Committee on Claims. A bill for the relief of X----. Be it enacted by the Senate and House of Representatives of the United States of America, in Congress Assembled, that the Secretary of the Treasury be and he is hereby authorized to pay out of any money in the Treasury, not otherwise appropriated, to X----, formerly a resident of W., in the State of Maryland, the sum of $45,600, being the amount of the loss sustained by said X---- in property and business while he was performing important service for the Government in the year 1863, and in recognition of valuable service rendered the United States, and compensation for loss resulting from his causing the arrest of a Confederate Spy, at the opening of the Gettysburg campaign, thereby defeating the Confederate plan to capture the two thousand or more government wagons loaded with the munitions of war of the Union Army, which sum shall be in full of all claims and demands upon the part of said X---- against the Government of the United States by reason of the premises."

The patient was soon apprehended and returned to the Government Hospital for the Insane, where he is at present.

In an extremely interesting brief of his case, prepared by the patient himself, which, unfortunately, is too lengthy to be given in its entirety here, he states, among other things:--

"I was indicted on the 2nd of April, 1906, by the grand jury of said

court, for perjury; the grand jury was about to adjourn, as they had
no evidence upon which to indict me, but they were called back to do
so in order to please the A. E. Company. The grand jury was authorized
to indict me in order to please the A. E. Company, as I was later told
by several members of that jury. I have also been told by numerous
detectives that they were hired by the A. E. Company to watch me." He
continues in his brief:--"I was kept in jail until the eve of the 13th
of February, 1905, when the jail doors were suddenly thrown open and I
was told to go home, the same as the circumstances related in the
Bible concerning St. Paul and Silas, who were in prison and during the
night their chains fell off, the prison doors opened and they were set
free by the hand of God. I believe the same thing happened to me; I
was released by the hand of God."

He further states:--"There are more than 17,000 newspapers in the
United States, and these people had it printed in 10,000 of them that
I had committed perjury. I sued them for slander, and a more just and
upright case or grievance for bringing suit could never be found."

Attention might be called here to the grandiose phase of his disorder.
His was no common slander; it was published in 10,000 newspapers.
Neither was his release from prison an ordinary everyday occurrence,
but resembled the Biblical episode of St. Paul's release from prison.
Later on, when through advancing years his intellect is becoming more
and more enfeebled, he expresses his grandiose ideas in a more direct
and naÃ¯ve manner. He tells the physician that he knows the law better
than any living authority; that none of the so-called judges around
town can compare with him; that he has made a brief of a case which
could not be duplicated by anyone. He is likewise the greatest
physician, and he will prove this when he gets to court. At this
writing he is beginning to show evidence of senile deterioration and
is no longer the keen manipulator of the law of years ago. He
endeavors now to gain his ends by more direct and extremely puerile

and childish methods. To illustrate:--His physician had left the institution about a year ago, and soon afterwards X---- produced an affidavit purporting to have been made by this physician in which he set forth that X---- was sound mentally; that this physician came to this conclusion after a thorough examination of X----, etc., etc. Upon the physician's return to the Hospital X---- was asked concerning this by him, but he stolidly maintained that it was genuine and given him by the questioner. This famous litigant has reached a stage where things simply are as he wants them to be. Whether this poor derelict will be permitted by his deluded or unscrupulous attorneys to end his days in peace at the Hospital, time alone will tell. Thus far his lunacy case has been carried by them to the Court of Appeals.

CASE II.--Y. was found guilty of libel in the Criminal Court of the District of Columbia, and while awaiting sentence was adjudged insane by a jury and admitted to the Government Hospital for the Insane, June 22, 1911, at the age of 56. Y. is an attorney by profession, comes from a prominent family in Ohio, and has received an excellent education. According to information obtained from his father and sister, it appears that one sister and a nephew are insane; that the patient himself has been considered insane by members of his immediate family since 1889, when, as the result of a court-martial for disobedience, he was discharged from the Navy, where he then held the grade of ensign. Immediately following this discharge he took up the study of law and began to specialize in maritime affairs, handling almost exclusively sailors' grievances against the Navy Department. He spent a great deal of time working up these cases, occasionally writing contributions to the Maritime Register, for which publication he was a regular correspondent for several years. In these papers he would constantly harp on the irregularities and illegalities of many of the government affairs. At home he always acted in a peculiar manner, never had much to say to anyone, was unreasonable, fault-finding and complaining; he always wanted things his own way. Several years ago he came to live with his sister, accompanied by his wife and child. Although he paid nothing for board and lodging for the three, he complained about the food and had something to say in criticism for every little inconvenience. He would frequently leave town without saying a word to any member of his family, and would reappear just as suddenly. He kept to his room almost constantly, leaving same only for his meals. On one occasion he wrote his wife, who at the time was staying with her child at his sister's house, that she should watch this sister, as he feared she might try to poison the child. Sometime in 1910, he came to his home town, had an interview with the Judge of the Probate Court, and left town without visiting any of his relatives, although they lived only four squares distant. At that time this Judge told the patient's father that he thought the patient was mentally unbalanced. He was always considered by his relatives as being of a morose disposition, vindictive and selfish. On a later visit to his parental home he acted very strangely about the house, disarranged things, kept the rooms in disorder, and was busy writing constantly. At this time he left home suddenly without taking leave of anyone. A few years ago, while home on a visit, he declared that his father was incompetent to manage his own affairs, instituted legal proceedings to have himself appointed committee for his father, petitioning the court on the ground of his father's insanity. In this, of course, he was defeated.

The patient himself states that he graduated from Annapolis in 1878, between which year and 1883 he traveled in Europe and South America as midshipman. In 1883 he entered the Cincinnati Law School, where he remained one year. After this he states he acted in the capacity of Judge Advocate General for a short time while on shore duty. He then went to sea again and finally resigned from the Navy in 1887, with the grade of ensign. (As has already been indicated above, the patient was dismissed from the Navy for disobedience and disrespect.) He then entered the practice of law in Cincinnati, at which he continued until his appointment to the Department of the Interior on June 1, 1904, at a salary of $1,000 per annum. Here he remained until 1908 in the capacity of clerk, when he resigned, receiving at that time the same salary. He says he was moderately successful financially as a lawyer, and did a good deal of literary work. He is especially proud of a case which he conducted in the Court of Appeals, where he obtained a decision setting aside a Naval court-martial. He says that this is the only decision of its kind ever rendered, and on that account he is very proud of this. According to his own story, he was always moderate in his habits, and prior to his marriage in November, 1902, he had never come in conflict with anyone. The latter part of this statement is contradicted by his relatives, who state that for more than twenty years past, the patient has exhibited an uncontrollable desire to sue people for all sorts of imaginary grievances, and that on this account he frequently came into serious conflicts. The patient is inclined to put all the blame for his difficulties to his wife, whom he describes with a great deal of rancor as the descendant of an insane and illegitimate grandfather and illy-favored mother. He thinks that his wife was slightly unbalanced, accuses her of being responsible for the death of their first child, and of various other misconduct. However, everything went tolerably well until April, 1906, when their second child was born. The doctor who attended Mrs. Y. during her confinement, a very prominent local physician, testified in open court at that time, that from his observation of the patient's acts he believed him to be insane. This, the patient said, precipitated a lot of trouble between him and his wife. He does not enter into details concerning the difficulties he had with the physician, but the details are extremely illuminating. It appears that the patient refused to pay this doctor's bill and was sued for the debt. At the time of the trial he gave as his defense the following two reasons why he should not pay this bill:--The first one was that inasmuch as this doctor lived in a part of the city which would necessitate the crossing of a railroad grade in order to reach the patient's house, and that on this account there was a possibility of his being detained at the crossing during an emergency call, he had no right to take the case in the first place, and therefore he was not entitled to payment. His second reason was that inasmuch as this doctor wore a beard, he carried more germs into the house than would otherwise have had access to it; therefore he should forfeit his fee. In 1907 his wife obtained a divorce on the grounds of cruelty and non-support, and was given the custody of the child; this had the effect of launching the patient upon a new series of litigation. His first retaliating measure was the abduction of the child, which brought about his indictment by a grand jury and subsequent arrest. The reason he gave for taking the child out of the District was that his wife lived in a house over an old abandoned cellar, and that it was therefore an unhealthy place for the child. Upon regaining his freedom he began to investigate the ground upon which the grand jury indicted him, and soon, he states, he discovered that the District Attorney's office committed a gigantic fraud by having maliciously misrepresented the case to the grand jury; this body, he says, was led to believe that the Ohio decree granting his wife the guardianship of the child held good in the District, whereas the law of the District specifically states that no extra-territorial decree should be recognized within the District. He further discovered that Mr. J., his wife's attorney, knowingly and maliciously became a party to this fraud, and he immediately proceeded to file charges of mal-practice against this attorney before the Grievance Committee of the District Bar Association. The result of this was that the patient was charged with libel in the Criminal Court. To his great surprise, he says, the Court recognized this charge and found him guilty of same. While awaiting sentence he was adjudged insane by a jury and committed to the Government Hospital for the Insane. He believes this commitment is the result of a deep-laid conspiracy on the part of the District Attorney's office and some of the District Judges. These officials, he believes, were afraid of him because at a hearing before a Senate Committee he started to expose their fraudulent conduct. The judges were prejudiced against him throughout, and it might be interesting to mention here that among the multitudinous bills which he had proposed for enactment into law since in the Government Hospital for the Insane, there is one which is intended to abolish entirely the Courts of the District of Columbia, so that unfortunates like him might get a chance before unprejudiced judges. This deep conspiracy against him, he is convinced, dates as far back as 1906, when the Ohio Courts appointed his wife guardian of his child.

No great difficulty need be experienced in forming an opinion of this man's mental status after having followed his history thus far, but when we further read that, during his sojourn in the Government Hospital for the Insane, he has evinced the most persistent tendency to weave into his delusional system every important occurrence of local or even national interest, that he sees a clear relationship between his case and the recent change of administration, and is fully convinced that many important officials held over from the last administration owe considerable gratitude to him; when he is seen in his self-assumed most important rÃ´le of the man of destiny, flooding Congress, the Courts and many high officials with petitions, charges, writs, and proposed investigations; when one sees the criminal code as transformed by him; then one begins to get a proper perspective of the grandiose phase of this man's mental disorder. It is impossible, of course, with the limited space at our disposal, to even give the briefest outline of his activities, but it might be stated that only within the past several months he has succeeded in very ingeniously getting his case before a considerable number of senators and congressmen and many other prominent officials. Among the bills which he proposes to have enacted into law, is one, as has been mentioned, to abolish entirely the Courts of the District of Columbia. Of course, courts which cannot administer justice, as he sees it, must be abolished.

On his admission to the Government Hospital for the Insane, he really welcomed the procedure, stating that at last he had the opportunity to be under the supervision of a trained physician who would soon discover that he was absolutely sane and would render a report to that effect, thus vindicating him. Unfortunately for the physician, he did not see his way clear to render such a report, and Y's amiability soon changed into a very bitter antagonism towards the one who had immediate charge of him, showing a great deal of rancor in his attacks upon him, in spite of the fact that he has been accorded all sorts of privileges. He has, of course, by this time consigned many hospital officials to life imprisonment, and the amount of damages which he expects to collect from them and the Government runs into fabulous sums. He soon began to solicit the grievances of his fellow patients, establishing, so to speak, a law office in miniature upon the ward; and whereas formerly these patients in the criminal department merely aired their grievances as they saw them, they now accompany them with quotations from the statutes concerning these points furnished by this legal missionary. Soon, however, even the insane patients on his ward began to distrust him, and at the present time there is hardly an attendant or patient in the building who cares to associate with Y. He missed no opportunity of playing upon the credulity of the younger and less sophisticated attendants in the criminal building, at first begging and urging them to carry his petitions to their destination in a surreptitious manner, and finding this of no avail threatening them with fines and imprisonment as accomplices in this gigantic crime of keeping him confined in a hospital. When not out walking he keeps himself constantly busy making out documents, briefs, petitions, bills, etc. He is very seclusive, keeping himself aloof from the other patients, as he considers himself very much their superior.

Now this master litigant, this profoundly diseased man, succeeds in making quite a normal impression in a casual interview, and in his writings he frequently succeeds in conveying the idea of being quite normal. Each isolated fact looks plausible enough to the casual observer. He talks quite rationally, shows a remarkably well-preserved memory, has never exhibited hallucinations or those gross disorders of conduct which to the lay mind form the *sine qua non* of mental disease. It is only after a close study of the entire life history, of the many fine shades of deviation from the normal which this man exhibits, that one discovers that his mind is very seriously affected indeed, and that because of his plausibility he belongs to a rather dangerous type of mentally diseased individuals.

The chief aim of this paper has already been indicated, and we shall adhere to our original intention of rendering it as free from purely didactic considerations as is consistent with clearness. For this reason the case histories given above were considerably abbreviated and only such an account rendered as would suffice to convince even a layman that the two individuals in question are seriously affected mentally. Of this there should not be the slightest doubt in anyone's mind, neither should one encounter here any diagnostic difficulties. The only difficult point, and a point which may become of considerable forensic importance, is the exact estimation of the duration of the illness in each instance. From the available data at hand it would seem that in the case of X----, the disease had its inception in the episode during the late Civil War, though the possibility of retrospective falsification must be kept in mind; while Y seems to have been launched upon his litigious career by his dismissal from the Navy. It is therefore but fair to assume that in both instances the disease has existed for a great number of years. Nevertheless, it was only when these individuals faced the bar as defendants in criminal suits that the disease was recognized in either case. One may readily see, therefore, how easily mental disease may remain undetected, especially if one neglects to take an inventory of the individual's past life. I have already alluded to the difficulty frequently experienced in having evidence of this nature accepted in a court of law, and here, it seems to me, is room for a good deal of reform in procedure. Thus far society's side of this problem has been chiefly emphasized; but what about these unfortunate derelicts, X---- and Y? Both of them are at present confined in the criminal department of the Government Hospital for the Insane with criminal charges pending against them. Assuming that our contentions with respect to their mental status are correct, what possible justification is there to hold them responsible before the law for their acts? Nevertheless, the same sort of procedure is constantly taking place; individuals are being sent daily to hospitals for the insane, presumably for the purpose of giving them the best possible chance for recovery, the best modes of treatment, while at the same time the law persists in carrying them as individuals charged with crime, thus throwing many obstacles in the way of proper care and treatment. With many of these individuals the mere fact that there is still a criminal charge pending against them seems to act in a deleterious manner upon their mentality, while in the great majority of instances, owing to the fact that they must be carried as criminals, unusual precautions have to be resorted to both in their confinement and in the matter of various privileges, thereby vitiating in a great measure all attempts at treatment.

These are some of the problems which present themselves from a study of life histories such as are here reported, a better mutual understanding concerning which between the lawyer and the physician would unquestionably tend to a more enlightened administration of the law.

NOTES

[1] MAUDSLEY: "Responsibility in Mental Disease."

[2] KRAEPELIN, E.: "Psychiatrie." Achte Auflage. Leipzig, 1910. Bd. 1.

[3] TANZI: "Mental Disease."

[4] BISCHOFF: "Lehrbuch der Gerichtlichen Psychiatrie." 1912.

[5] SANDER: Quoted by White. "Outlines of Psychiatry." Fourth Edition.

CHAPTER IV
THE MALINGERER: A CLINICAL STUDY

I

The following study is undertaken less for the purpose of discussing the psychology of malingering than with the object in view of illustrating by means of clinical records the type of individual who malingers. The opinion is a general one that malingering is a form of mental reaction to which certain individuals resort in their effort to adjust themselves to a difficult situation of life. Being a form of human behavior, it should have been approached, therefore, with the same attitude of mind as any other type of behavior.

A perusal, however, of the literature on the subject, especially of the contributions of the older writers, reveals that with certain isolated exceptions the subject was viewed primarily from the standpoint of the moralist. Even today one sees in certain quarters a good deal made--certainly a great deal more than the facts would justify--of the "insanity dodge" in criminal cases. It is true that today, notwithstanding the still broadly prevalent tendency to view with suspicion every mental disorder which becomes manifested in connection with the commission of crime, the danger of error in this respect has been reduced to a minimum owing to the more advanced stage of psychiatry, and therefore the practical importance of the subject of malingering is not so great as it was formerly. We find, nevertheless, justification for the further study of this subject in the fact that, aside from its purely psychiatric importance, the more intensive study of the malingerer offers a solution for some of the important problems in criminology. As one of the results of this more intensive study may be mentioned the gradually-gained conviction that malingering and actual mental disease are not only not mutually exclusive phenomena in the same individual, but that malingering itself is a form of mental reaction manifested almost exclusively by those of an inferior mental make-up; that is, by individuals concerning whom there must always be considerable doubt as to the degree of responsibility before the law. As a result of this recognition cases of pure malingering in individuals absolutely normal mentally are becoming rarer every day in psychiatric experience.

The conviction was further gained that malingering as well as lying and deceit in general, far from being a form of conduct deliberately and consciously selected by an individual for the purpose of gaining a certain known end, is in a great majority of instances wholly determined by unconscious motives, by instinctive biologic forces over which the individual has little or no control. This is one of the factors which determines the growing realization among present-day psychiatrists of the extreme difficulty to state in a given case which is malingered and which genuine in the symptomatology. That such views should encounter opposition among our jurists is perfectly natural, threatening as it does with complete annihilation that wholly artificial concept of the "freedom of will" upon which our laws are based.

In touching upon the subjects of "responsibility" and "freedom of will" I incur the danger of adding to the general misunderstanding which still exists between the physician and jurist concerning crime and the criminal.

Speaking from personal convictions, I see no real justification whatever for this misunderstanding, unless it be the difference in the mode of approach to the subject on the part of the two. The jurist is compelled by existing statutes to look upon crime largely in the abstract--not as it concerns the individual who committed the deed, but as it is affected by the statutes covering it. The physician, on the other hand, sees in the criminal act a form of reaction to an intrinsic or extrinsic stimulus by a feeling, willing, and acting human being, and proceeds accordingly to analyze in a concrete manner the forces which brought about this particular form of reaction in this particular individual. As a result of this mode of approach to the subject he is enabled to conceive of "responsibility" as something fluid, something extremely variable, and which may be affected by a thousand-and-one things, and not as something absolutely fixed and invariable and which may be definitely foreseen by a set of statutes.

Any attempt to bring about this most desirable uniformity of approach to the subject of criminology between the jurist and the physician must be based primarily upon intensive study of the personality of the criminal. Such is the aim of this paper.

II

In the last analysis malingering is to be looked upon as a special form of lying, and its proper understanding will necessitate a clear insight into lying in general.

Lying, a very natural and generally prevalent phenomenon, may manifest itself in all gradations--from the occasional, quite innocent "white lie" as it occurs in a perfectly normal individual to the pathological lying exhibited in that mental state known as "pseudologia phantastica." Its proper understanding, however, no matter under what circumstances and to what degree it be manifested, will be possible only through a strict adherence to the theory of absolute psychic determinism.

Lying, like every other psychic phenomenon, never occurs fortuitously, but always has its psychic determinants which determine its type and degree.

Naturally many of these determinants are quite obvious and readily ascertainable. One has only to recall the lying and deceit practiced by children. But many others, if indeed not most of them, are active in the individual's unconscious motives and accessible objectively as well as subjectively only with great difficulty and by means of special psychological methods.

The degree of participation of unconscious motives in lying will be determined in the individual case by the extent of repression necessitated because of social, ethical, and Ãsthetic considerations. It is for this reason that lying is most prevalent and exhibited with the least amount of *critique* in those individuals who either have never developed those restraining tendencies which a normal appreciation of social, ethical, and Ãsthetic consideration demands, or in whom these restraining influences have been weakened or abolished by some exogenous insult to the nervous system--as, for instance, the tendency to fabrication dependent upon chronic alcoholism or morphinism. A beautiful illustration of the latter type is furnished by General Ivolgin in Dostoieffsky's "Idiot."

The child's tendency to lying and deceit is dependent to a large extent upon the undeveloped state of those restraining forces. To state, however, that this is the sole mechanism underlying the phenomenon of lying would be to state only half a truth. For it is an undeniable fact that, no matter how strongly endowed an individual may be with ethical or moral feelings, still there comes a time when these are entirely forgotten and neglected; when, finding himself in a stressful situation, the instinctive demands for a most satisfactory and least painful adjustment, no matter at what cost, assert themselves. It is then that the lie serves the purpose of a more direct, less tedious gratification of an instinctive demand. The resort to this mode of reaction, to evasion of real issues for the purpose of gratification of instinctive demands, is not characteristic of man alone, but is quite prevalent even in some very low forms of life. We will have more to say about this later. It is an important tool in the struggle for existence among all living beings; it is one of the mechanisms by means of which the weaker inferior being escapes annihilation at the hands of the stronger, superior being.

Malingering, it will be seen later, appears to certain individuals to be the only possible means of escape from and evasion of a stressful and difficult situation of life. The lack of *critique* which permits such an abortive attempt at adjustment and the inherent weakness and incapacity to meet life's problems squarely in the face which drives them to resort to such a means of defense are some of the traits of character which serve to distinguish these individuals from what is generally conceived to be normal man.

The extent to which lying and allied behavior depend upon unconscious motives has never been so well illustrated as in recent psychoanalytic literature, especially in a paper by Brill.[1] This author is so thoroughly convinced of the value of conscious lying as an indicator of unconscious strivings and motives that he frequently asks his patients to construct--artificially--dreams which he finds to be of valuable aid in the analysis of the patient's unconscious. After citing a number of examples Brill states: "These examples suffice to show that these seemingly involuntary constructions have the same significance as real dreams, and that as an instrument for the discovery of hidden complexes they are just as important as the latter. Furthermore, they also demonstrate some of the mechanisms of conscious deception. The first patient deliberately tried to fool me by making up what he thought to be a senseless production, but what he actually did was to produce a distorted wish. He later admitted to me that for days he was on his guard lest I should discover his inverted sexuality, but it never occurred to him that I could discover it in his manner. That his artificial dreams have betrayed him is not so strange when one remembers that *no mental production, voluntary or involuntary, can represent anything but a vital part of the person producing it*."

Were this thesis on malingering to succeed in nothing else than in bringing home to our legal brethren this important truth of absolute psychic determinism, that a man is what he is and acts as he does because of everything that has gone before him--because of ontogenetic as well as phylogenetic instinctive motives--it will have fully established its raison d'Âªtre. For a realization of this truth would at once annihilate from our minds that deceptive notion of the "freedom of will" upon which our laws are based, and will be certain to bring about a more enlightened solution of the problem of the criminal, all attempts at which, we are constrained to state, have thus far[1]

---

[1] Intimate contact with members of the legal profession, both professionally and socially, for some years past has convinced me that the average lawyer still looks upon the ideas concerning crime and the criminal expressed by physicians of a forensic bent as totally unpractical and visionary. It would take only a brief visit to a criminal department of any modern, well-conducted hospital for the insane to convince any fair-minded individual that the physician handles the problem of the criminal not only in a more scientific and rational manner than does one not possessed of this particular training, but also in an eminently more practical manner, even so far as dollars and cents are concerned. I have frequently had patients come under my observation who for a great number of years had been oscillating between penal institutions and hospitals for the insane, in whom each additional sentence did not only fail to bring about the hoped-for reformation, but served to render them more depraved and criminally inclined, and who would have undoubtedly continued this checkered career throughout life, had not their true, unreformable nature been discovered and thus caused

undeniably been huge failures.

The psychic mechanism of lying is the same both in the occasional and in the pathological liar--in both it is the expression of a wish--but the difference in the personalities of the two is a very decided one. On the one hand we have an individual who closely approaches normal man, while on the other hand one who is closely allied to the mentally diseased. The difference between the pathological liar and the habitual criminal, aside from the moral phase of lying, is perhaps but a very slight one, when we keep in mind that in both instances we are dealing with individuals who habitually resort to a form of reaction in their attempts at adjustment to reality which aims at a direct, simple, and least resistant means for gratification. In both we are dealing with a type of mental organization which is primarily incompetent to face reality in an adequate, socially acceptable manner, and therefore has to resort to constant deceit and lying, and in which those inhibitions determined by social, ethical, and Ãlsthetic considerations are equally impotent. The marked egotistic trend which constantly comes to the surface in the habitual liar when he attempts to play the part of the hero and central figure in the most fantastic, bizarre, and impossible adventures is likewise frequently at the bottom of the escapades of the habitual criminal. The two traits are frequently, though by no means always, concomitant manifestations in the same individual.

When, in 1891, Anton DelbrÃ¼ck[2] published the first comprehensive study
of the pathological liar, he not only succeeded in very accurately delineating a more or less distinct psychopathological entity, but also

their permanent isolation from society, not by the jurist but by the physician. Should reformation ever take place in any of these individuals it is safe to assume that the one who was clear-visioned enough to discover the cause of their antisocial existence would likewise be competent enough to know when this cause has disappeared.

furnished additional proof in substantiation of the fact, well known in psychiatry but as yet unrecognized by the legal profession, that the transition from mental health to mental disease is not a sudden one; that any dividing line which would have for its purpose the strict separation of the mentally sound from the mentally diseased must of necessity be a purely imaginary one, and one not justified by existing facts.

The transition from absolute mental health to distinct mental disease is never delimited by distinct landmarks, but shows any number of intermediary gradations. Nowhere is this better illustrated than in the pathological liar. Here one sees how a psychic phenomenon regularly manifested by perfectly normal individuals may gradually acquire such dimensions and dominate the individual to such an extent as to render him frankly insane.

To endeavor, however, to definitely state where normality leaves off and disease begins would be, to say the least, to attempt something well-nigh impossible. And yet this is just what the jurist constantly demands of the alienist. The law as it is laid down in the statutes, especially in this country, does not permit of any intermediary stages between mental health and mental disease. An individual, according to law, must either be sane or insane. This point seems to me to be of very vital importance, and I shall have occasion to refer to it again in the consideration of our clinical material.

The part played in lying by disturbances of the apprehensive, retentive, and reproductive faculties will not be discussed here in detail. These undeniably have their influence in facilitating the mechanism of lying. But to attribute this phenomenon wholly to disturbances of this nature would be to assign to it a purely passive rÃ´le, whereas experience teaches that back of every lie are active forces, either conscious or unconscious, which give birth to it and determine its type and degree.

The following two cases will illustrate better than any formal description could what is meant by pathological lying, a psychopathological state for which DelbrÃ¼ck proposed the term "Pseudologia phantastica":

E. W. S., a colored male, aged thirty-two years, was admitted to the Government Hospital for the Insane from Fort D. A. Russell, Wyoming, on January 29, 1912, on a medical certificate which stated the following: "Patient is a native of Porto Rico; has been sailor and soldier; has occasionally used alcoholic beverages, but usually the light wines or beer; is very good-natured, occasionally melancholy and lachrymose; gave a history of 'fits', and was previously discharged from the army on this account. He was thought to be 'queer' in his organization and had more or less trouble with the men, who made fun of him. He was sent to the hospital from the guard-house in October, 1911, and his mental condition noted at that time. His present symptoms were described as delusions of grandeur: 'Queen Victoria was his instructor in English', 'King Edward of England was his school chum.' He thinks he was royal interpreter. He does speak a number of languages fluently and, so far as we can learn, with fair correctness (?)."

On admission to this hospital the patient was in excellent health physically; Wassermann reaction with the blood-serum negative. Mentally he was clearly oriented in all respects and fully in touch with his immediate environment. He comprehended readily what was said to him, and his replies, aside from his extreme tendency to fabrication, were coherent and to the point. Intelligence tests showed him to be intellectually about on a par with the average negro of his social and educational status.

When asked to give his family and past personal history, he recited the following: He knew nothing of his grandparents or parents, and denied having any living sisters or brothers. One brother died in Chicago in 1906; thinks he must have been murdered, because he himself was almost murdered in November, 1911, when they attempted to assassinate President Taft out in Wyoming. King Mendilic, of Cape Town, Africa, now dead for seven years, was his cousin. The patient himself was Prince of Abyssinia, where he reigned for eight years, having remained in that country from 1896 to 1899, and conducting the affairs of state the remaining five years by correspondence, with the approval of Lord King Edward. He stated he was born in Porto Rico in 1876, and calculates his present age as thirty-four, as this is 1912. About two months ago he received a letter from Queen Alexandra of England telling him he was thirty-two years, ten-twelfths and two days old, or thirty-two years, two months, two weeks, and two days. Asked how much ten-twelfths of a year was, he said: "Three months, three and two days." When told that ten-twelfths of a year equaled ten months, he replied: "The calendar of the English era, which is 'our calendar', does not correspond with the American calendar, but, being in America, I believe I ought to figure from their standpoint." He left Porto Rico at the age of six; does not know who took care of him up to this time, as he never knew his parents, stating that he was just thrown on the mercies of the country. At the age of six, upon the recommendation and advice of King Alfonso of Spain, he was taken to England by Queen Victoria, who came to Porto Rico especially for this purpose. When asked his opinion as to why Queen Victoria should have taken so much interest in him he stated that he did not know positively, but it may have been because he was related to King Solomon of Bible fame. Requested to explain this relationship to King Solomon, he traces it in the following manner: He was a cousin of King Mendilic, who in turn was the "third reigning seed" or stepson of King Solomon. Queen Victoria, whom he calls "Mother Victor", because she took the place of his mother, sent him to "Hammenotia School" in Oxford University, which he attended for four and a half years, received his diploma, and was transferred to Cambridge College. Here he attended for four years.

At the former school he learned the alphabet, went up to the seventh grade, learned some medicine about herbs, etc. "I learned some medicine, not all of it. I didn't practice it much; just practiced it enough to do the country good. At that time we didn't have any doctors." At Cambridge he learned "The Reigning of the Thornes", or the laws of the country. Upon request he described in minutest detail the city of Cambridge. When asked whether he remembered a large oak tree which grew on the banks of the river flowing through the city, he replied: "I should say I do; many a time I sat on the banks of this river during my student days." Earlier in his student days at Cambridge he learned German, French, and English. It should be remarked here that the patient actually did know a few common phrases in several languages which he picked up during his sailor days. But he always insisted that he knew thoroughly twenty-two languages, and when asked to enumerate these he found himself in deep water and was obliged to invent the languages for the occasion. Nevertheless he stuck to this story, and was always ready to launch upon the task of enumerating his twenty-two languages.

After his four years' sojourn at Cambridge, Mother Victoria sent him to "Saint Palestine", Jerusalem, where he remained for fourteen months, learning the constitution of the country, by-laws, etc. Mother Victoria and Father Edward (Queen and King of England) brought him up so that he could properly reign over Abyssinia. He states that he saw Queen Victoria frequently, and was at her funeral in August, 1910, shortly after the death of Pope Leo. Lord King Edward died about three months later. The Queen died about the age of seventy-six, as did King Edward at the same age, from grief and senility. Here he adds that his maternal grandmother was sister to Queen Victoria. While at the English Court he held the position of "Prince of Escorts." He left Jerusalem to go to school at Sydney, Australia, for one year. He then went to sea on Lord Edward's naval reserve boat, which he had permission to use. Remained at sea for three years and four months, visiting China, France, Japan, Germany, Austria, Turkey, Italy, Havana, Archipelago. When asked to repeat these countries, he omits some of them and adds others.

He then came to the United States for the purpose of electioneering, stump-speaking, etc., all to benefit the government. He then became a United States interpreter in the Philippines from 1896 to 1902, at a salary of $75 per month and expenses. He then returned to Porto Rico, where he remained until 1910. Following this he attended the funerals of Queen Victoria, Pope Leo, Lord Edward, and his cousin Mendilic, and finally came to Chicago, where he enlisted as first-class sergeant in the United States Army. He was sent to Fort D. A. Russell, Wyoming, to serve in the Hospital Corps, at a salary of $48 per month and maintenance. There everything went well until he got to worrying and crying, so they sent him here. He acted thus because he was ill-treated, was not treated right for a man of his abilities, was sworn at too much, and called bad names by the enlisted men. They did this because they were jealous of his "politicalness", his education; he never swore, drank, or gambled like the others did. Was robbed of his every possession in Cheyenne, Wyoming, by members of the Ninth Cavalry and Eleventh Infantry. Lost $1400 in the past five months in cash and property. They robbed him of his horse, buggy, clothes, and jewelry, including chain, watch, finger ring, a pair of jasper earrings. He could hear them talking about him day and night; feared to leave his room, for he was continually threatened. They were going to kill him. On this account he was taken to the hospital and kept under close guard, because they could protect him. He had to leave at night. He did so after having received a telegram from the Surgeon-General of the Army, asking him to report to the Hospital Corps at St. Elizabeth's Hospital, Washington, D.C. As one of the main reasons why they had it in for him he gives the following: There was a car line running from Fort D. A. Russell to Cheyenne, the fare being ten cents. The men wanted it reduced to five cents. As the one in charge of the canteen he had it in his power to approve or disapprove of this reduction. He disapproved of it because he didn't think that ten cents was an excessive charge for a three-mile ride, especially since they spent so much money on drink, etc. He had a runabout motor car, so they thought this was why he disapproved of it. "In consequence they were on my trail." Part of the way to Washington he came in a private car, but this they deprived him of at Omaha, Nebraska. Perhaps they did this because they thought it was too large for him, but, inasmuch as it was assigned for his private use, they had no business taking it away from him.

During the recital of the foregoing the patient was bright and alert, and his attention was easily gained and very well held. He quickly understood everything that was said to him, and replies were prompt, relevant, and coherent, though, of course, entirely colored by his bizarre fabrications.

During his sojourn at this hospital he was a model patient in every respect, worked diligently with a farm gang, though frequently dilating upon the fact of having the responsibility of the whole gang on his shoulders. On several occasions he gave evidence of being of a highly sensitive make-up, becoming readily insulted, but he always reacted to these real or imaginary insults in a mild and kind sort of way, always preferring to go out of people's way rather than retaliate. Hallucinatory disturbances were never manifested.

The story of his past life was gone over with him on a number of occasions, but on each occasion he gave a different, highly fantastic recital of his past adventures, always using high-sounding words and phrases and high-sounding names, many of which he mispronounced. Many of the words used by him were of his own coinage, if one were to judge by the sound of them. He was always very pleasant and agreeable, and enjoyed reciting his past immensely. In all these bizarre and marvelous adventures he played the chief rÃ´le and occupied the center of the stage.

He was finally induced to give an explanation of his extreme love for lying, which he gave as follows: "It isn't because I don't know better, doctor, but because I think it will make me feel better, that's all. When I tell of all these big things it makes me feel that I am a little above the common herd of negroes, and then I never tell anything to hurt anybody."

He stated that he couldn't really separate the true from the false in his stories, and that he seemed to have little or no control over this tendency to exaggerate things and to weave into real occurrences all sorts of manufactured detail. "I know one thing, doctor; that it's been a habit of mine all my life. I have always tried to exaggerate a bit. It makes me feel, for the time being, that I'm above the other negroes, that's all. I know I always try to make an honest living, and this habit of mine never interfered with me."

A good deal more could be furnished from the records of this man's case in illustration of his pathologic disposition to lying. An ordinary negro soldier, he succeeds in projecting himself, by means of his ready and very fertile fantasy, into the most wonderful situations and in rubbing shoulders with royalty. If we inquire into the causes operative here we first of all see in the fabrications of this individual an unbounded craving for compensation for a natural deficiency--in this instance a racial deficiency. What this man lacks in reality he endeavors to substitute in his fantasy. There can be no doubt that the tendency to lie has reached such dimensions and intensity in this man's mental make-up as to make him absolutely believe in his own impossible fabrications, to render him absolutely helpless in the mazes of his fantastic creations. He is assisted in this by his craving for self-esteem, by his extreme need of compensation for a real deficiency,

by his ready and fertile fantasy, one absolutely devoid of *critique*,
by his extreme suggestibility, and, lastly, what is of great importance,
by his extremely defective apperceptive faculties and consequent
falsifications of memory.

The latter defect was particularly well illustrated in the following
note from my records of the case. He was asked, in the course of my
examination, to repeat a simple story known as the "Shark Story", which
I shall reproduce here in full for the sake of making clear my point:--

"The son of a Governor of Indiana was first officer of an Oriental
steamer. When in the Indian Ocean the boat was overtaken by a typhoon
and was violently tossed about. The officer was suddenly thrown
overboard. A life preserver was thrown to him, but on account of the
heavy sea difficulty was encountered in launching a boat. The crew,
however, rushed to the side of the vessel to keep him in sight, but
before their shuddering eyes the unlucky young man was grasped by one
of the sharks encircling the steamer and was drawn under the water,
leaving only a dark streak of blood."

In reproducing it he said:--

"The son of a Governor of an Oriental steamer was the captain. Now,
doctor, I can't think of those little stories. It isn't because I
haven't brains enough; it's because I'm so poor a scholar at reciting.
I always was." "What happened to the captain?" "That I can't
recollect, neither." "What happened to the ship?"

Here, instead of answering my question, he said: "Doctor, I suppose you
have heard about the big wreck that happened out on the ocean." (This
was when the terrible *Titanic* disaster was on everybody's lips and the
papers were full of the tragedy.) The patient regularly read the papers.
"Tell me about this wreck."

"Well, the steamer was 1200 miles from the land--north-northerly course. It was first reported that 1800 lives were lost; afterwards they found out for certain, through the communication with General Wood, that it was only 1300. Mrs. Zelia Smith, she was on the vessel." (Patient's name is Smith.) "She is Commissioner Hodges's daughter. She was counted lost, for instance, and was found alive. I knew her well; I knew a good many other people on that boat." "About how many people did you know?" "Well, I just only remember some. For instance, Major B----; I knew him well, of course. I dare say I knew all the others, but I knew him best. The boat was in charge of E. C. Smith." "Did you know Captain Smith?" "Yes, sir; I knew him. I didn't know him personally; I only made one voyage with him from Angel Island." "When was that?" "In 1907." "What was the name of the wrecked ship?" "I can't recall that, neither; *Tripoli*, I think it was; she is close on 1500 feet long." "How much money was she supposed to be worth?" "I don't know, sir; there were several heirs who had charge of the ship. She was called the sister-ship *Trinic* and was worth about $25,000. That, perhaps, may not cover her upper-deck cabins." "Did you ever travel on her?" "No, sir; I never was on her. I was on the *Trinic*, the sister-ship. The White Star people own these boats. I used to run a transport between the White Star Line and the Yellow Star Line." Here he was told that the examiner did not know of the existence of a Yellow Star Line, and he replied: "Oh yes, doctor; you heard of the Flying Squadron that reports all these disasters and signals the other ships."

Thus we see that with partial truths, with facts only partially and imperfectly recalled as a framework, he builds his fantastic tales. He read the newspapers regularly, but could not even recall the name of the ill-fortuned ship, or any particulars about the accident. But what of that?--he could readily fill in the hiatuses with his fabrication. He failed entirely in the attempt to reproduce the story given him, and used the talk about the *Titanic* disaster as a subterfuge--as a ready means of escape from the difficulty in which he found himself.

He himself threw some light upon the part played by his craving for self-esteem in his statement: "When I tell of all these big things it makes me feel that I'm a little above the common herd of negroes." He unquestionably believes in these tales, if they are real enough to make him feel above the common herd of negroes. His suggestibility was well illustrated by the suggested river at Cambridge, "on the banks of which he sat many a time during his student days."

The facility with which his imagination, his fantasy, works was demonstrated by the "ink-blotch" test to which he was subjected. This test, in brief, consists of a series of ink blotches which are shown the patient, with the request to describe them as they appear to him. The following are several of his replies: (1) "A woman sitting on a man, seems like she's got a little weaving in her hand; a little stick, sticking out from the weaving, seems like the man's elbow is sticking out back of the shawl." (2) "It seems to me I have seen a volcano that looks like that. I think it is a ship out at sea. I can see the lifeboats lashed to the side, several ripples of water behind." (3) "A figure of a woman with a hand purse or a disfigured arm near the wrist. Her mouth is open and she is looking around. The wind carried her hat off; she has a muff on her right hand. Seems like there is a neck-piece around the muff."

Notice the detail with which he describes the blotches. In this one ordinary speech seemed to have been insufficient to describe the blotch, and he had to resort to a neologism. "Is that supposed to be a 'perpendicament'? It's got a head like a sea devil; the upper part seems like a peacock trying to peck him in the back of the head."

There remains one other thing to be inquired into in this case, and that is the history of epilepsy which accompanied the patient. He was never observed in an epileptic seizure at the military post from which he came to us, and no seizures were observed in this hospital. His own statements concerning this are, like everything else he said, quite totally unreliable. But in repeated examinations he persisted in his statement that he had had but one "spell" in his life, but that he frequently suffered from fits of melancholy. In all probability this one seizure was hysterical in nature, phenomena of which type not infrequently manifest themselves in the pathological liar, as will be seen in the next case.

Here one sees how lying, a mental phenomenon which is looked upon as quite a normal manifestation in a great many people, has reached such dimensions in this individual and has succeeded in dominating his personality to such an extent as to definitely remove him out of the pale of normality and place him within the sphere of the mentally diseased.

There is, of course, no question here about the genuineness of his lying as a symptom of mental aberration; *i.e.*, the fabrication as manifested by this individual is something over which he has no more control than the dementia prÃ¦cox patient has over his delusions. In both instances the symptoms are spontaneous and genuine expressions of a pathological mentality. And yet when such pathological phenomena become manifest in association with some concrete difficulty in the individual's life, say in connection with a threatened punishment for a crime committed, the genuineness of the symptoms is frequently doubted.

One, of course, can readily see with what facility an individual of the type under discussion could malinger mental symptoms. Reality and fiction have about identical values in this type of mental make-up, and it is frequently impossible to separate the genuine from the fictitious in their mental productivity.

It is likewise quite easy to divine why an individual of this sort would resort to malingering in his effort to extricate himself from a difficult situation which he is organically unable to meet squarely in the face. On the contrary, it would be strange indeed were an individual of this type to refrain from resorting to this form of defense. Of course, even the man whose history we have just quoted may still be considered mentally responsible before the law were we to judge him by the legal standards of responsibility. But as physicians we need not on this account refrain from attempting to delineate these mental types in their true colors.

The situation is well illustrated in the following case. Here the symptom of pathological lying is associated with pathological swindling and criminality and offers a fertile field for seeds of malingering.

E. D. C., a white male, aged thirty-four, came to us on April 16, 1914, from the penitentiary at Stillwater, Minn., where he was serving a sentence of ten years for white slavery. He was admitted on a medical certificate which stated that his father was supposed to have died from pulmonary tuberculosis. The patient gave a history of epilepsy until fourteen years of age, likewise of having been a patient in a Vienna hospital for the insane for one and a half years, in 1900 and 1901. So far as was known to the prison authorities, he was mentally depressed and had delusions since his arrival at the Minnesota State Prison on October 11, 1913. The present symptoms were described as mental depression; says that everybody is persecuting him; also has the delusions that he has or can invent a wonderful electric machine which he wants to sell to the government for a hundred million dollars; said he would shoot himself and die in prison. Physical condition was not good. Patient suffered from obstinate constipation, peculiar shuffling gait, suggesting partial loss of control of legs and feet. Complained of constant headache on the top of his head. No fever.

On admission to this hospital the patient was in poor physical health
and very anÃ¦mic. He was quite slender in stature and somewhat
effeminate in manners and speech. He walked with a very marked limp of
the right leg, stating that he had been afflicted in this manner ever
since his first attack of mental trouble at the age of nineteen.
Patellar reflexes were markedly exaggerated on both sides, the left
more so than the right, and ankle clonus was present on the left side.
Babinski phenomenon was absent. While the reflexes were being tested
he volunteered the information that his left patellar reflex was very
much stronger than the right. He was a very glib talker and spoke
fluently in five foreign languages. He gave his name as E. J. B.,
Count de C., the son of the chamberlain to the Austrian Emperor and of
a famous Austrian countess. In the official papers which accompanied
him to the hospital the above name was followed by several aliases. He
talked in an affected, whining manner, constantly complained of
various bodily ailments, and showed a marked tendency to
hypochondriasis. He spoke of himself as a poor, down-trodden, and
persecuted unfortunate who is being constantly misunderstood. The
whole "white slavery" episode for which he is unjustly made to suffer
ten years' imprisonment was a trumped-up affair on the part of the
sheriff, who was bound to make a case out of it. He married the girl
with the best of intentions, and when arrested was with her on the way
to the Atlantic coast, preparatory to sailing for Paris, where he
intended to give her a splendid time. She testified against him at the
trial because she was scared into it by the officials, and, being
naturally of a weak nervous organization, she gave in. He was certain
he was going to die if he had to serve out his sentence, because
prison life is so different from the life he has led in the past. He
is entirely too refined to be able to stand the rough life of
imprisonment. Referred the examiner to the Austrian Embassy, which
could readily establish his noble descent and get him out of this
terrible predicament. When, later in his sojourn here, he was
interviewed by several gentlemen from the Austrian Embassy he

maintained the same attitude of wronged innocence, notwithstanding the fact that these gentlemen confronted him with an undoubtedly genuine photograph of himself, obtained from the Austrian police. It seems that he was quite a famous character in Austria, and had served a sentence there under a different name for a similar offense (white slavery). Soon after his arrival at the Government Hospital for the Insane he began to scheme for his escape, and on one occasion attempted to saw the guards in his room with an improvised saw. He likewise began to associate freely with the more dangerous element of the criminal department of this hospital, quite likely with a view towards getting assistance for his escape. He spoke with reluctance of his ideas concerning the inventions, adding that he had decided to quit talking about these things, because, although he is quite convinced of the extreme value of these original ideas of his, people have told him he was crazy wherever he expressed them. As an illustration of some of these extremely valuable original ideas the following may be mentioned. It concerns a bed-bug trap which he invented, and which he described as a paper pocket which is placed in the bed and scented with oil of pine so as to attract the bed-bugs. These make their home in this paper pocket and lay their eggs there, after which it is removed and burned. In the course of time (about two months) he fully recovered from that serious leg affliction from which he stated he had been suffering since the age of nineteen.

When an attempt was made to obtain his past history it was soon discovered that it was so fantastically colored with fabrications as to be entirely worthless, so far as a reliable account of his past life is concerned. As an instance of pathological lying, however, it was a masterpiece. He was requested to write out briefly his past life history, and in this abbreviated form it covered twelve closely-typewritten pages. We will not burden the reader with a complete reproduction of his story, although I assure you it makes very interesting reading material, but will simply review it briefly.

He speaks of the confession made to him several years ago by the lady whom he had always looked up to as his mother. She told him that she was only his foster-mother, and that in reality he was the son of the Austrian chamberlain and a famous countess. The latter turned him over into this lady's care when he was quite young, following her divorce from the chamberlain. She furnished him with the authenticated proof of the fact that he was entitled to a fabulous fortune left by his parents. Unfortunately the lady died after a brief illness, during which he practically sacrificed his life to save her, and thus his most important witness is forever inaccessible. The papers which could readily prove his noble descent were, most unfortunately, taken from him when he was arrested and are probably destroyed by this time.

His foster-mother, he states, was regularly supplied with funds by his real mother, gave him an excellent education and traveled with him extensively. In a plea for clemency he dwells upon the fact that his father died insane, that he himself suffered from epilepsy in his youth, and that at the age of twenty he spent a year in an insane asylum in Austria.

As an instance of his tendency to dramatization, of the part his ego plays in the recital of his past exploits and of the tendency to crave sympathy and compassion, a characteristic quite common to these pathological swindlers, the following, his own description of the circumstances which brought about his admission to the Vienna Insane Asylum may be quoted:--

"While on vacation, I met at Wertersee, which is a fashionable summer resort, a girl with the name L. Adle von D. I had left my tutor behind. She was the first girl I met, and my romantic character, my easily-excited nervous system, overpowered me and I fell in love, in love as deep as a man can fall. A few months after that I was engaged to her, and we should have been married on the 23d of April, 1899. On

the 22d of April my beautiful beloved bride was riding horseback with
me in the park, when at once her horse frightened, threw her off,
dragged her for a distance and then left her behind, a motionless,
bleeding mass. I saw right away that she was dead, lost to me, lost
forever; there was but one way not to lose her, and that was to follow
her soul, and that as quickly as possible. There in the park beside
her I took my pistol and shot myself. The public had gathered and
stopped me, and then I don't know what happened. I only remember that
I was ill for a long time, and then I was ill again, and they told me
L. was alive, and then I found out that she was not alive and I was
ill again."

Of course, the entire episode is a fabrication. The patient admitted
quite as much, but the interesting thing in this episode is the fact
that it illustrates how rigidly dependent lying is upon unconscious
motives. Had this episode really taken place, the patient, because of
his particular make-up, would have acted, in all likelihood, just the
way he behaved in his fantastic adventure.

After his year's confinement in the insane asylum his foster-mother
traveled with him in France, England, Egypt, and Turkey, in order to
divert his mind. Finally arriving at Transylvania, he became infatuated
with a poor girl named P., whom he christened L. in memory of his former
love, and married. The highly dramatic adventures of this second
matrimonial venture are altogether too numerous to describe in detail.
He describes in a very dramatic style how this lady was kidnapped from
him by a family of New York artists and spirited away across the ocean;
how after awakening from his unconsciousness, induced by some dope
administered to him in a tea which he had with these artist-friends the
night before, he at once made for the dock, arriving there just as the
ship carrying his wife was disappearing from sight; how he pursued them
across the Atlantic, to England, the continent, and so on, finally
locating them in Cape Town, South Africa; how upon arriving there he was

mortally wounded to find his beloved wife performing upon the stage of a cheap, dirty place. An excerpt from his description of this eventful voyage is as follows: "We passed Las Palmas, Asuncion, and St. Helena. Christmas and New Year's were celebrated on board the ship, but I did not care much for it. I was too much in distress. Would I find her there? Would I reach her in time? How would I find her? Would she be alive? My excitable fantasy awakened in me the most terrible suspicions. I suffered dreadfully, and it seemed to me we would never arrive. But we did at last, and some time in the beginning of January, 1906, I landed in Cape Town." This is how he discovered her: "I knew I was going to see something terrible, but I remained there--I had to. There were the rope dancers, the clowns, and the music, but I had no interest in them. I was waiting for L., my wife, and she came. On a small, mean stage L., my beloved wife, appeared with painted cheeks and shining eyes, dressed up in tights. She was dancing a mean dance and singing an obscene song before an audience consisting mostly of drunken sailors. So I found my wife L. and the music played. It was surely wonderful that I could control myself at such a moment. At once it seemed to me that I had no reason to be astonished. I was quiet and decided and waited until the show was over, and after the show I went behind the stage, and when my wife came out, laughing and happy, with a couple of other girls, I stepped near her and said simply 'L.' She gazed at me and fainted." Thus he finishes another tableau in his adventurous career. Several other similarly dramatic adventures follow in his history, the last of which landed him, wholly unjustifiably, in prison for ten years. When asked why all his love adventures ended so disastrously, he replied: "Doctor, all my life I have been suffering from a 'superaltruistic monomania to help girls in distress,' and that is how I'm repaid."

Any discussion on "freedom of will" and responsibility in connection with an individual of this type is, of course, quite futile and really of no practical importance. This man ought to be permanently isolated from the community, but not because he happens to have violated a given statute, but because his grave mental defect--in all probability an incurable defect--tends to express itself in criminal traits.

Back of this fantastic lying we see again that instinctive craving for compensation by means of a resort to the imagination and fantasy, a subterfuge rendered easy by those inherent defects enumerated in connection with the preceding case.

All the frankly psychotic manifestations, such as his delusional ideas and his grave affection of the lower extremity which served to put him in a hospital for the insane, were, of course, entirely malingered.

This brings us to the subject of malingering proper.

III

In malingering we see the application of deceit and lying to a definite situation. That which is a habitual type of reaction in some individuals, as was illustrated in the foregoing cases, comes to the fore in others only under certain stressful situations of life. While in the habitual fabricator the most prominent motives are those of an egotistic nature, a craving for self-esteem as compensation for an inherent defect, in the malingerer we see a resort to this form of reaction as a means of self-preservation, as a means of escape from a particularly painful situation.

There was a time in the history of psychiatry when malingering was a frequent subject of discussion in psychiatric literature. This was due not so much to any inherent practical importance of the phenomenon of malingering as such as to the faulty conception that this phenomenon was something which by its very existence ruled out the existence of mental disease. More scientific studies of personality which led to a direction of our attention to the malingerer rather than to malingering as an isolated mental phenomenon brought with it a complete change of attitude towards the entire subject.

Today, far from harboring the notion that malingering and mental disease are mutually exclusive, we are beginning to look upon malingering itself as the expression of an abnormal psychic make-up. Furthermore, far from believing, as of old, that the proverbially insane is supposed to be totally devoid of discretion in his conduct, we know that there may be a good deal of method in madness, and that even the frankly insane malinger mental symptoms when the occasion requires it. No experienced psychiatrist would today, for instance, consider the oft-quoted story of the alleged madness of Ulysses as evidence of malingering.

The story is told that Ulysses, in order to escape the Trojan war, feigned insanity. He yoked a bull and a horse together, plowed the seashore, and sowed salt instead of grain. Palamedes detected this deception by placing the infant son of the King of Ithaca in the line of the furrow and observing the pretended lunatic turn the plow aside, an act of discretion which was considered sufficient proof that his madness was not real. Without attempting to pass upon the case of Ulysses, we may say without fear of contradiction that no one would today depend upon such criteria. Experience teaches us that an individual may be very seriously mentally affected and at the same time show sufficient discretion of conduct to avoid threatening danger and to seek those means which best subserve his immediate needs and wants. Not only is this true, but we have arrived at a stage where we are prone to look upon a great many of the psychoses as the direct expressions of the individual's wish--as a haven sought out by himself within which he seeks shelter from the tempests of life. One of my patients tells me that the gun which he used in the alleged homicide was not loaded with bullets, but with paper wadding put there by his enemies, hence his alleged victim could not have been killed; in fact, he knows that this man is alive and having a good time on the money furnished him by his, the patient's, enemies. Another instance is that of a colored man who is serving a life sentence for murder. Among the many symptoms which this fairly advanced dementia prãcox case shows is the one that he considers himself a white man; that his dark color is due to some paint which he used in order to disguise himself; and that, inasmuch as the murder with which he is charged was supposed to have been committed by a colored man, he is not guilty of it. The motives here are quite obvious. Both these individuals find life much more bearable believing, as they do, in their innocence of the crimes imputed to them. Many other examples could be cited to prove that symptoms in mental disease do serve a definite purpose; that there may be indeed considerable method in madness.

Nevertheless, the observation is not uncommon that whenever such method is detected under circumstances where some ulterior motive may be ascribed to it the lay mind, and not infrequently psychiatrically-trained physicians, are at once ready to question the genuineness of the symptoms. It is the more curious that the so-called "insanity dodge" cry is frequently raised under circumstances where it would seem to be the least justifiable, as, for instance, in the case of an individual battling for his life before the bar of justice.

A little inquiry, however, into this phenomenon will help us to understand it better. It has its root primarily in that very common tendency of man to impute to his neighbor a type of behavior, a form of reaction, of which he would gladly avail himself were he in his neighbor's place, and the weapon he would use under the circumstances would very likely be that exquisitely human trait, deceit, malingering. It is a weapon which has played a tremendous part in the evolutionary struggle, not only of man but of all living things; in a broader sense, it may be looked upon as an organic function, as an endowment, thanks to which the weak, inferior being is able to avoid the danger of becoming the prey of the stronger, superior being. This function is very well illustrated in those animals which are able to acquire the color of their immediate surroundings in order to render themselves more difficult of detection. It is common among various insects, reptiles, and amphibians. The chameleon may be especially mentioned in this connection. Even the eggs acquire, in the process of natural selection, the color of the place where they are deposited, and the cuckoo which is about to cheat a couple of another species by placing her eggs in their nest for them to hatch selects that species the color of whose eggs most closely resembles that of her own, in order to assure herself of the success of the deception. The simulation and malingering practiced by the fox is common knowledge. Malingering, an instinctive function originally, has, in the process of evolution, become an act of reason with certain animals. One is forced to believe, from a survey of mythological writings, that primitive man must have had recourse to simulation and all else that this term stands for whenever he was confronted with an especially difficult problem in his struggles for existence. To the gods was attributed, among other special propensities, the ability to assume any shape or form, else how could they have performed all those miraculous escapades? Thus we are told that Jove transformed himself into an eagle when he carried off Ganymede. Achilles, the son of a goddess, sought to avoid the iniquitous fate which drove him to Troy by disguising himself as a woman. Deception is a common weapon of defense with the savage and with the inferior races of today. It is the tool by means of which these individuals render things as they want them to be; it is with them the means for a more direct, less difficult, less tedious solution of the problems of life.

The child in whose development the various steps of phylogeny are recapitulated shows this tendency to deception, to simulation, and dissimulation in a very pronounced degree. Lombroso, who was the first to demonstrate that so-called moral insanity is but a continuation of childhood without the adjunct of education, cites many facts, not excepting his own example, to show that the child is naturally drawn to fraud, to deception, to simulation. The child simulates either because of fear of injury and punishment or because of vanity or jealousy. Ferrari,[3] in his excellent work on juvenile delinquency, discusses the various motives for deception and malingering in the child. According to him, deception is, first of all, instinctive with the child. It malingers because of weakness, playfulness, imitation, egotism, jealousy, envy, and revenge. Deception frequently forms for it the only available weapon of defense against the parents and teachers.

Penta[4] cites many well-authenticated cases of malingering of mental symptoms in children. Of special interest is Malmstein's case of a girl of eight years who, in order to deceive her father and render him less severe in his treatment of her, and in order to gain the sympathy of those in the house who were in the habit of giving her sweets, feigned complete muteness for five months, after which time, no longer able to resist the desire to speak, she went into the woods, where, believing herself unobserved, she began to sing. St. Augustine, in his confessions, speaks of his childhood in the following manner: "I cheated with innumerable lies my teachers and parents from a love of play and for the purpose of being amused."[2] Penta, after a thorough discussion of the subject of malingering in children, comes to the conclusion that children use all the diverse forms of fraud, from simple lying to simulation, much more frequently than is believed or known. It may with them as with some lower animals simply be an instinctive playfulness, a habit or a necessity, as a weapon consciously and voluntarily wielded. This inherent tendency is, of course, modified to a considerable extent by the environment under which the child was brought up. Finally, the independence which the growing human being acquires from this form of reaction is in direct proportion to the ability he has acquired through education and precept to meet life's problems squarely in the face. We will see, later on, how the type of individual who is most likely to malinger has in reality never fully outgrown his childhood; that his

---

2   Cited by Penta.

reactions to the problems of everyday life are largely infantile in character.

Thus we see that malingering has its raison d'Ãªtre; that, after all, it is not at all strange that the suspicion of its existence should be so frequently raised by our legal brethren--yes, and medical brethren, too; that in reality it ought to be a very common manifestation. Nevertheless, paradoxical though it may seem, cases of pure malingering of mental disease are comparatively rare in actual practice. Wilmanns,[5] in a report of 277 cases of mental disease in prisoners, cites only two cases of pure malingering, and in a later revision of the diagnoses of the same series of cases the two cases of malingering do not appear at all. Bonhoeffer,[6] in a study of 221 cases, found only 0.5 per cent of malingering. Knecht,[7] in an experience of seven and a half years at the Waldheim Prison, did not observe a single case of true malingering. Vingtrinier[8] claims not to have found a single case of true malingering among the 43,000 delinquents observed by him during his experience at Rouen. Connolly, Ball, Krafft-Ebing, Jessen, Siemens, Mittenzweig, and Scheule are quoted by Penta as having expressed themselves that pure malingering is extremely rare. Penta, on the contrary, observed about 120 cases during his four years' service in the prison in Naples. He gives as the reason for this unusually high percentage of cases observed by him the fact that two-thirds of the inmates of the prison belonged to the Camorra, an organization whose members are gleaned from the lowest and most degenerate stratum of society, and in whom the tendency for deception and fraud in any form is highly developed.

The question naturally arises, What is the reason for this rarity of cases of malingering? Is it because man has reached a state of civilization where he no longer resorts to deception? Decidedly not. The reason lies almost wholly in our changed attitude of today towards this question. As we acquire more real insight into the workings of the human mind we are prone to become more tolerant towards the human weaknesses, and in our study of the malingerer it is the type of individual, his mental make-up, which interests us most, rather than the malingered symptoms. It is for this reason that today the number of authorities is indeed small who do not look upon malingering per se as a morbid phenomenon, as an abortive attempt at adjustment by an individual who is quite incapable of adequately coping with the vicissitudes of life. In my own limited experience of several years with insane delinquents I have yet to see the malingerer who, aside from being a malingerer, was not quite worthless mentally.

Our discussion of malingering,--i.e., of the exhibition of a fictitious mental state by an individual for the purpose of rendering more bearable or more pleasant a particularly painful or difficult situation of life, or for the purpose of entirely annihilating such a situation and of removing it from consciousness by substituting for it a state of affairs wholly created from the individual's fantasy,--would indeed be incomplete if we were to omit from our consideration at least that much of Freud's psychology as pertains to this subject.

Thus far we have considered principally the views of what may be termed the descriptive school of psychiatry, though we have briefly touched upon the instinctive biologic roots of this primitive mode of approach to the problems of life, malingering of mental symptoms.

With the consideration of the Freudian psychology we enter upon the interpretative phase of psychiatry and to a very large extent of mental life in general.

Freud holds that a great part of mental life can either partially or entirely be summarized under two principles, which he terms the "pleasure principle" and the "reality principle" respectively.[9] These two opponents are constantly facing one another in our inner life. The former represents the primary, original form of mental activity, and is characteristic of the earliest stages of human development, both in the individual and in the race; it is, therefore, typically found in the mental life of the infant, and to a less extent in that of the savage. Its main attribute is a never-ceasing demand for immediate gratification of various desires of a distinctly lowly order, and at literally any cost. It is thus exquisitely egocentric, selfish, personal, and antisocial. The activities of this "pleasure principle", however, constantly come into conflict with the "reality principle." The rigid requirements of our environment, of the social system in which we live, deny us the fulfillment of many, if not most, of our most dearly coveted desires, without, however, being able to abrogate these entirely.

There are two ways in which these forbidden desires may become satisfied. On the one hand, the instinctive striving, finding it quite out of the question to gain expression through the desired channels, may become sublimated into a form which is in accord with our social and ethical requirements, or the forbidden strivings and desires may find gratification in the individual's fantasy. We are here particularly concerned with the latter mode of psychic adjustment. This mode of adjustment is the usual way in which conflicts with reality are solved by the child and the savage. For them a rigid recognition of reality, such as is necessitated by the normal adult in his struggles for existence, does not take place. In fact, the evolution from childhood to adult life, from savagery to civilization, consists in nothing else than in the progressive recognition of reality and the adjustment thereto. One of the forms of getting away from reality, or a falsification of conditions as they actually exist, was expressed by one of Freud's patients as the "omnipotence of thought" (Allmacht der Gedanken). It is a state of mind in which the individual believes in the omnipotence of his thoughts; that his mere thinking possesses tremendous power; that no sooner he thinks of a certain deed than the same is accomplished; that an enemy, for instance, is actually harmed by merely wishing him harm. This mode of thinking forms the basis for many magic ceremonials. It is this latter mechanism,--i.e., the endowment of one's own thoughts with an omnipotent power,--which is also frequently illustrated in malingering. It is sufficient for the type of individual who malingers to merely say the word, and the most fantastic creation of his fancy immediately becomes a reality and is apperceived by him as such. A mere verbal denial of guilt on his part is sufficient to make him believe fully in his innocence and act accordingly. When we inquire into the origin of this facility in transforming fantasy into reality, for this omnipotence of the mere word or thought, we find it in the totally unreasonable overcompensation of these individuals for their feeling of impotence and weakness. This feeling of weakness and helplessness naturally becomes more acute under especially stressful situations of life, and hence it is that the criminal, especially the habitual criminal, who always uses deceit and simulation in his vain attempts at meeting life's difficulties squarely in the face, regularly resorts to malingering when confronted with a serious criminal charge or when life in prison becomes especially unbearable to him. A good illustration of an attempt at falsification of reality for the purpose of annihilating a particularly stressful situation by means of a mere assertion of a state of affairs such as he would wish them to be, with a total disregard for the real facts which constantly stare him in the face, is furnished by the following case:--

M. came from a good family and led a normal life, earning a substantial livelihood as printer up to the age of about thirty-eight. At this time one of his children died, and this, together with poor physical health, is said to have brought on a severe depression, during which he was actively suicidal and very self-accusatory. Several months later he lost another child by fire, and at this time also claimed to have obtained positive proof of his wife's infidelity. His mental depression became very much more aggravated; he attempted suicide on a number of occasions, was very suspicious and apprehensive, developed persecutory delusions, feared he was going to be burned to death or suffer some other horrible fate. This condition finally necessitated his admission to the Government Hospital for the Insane on May 28, 1897, at the age of forty. Here he gradually improved, and was discharged into the care of his father on October 22, 1899.

On February 19, 1903, he was readmitted as a D.C. prisoner, having shot and killed a man who seduced one of his daughters. Some idea concerning the type of individual we are dealing with here can be had already when we keep in mind his mode of reaction to the various stressful situations in his life enumerated above. All went well with him so long as he was not called upon to make a difficult adjustment, but with the loss of his child he develops a mental disorder. That he should have reacted to his daughter's injury with murder is quite in line with his general inability and incompetency for proper adjustment, and the development of a mental disorder which has kept him in an institution for the past twelve years and will in all probability keep him there the rest of his life, in reaction to the committed murder, further emphasizes the general vulnerability of his nervous system. Let us see how he attempts to adjust himself to the situation; how he faces reality in his psychosis.

He does just what primitive man has done and what the child of today does. Not being able to face reality, he annihilates it and substitutes for it a world created out of his fantasy, in which he plays every conceivable rÃ´le but the real one,--i.e., that of a patient accused of murder. We will see that he does this by the mere fiat of his word--that magic dexterity which has served so well primitive man in his struggles with reality.

Let me reproduce some of his letters, of which he hands me at least one daily. Here is one addressed to King George V:

DEAR SIR: I wish to return at once to England to the Cissel Hotel. You told me not to take my wife back after the courts here had granted me a divorce, so I look to you to just please come on here in person and have me released, as the United States Senate has given permission for you to come and release me. I am the young man that rescued you from drowning at River View, and after telling you my case you advised me to get a divorce. The guests from the hotel were wishing for me to return when on here, as also my family.

Please find enclosed check for your expenses and give prompt action.

  Very respectfully,
    (W. H. M.) HOWARD HALL,
      Washington, D.C.

The check:--

U. S. Treasury,
Pa. Ave. and 15th Street.

        WASHINGTON, D.C., October 1, 1914.

Please pay to King George of England Ten Thousand Dollars for professional services.
$10,000   W. H. M.

Thus by the mere stroke of the pen he, a poor mortal accused of murder and indefinitely confined to an institution, succeeds in putting himself in touch with King George, in drawing *ad libitum* upon the United States Treasury, in ridding himself of the wife whom he accuses of infidelity, and in annihilating old age by styling himself "The young man," when in reality he is fifty-seven years of age at present.

His belief in these statements is absolutely unshakable, notwithstanding the fact that he retains a clear orientation concerning his immediate environment, and thus has the actual state of his affairs constantly forced to his attention.

His grandiose compensation has such dimensions as to gratify every imaginable wish of his. He came here because he was divorced from his wife, not because of any crime he had committed. He is the son of the supervisor in charge of this building. He owns this institution and built it for a place in which he could count his money. He had forty-six wagon-loads of this. He will live 250 years, because he has taken the severest punishment to secure this. He refuses to assist with the ward work, because he pays $1.50 a day for board and is not supposed to do any work. He was brought here to select a woman for his wife. They brought him a lot of blue-eyed blondes and also a lot of Baltimore and St. Louis beauties, etc.

W. H. M., Owner, Washington Asylum, 5000 Branch Hospitals, five million employees.

ANACOSTIA, D.C., Fri., Nov. 6, 1914.

DEAR MR. PRESIDENT:

I came over here to take out forty-six wagons loaded with greenbacks. I respectfully had it arranged to have the Senate hold me here on account of so much wealth until I thought it safe to return. Please sign this and return it by mail. The Senate ordered me to write it to you, as there is no crime against me.

WASHINGTON, D.C., Fri., Nov. 6, 1914.

DR. W. AND STAFF OFFICERS OF WASHINGTON ASYLUM:

Please allow Mr. W. H. M. to pass out the gate at once free.

Very respectfully,
W. W.

Please don't delay this one minute.

Thus we see that the entire content of this man's delusional fabric is intended, first, to serve the purpose of annihilating the painful reality, and, second, to substitute for it a beautiful world in which he finds himself free and young again, enjoying his fabulous riches and many blue-eyed beauties. It is the only compromise possible for him, and the fact that it is nothing but a day-dream does not in the least detract from its compensating possibilities for this individual's painful reality. This man's mental disorder has been so obvious ever since its inception that the question of malingering never suggested itself to anyone, and yet the underlying mechanism in this case differs in no particular essential from the cases usually considered as malingerers. In both instances the psychosis represents an attempt to get away from a painful reality by individuals who are quite incapable of meeting such reality face to face.

A more detailed consideration of Freudian psychology, especially such as concerns the subjects of determinism, defense, and compensation, would give one a still clearer insight into the subject under discussion, but to do so would lead us considerably beyond the scope of this paper. From what has been said thus far it will be seen that the mental processes underlying the mental state of malingering differ in no essential from those operative in the human mind generally; that man in his endeavor to reach a satisfactory compromise between the two underlying principles of his conduct,--i.e., that of pleasure and reality,--frequently resorts to his fantasy; that malingering in its broader sense,--i.e., the attempt to evade reality,--is a common mode of reaction in primitive man, the child of today and in the undeveloped mind, in all of these instances signifying an inability to meet stern reality in the face, and that, therefore, malingering, when it does occur, should at least not be looked upon as an aggravating circumstance, which is not infrequently the case when the malingerer happens to be facing a court of law.

That this mode of reaction is at times resorted to by individuals who had always been looked upon as being far from incompetent only proves that under special stress, especially mental stress, man readily sinks to a lower cultural level and resorts to the defensive means common at this level.

Clinically, malingering is to be considered from three distinct viewpoints:--

1. Malingering in the frankly insane;

2. Malingering in those apparently normal mentally; and

3. Malingering in that large group of border-line cases which should rightly be looked upon as potentially insane and as constantly verging upon an actual psychosis.

It may be difficult to convince the lay mind, and especially the legal mind, that an individual may be suffering from an actual psychosis and at the same time malinger mental symptoms. It is the legal mind especially, working as it does with well-differentiated, sharply-defined, and wholly artificial concepts, that demands a sharp, strict differentiation between the mentally well and the mentally sick. By means of man-made statutes a line has been created, on one side of which they would place all the mentally well and on the other side all the mentally diseased. By the same token they cannot conceive how an individual placed on one side of the line may be able to manifest a type of reaction, a form of conduct, which is by common consent considered as being something essentially characteristic of the man on the other side of the line, losing sight of the fact that in the evolution of the human mind Nature is far from drawing such sharp differentiations as are exemplified by legal statutes. It would certainly be very convenient, and expert testimony would certainly have been spared the disrepute into which it has fallen, were Nature more accommodating in this respect. But Nature does not work in this fashion; differentiation in Nature takes place through infinite gradations, and between the absolutely well mentally and the frankly insane there is a host of individuals concerning whom it is almost next to impossible to state to which of the above two groups they belong. Thus it is that the frankly insane at times manifest conduct which taken by itself differs in no way from normal conduct, and that the so-called normal individual at times exhibits a type of reaction which is essentially of a psychotic nature.

To the psychiatrist it is a matter of common occurrence to see the mentally diseased not only dissimulate very ingeniously and tactfully mental symptoms so that it is frequently impossible to convince a jury of laymen of the existence of mental disorder, but at times, when the necessity arises, they consciously accentuate their symptoms or frankly malinger.

There is nothing strange about this. There is absolutely no reason why the insane, in his desire to gain expression for his wishes and strivings, should not avail himself of the same means that normal man uses.

The following case illustrates this very clearly:--

W. J. C., a well-educated, fairly efficient newspaper reporter, after a period of indefinite, vague, neurasthenic complaints lasting several weeks and which brought about his discharge from the staff of a local newspaper, awoke one July morning, picked up his infant child and, throwing it against the opposite wall of the room, inflicted fatal injuries upon it. After this he turned his face to the wall and remained quietly in bed. There was no ascertainable cause present for this act. The child was in the habit of entering the patient's room every morning and playing with him before he arose from bed. It was apparently on the same errand on this fatal morning. Shortly after getting up the patient wanted to leave the house in his night clothes, but was prevented from doing so and held until the police arrived. Six and one-half hours later,--i.e., on July 27, at 12.30 P.M.,--he was seen by me at the Government Hospital for the Insane.

On admission to the hospital he was very restless and anxious, walked up and down the room, hands in his pockets, would sit down for a few minutes, then walked the floor again. Later in the day he was visited by a newspaper reporter, a friend of his, with whom he conducted a clear and coherent conversation, and when told by the latter that the child was dead he assumed a markedly depressed facial expression. In reply to my questions intended to bring out his attitude towards the whole affair, he usually stated, "I don't know," and on one occasion in a very agitated manner said, "So help me God, doctor, I don't know anything about this." Later in the day he gave a clear and coherent account of his past life, and a detailed mental examination failed to bring out any gross mental disorder. He showed, however, considerable uncertainty about the length of time certain events of the preceding day consumed. He could not tell exactly when he retired the previous evening. He remembered, however, going to bed, likewise that his wife came to his room sometime during the night and asked him to fill the babe's milk bottle. He didn't remember whether he did this or not. The next thing he remembered was sitting in the parlor of the house, sometime in the morning, and was able to describe accurately those who were present.

During the remainder of the afternoon he was morose and depressed, refused to eat his supper, and continued in a restless state. He was again seen by me at 7.30 in the evening in company with two other physicians. The patient approached one of the physicians, extended his hand to him, and in a familiar manner said, "Hello, Mr. C." When told that this was not Mr. C., patient exclaimed "Oh!" in a confused and astonished manner, said, "Where am I?" and reeled over on the floor as if in a swoon. He was told to sit up in the chair, which he did.

"What date is this?" "August 26, 1910" (July 27, 1910).

"How long have you been here?" "Since July 25, 1910."

"How long a period would that make?" "One month--oh no, one day; this is August 10, 1910."

"What were you sent here for?" "Don't know."

"Who brought you here?" "Don't know--oh yes, two policemen."

"What is your babe's name?" "Don't know."

"What is your wife's name?" "Don't know."

He was then given a newspaper clipping in which the whole affair was fully described. He read the account through, but without exhibiting the slightest emotion, and said, "Isn't that awful, doctor?"

"How do you feel about this affair of your babe being dead?" "I don't know anything about it."

"How much is 2 times 3?" After considerable delay and in an absorbed mood he said, "70."

"How much is 6 times 7?" After a long pause he said, "Don't know."

"Which is the largest newspaper in Washington?" "Don't know." (Patient was on the staff of a local newspaper.)

When we remember that only several hours before this the patient gave a coherent account of his past life and showed nothing grossly psychotic, the foregoing symptoms, such as the lack of knowledge of his wife's or babe's name, inability to solve problems such as 2 times 3, the fainting spell, etc., must be looked upon as unquestionably malingered. When examined the following day he showed still further signs of malingering, the detailed account of which must, however, be omitted on account of lack of space, and yet this man was unquestionably insane; the act itself (the infanticide) was unquestionably an insane act, as will be shown later. We have mentioned the fact of his neurasthenic symptoms and how as a result of these he lost his position. The physical examination of the patient revealed certain neurological signs, such as exaggeration of the patellar reflexes, lateral nystagmus of both eyes, which determined us to look further into the question of his physical state, especially in view of a history of luetic infection five years before. A spinal puncture was accordingly performed, and the spinal fluid findings were as follows: Fluid clear, pressure moderately increased, Noguchi butyric acid reaction positive, a rather uncommonly heavy granular type of precipitate, cells per cubic millimeter 129. Differential cell count: Lymphocytes, 94 per cent; phagocytes 2.2 per cent; plasma cells, 0.25 per cent; unclassified cells, 2.25 per cent. Wassermann reaction with spinal fluid negative, both active and inactivated. Wassermann reaction with the blood-serum negative. This, however, became positive later on in the disease. The above findings indicate unquestionably that he was suffering from cerebral syphilis.

It is not necessary to enter into further detail concerning the progress of this case. Suffice it to say that with proper treatment he entirely recovered and was so discharged on June 14, 1911.

There can be no doubt that this man malingered mental symptoms, neither need there be the slightest doubt about his having suffered from an actual mental disorder. The motive for his malingering is perfectly obvious. Finding himself suddenly confronted with a charge of infanticide, and rent by the various conflicting emotions which a realization of this carries with it, he resorted to the common weapon of defense, malingering of mental symptoms. We have seen that he deceived no one but himself; that in reality he was a very seriously affected individual. It was fortunate for him that because of some lucky turn of events he landed in a hospital instead of in jail.

A more or less similar case recently received the maximum sentence of life imprisonment for manslaughter. In this instance the case was chiefly observed by jail officials instead of physicians in its early course.

The foregoing case, it seems to me, illustrates very well that, while we are fully justified in assuming a relationship of cause and effect in many cases of malingering, in many others malingering and actual mental disease are concomitant phenomena, having a common root in the same diseased soil. Thus Pelman[10] holds simulation in the mentally normal to be extremely rare, and he always finds himself at a loss to differentiate between that which is simulated and that which represents the actual traits of the individual. My own experience prompts me to agree with Pelman. This confusion and difficulty of differentiation between actual mental disease and malingered symptoms may manifest itself in two ways. The same individual may be suffering at one time from a frank mental disorder, and at some later period, finding himself in a stressful situation, malinger a psychotic state, or, as we saw in the preceding case, malingering of symptoms may manifest itself during the course of a frank mental disorder, as will be further illustrated in succeeding cases. Pelman's statement, however, applies most forcibly to that mass of border-line cases which will be discussed later.

T. W. was admitted to the Government Hospital for the Insane from the United States Penitentiary, Leavenworth, Kan., on June 16, 1910, at the age of twenty-nine. He was serving at the time a sentence of eight years for post-office robbery. His own version of his family and past personal history is unreliable. He claimed to have suffered from a paralysis of both arms from March, 1904, until March, 1906, and that he was at that time confined to a sanitarium. He would not give the name of that institution, and the whole story may have been fictitious. At any rate, if he did suffer from this paralysis it was very likely functional in type, as at the time of his admission here, four years later, he showed no traces whatever of this. He admitted having been arrested several times before for drunkenness and disorderly conduct. His industrial career was very irregular.

The onset of the present attack, as described in the medical certificate which accompanied him on admission, was as follows:--"On the evening of April 17, 1910, patient suddenly began to shout, sing, and pray, claiming that the spirit of God had entered his heart and that he had a mission to perform. This mission was to go among the prisoners and preach the Gospel. He then manifested this in a very erratic manner; ideation was disturbed and disconnected, and there was present psychomotor restlessness. A probable diagnosis of manic-depressive psychosis was made by the prison physician."

On admission to this hospital the patient was well nourished physically, talked readily and coherently, was clear mentally, although he stated he did not know the nature of this hospital, adding spontaneously that he knew it was not an insane asylum. His productivity was chiefly of a religious nature. He stated he was the real Elijah III, the real prophet; that the vision of Jesus Christ came to him in his cell, handed him a cross, and told him to pick up his clothes and follow Him. The warden at the penitentiary was jealous of his ability to preach the Gospel, and in consequence tried to get two men to kill him, but these could do him no harm, because he had the spirit of God in him. The warden also tried to poison him. He complained of a fever in his stomach from the food the warden gave him, stated he could see crosses in the corner of his room, and was continually mumbling something to himself in a low voice. He rested well on the first night of his sojourn here, and the following morning told the attendant that he had seen God standing behind him at intervals during the night. On June 28, 1910, he developed a marked religious excitement, preached loudly while out in the yard, and wildly gesticulated in a manner as if he were addressing someone above. He continued intermittently excited until the early part of August, 1910. It should be noted here that at this time there were two other cases confined in the same building, two cases of dementia prÃ¦cox, who manifested similar religious excitement. It is of importance to note this, inasmuch as suggestion plays a considerable rÃ´le in the choice of the malingered symptom, and because one of the characteristics of the type of individuals under consideration is a high degree of suggestibility.

In his conduct in the ward he was quiet and orderly, frequently talked in a rational and coherent manner, but invariably brought into the conversation his delusional ideas. In his demeanor towards me he was very evasive, suspicious, and showed a marked disinclination to enter into a protracted interview. Soon after an unsuccessful attempt to examine him more thoroughly he handed me a letter addressed to Judge Landis at Chicago, in which he ordered said Judge to remove Voliva from Zion City and turn the latter over to him, the patient, as the rightful heir and the only real Elijah III. Following this there was another tranquil period, during which the patient's conduct was quite good. About a month later another attempt was made to examine him in detail, but so soon as he noticed my intention to take notes of the examination he became very suspicious and evasive and absolutely refused to coÃ¶perate. This episode was likewise soon followed by a letter as follows. The letter was addressed to the warden of the United States Penitentiary at Leavenworth, Kan., and he requested that it be mailed immediately, as it was very important. It was correctly dated and read:--

"DEAR SIR: When you receive this letter you will immediately take steps to have me returned to the penitentiary, where I have a divine mission to perform. You old ... do you realize that you are fooling with the prophet Elijah, the Lord's chosen? Have you no fear of the wrath that God shall bestow on you if you even dare to offend His divine servant? Don't you ever for a minute think that you can connive to beat me out of my property in Zion City, you and that interloper, L. L. Voliva. I shall have it all just as the Lord meant I should, and I shall carry on the work just as the Divine Master meant I should. For what matter it if the world is against us, so long as God is for us? Now, you old reptile, on receipt of this you will immediately discharge the chaplain; he has no business there. When I get back I'll take his place, for I am Elijah III, the Lord's anointed.

(Signed) "T. W. ELIJAH III, Station L, Washington, D.C."

In the meantime it was noted that the patient was very shrewd in his various schemes for making his escape from the hospital; that he very ingeniously managed to manufacture all sorts of weapons, and that he seemed to be especially delusional when in conversation with the hospital officials.

Soon after the patient planned and executed a very daring escape, taking with him two other patients, but was soon apprehended and returned to the hospital. All of this led me to suspect that the patient was simulating a good many of his symptoms, and that, at any rate, he was very much exaggerating his psychotic state.

However, there was a certain element of contradiction, a certain lack of consistency, present in his behavior which is entirely atypical of the pure malingerer. His explanations of his ideas were flat and somewhat dilapidated, and resembled to a certain extent the explanations of a dementia prÃ¦cox case. In other words, there was no doubt that the patient malingered, but there was likewise no doubt that he suffered from a psychosis. On several occasions he refused to take nourishment for several days at a time in reaction to his delusional ideas.

Upon his return from his elopement it was felt that, owing to his dangerous tendencies, a more thorough attempt at evaluating the relative importance of the genuine and the malingered in his case ought to be made with a view to returning him to the penitentiary.

He was accordingly again thoroughly examined on April 8, with the following results: He reiterated his delusional ideas substantially as given above. He insisted that he was not insane; that he was railroaded to this hospital because the warden of the penitentiary and other United States officials are trying to rob him of his property in Zion City. "God Almighty meant that Zion City should belong to me." This was decided on the night when he saw the cross.

"How many months in a year?" "Twelve."

"How many days in a week?" "Seven."

"Name the months." "March, April, June, July, August, October, November, December, January, and February."

"What is the last month of the year?" "October."

"What is the first month of the year?" "March."

"Which is the Christmas month?" "I'm not certain, but I think it's January."

"How does vinegar taste?" "Sweet."

"How does a lemon taste?" "Sweet."

"What is the color of an orange?" "Blue."

"Count from 1 to 20." Counts very slowly and deliberately, omitting 11 and 15.

"$4 \times 2 = 8$; $8 \times 4 = 28$; $9 \times 3 = 27$; $7 \times 4 = 24$; $6 \times 4 = 22$; $6 + 7 = 13$; $19 + 11 = 30$; $7 + 8 = 14$; $3 \times 3 = 9$; $4 \times 2 = 12$; $6 \times 4 = 14$; $5 \times 2 = 10$; $1 + 9 = 10$; $9 + 11 = 21$; $11 + 9 = 18$; $50 + 5 = 11$; $8 \div 2 = 4$; $27 \div 9 = 4$."

"Name the days of the week." "Tuesday, Wednesday, Thursday, Friday, and Saturday."

"Name them again." "Monday, Tuesday, Thursday, Friday, Saturday, and Monday."

In repeating a very simple story he changed the content entirely, and omitted some of the most important details of it.

When we remember that this man was far from being as ignorant as some of the above answers would suggest, and that, while he unquestionably suffered from a psychosis, his state of consciousness was altogether too clear to justify a degree of lack of touch with his environment such as his replies would indicate, it becomes quite obvious that he malingered. This, together with his dangerous tendencies, determined us to return him to the penitentiary, which was done on April 11, 1911.

He reached the penitentiary on April 13, and on the night of April 20 he began preaching in a loud tone of voice, claiming that he was the son of David, and that he was called upon to go forth and preach to the world. He was removed from his cell to the isolation building, where he refused to take nourishment until April 23. During this period he spent most of the time preaching and singing religious songs, and at times would hold long and heated arguments with some imaginary person, always on religious topics. From the above date until his transfer to the Government Hospital for the Insane on September 24, 1911, he continued in a very disturbed and destructive state, refusing food frequently for several meals in succession, preached, sang, and cursed in turn, gave voice to the various delusional ideas manifested above, and gave objective evidence of suffering from hallucinations. Throughout he strongly maintained that he did not want to return to the hospital at Washington, as there was nothing wrong with him mentally.

The prison physician who examined the patient at the penitentiary before his second admission to this hospital made the following notation in the case: "The mental examination of T. W. reveals inconsistencies that are strongly suggestive of simulation, and I believe there is in this case a degree of malingering, frequently associated with prison psychoses, yet that there is a psychosis, in my opinion, there is no doubt."

Upon his return to this hospital he became involved in fistic encounters, on the way to his ward, for which there was very little provocation. For several weeks following this he was very surly, dissatisfied, moody, and inaccessible, but showed no other psychotic symptoms. Four days after admission he subscribed to a local newspaper, which he read regularly and kept himself well informed on ordinary topics. He was clear mentally, well oriented in all respects, and adapted himself readily to his new environment, except that he absolutely refused to eat the regular food furnished the patients. For about three weeks he lived practically on fruit and candies which he purchased, persisting in his determination to starve himself unless he were given a special diet. This was furnished him, and he had no further dietetic troubles. No delusions or hallucinations were manifested, intellectual examination revealed no intelligence defect (gross), and, aside from his surly mood and his tendency for rather frequent endogenous depressed periods, he showed no abnormal manifestations.

In this state he required no special hospital treatment, and, as he promised to conduct himself properly if he were returned to the penitentiary, he was transferred back on February 20, 1912.

Upon his return he continued, however, to manifest periodic excitements, with destructiveness, always, however, in reaction to some environmental irritation. He nevertheless managed to remain in the penitentiary until the termination of his sentence.

It is highly doubtful whether proper means will ever be evolved to enable one to differentiate accurately between that which is genuine and that which is malingered in cases like, for instance, the foregoing.

This man unquestionably suffered from a psychosis, and yet there is likewise no doubt that he malingered. The question of the accurate differentiation between the genuine and the shammed seems to me, however, to be strictly an academic one and of very slight practical importance. What is of importance is the recognition that malingering and mental disease are here the expression of the same diseased soil, and that the same source should perhaps be also attributed to this man's criminalistic tendencies. Crime, mental disease, and malingering should perhaps here be looked upon as different phases of a mode of reaction to life's problems which belongs to a lower cultural level, which is largely infantile in character.

That this infantile way of facing reality is dependent upon some constitutional inherent anomaly is attested to by the circumstance that these individuals practically always react in this manner when forced to form new adjustments, new adaptations. This repeated recourse to mental disease as a refuge from a stressful situation is amply illustrated in a series of cases reported elsewhere.

The other form in which malingering may be so intertwined with actual mental disease as to render accurate differentiation quite impossible is where the individual may be suffering from a psychosis at one time, and at some later period, finding himself in a stressful situation, malinger a psychotic state. In these cases the danger of ever committing a habitual criminal to a hospital for the insane is especially apparent.

Finding, as these individuals do, a successful and convenient refuge in a psychosis, it is but natural for them to again seek this refuge when they find themselves in conflict with the law. But that which was at one time a spontaneous, unconsciously motivated mental reaction may later become a conscious volitional act, an only available means of escape--malingering of mental symptoms.

J. E. M., aged twenty-seven on admission, June 15, 1912. Family history obtained from the patient four days after admission is quite unreliable. He knew nothing of his grandparents, who died in Ireland.

Father was living when last heard from, four or five years ago. He is moderately alcoholic; a stableman by occupation. Mother died at fifty-five in Bellevue Hospital, New York City, from some unknown cause. One brother was drowned. One sister died of tubercular adenitis. No instance of epilepsy, insanity, or nervous disorder in any form is known to have existed among his relatives.

Patient stated that he was born in Ireland on October 12, 1884. He never attended school, but has learned to read and write a little. Childhood was uneventful, so far as known. He came to this country at the age of four, and at twelve or thirteen years of age began selling newspapers in the streets of New York. His occupational career since then has been chiefly that of a steamboat and longshoreman laborer along the docks of New York City. He said he enlisted in the Navy in 1907 or 1908, was not quite certain as to which year, at San Francisco, Cal. He served on the U.S.S. *Buffalo* as coal-passer; was dishonorably discharged for drunkenness. He then reÃ«nlisted and served as fireman, first class, on the *Milwaukee* for about three and one-half years. Says he got along well on the *Milwaukee*, until he got into his present trouble. He was convicted of sodomy and sentenced to prison for ten years, January 15, 1911. Patient did not see the discrepancies in the dates as given by him, but, as stated before, the history is quite unreliable.

A letter received from the War Department on June 28 requested identification of J. E. M. for the purpose of detecting whether or not he is the same man who under the name of Lee deserted from the Army, January 14, 1909. The photograph accompanying the letter was that of the patient.

He had measles and mumps during childhood, from which he made good recoveries. GonorrhÅ"al and syphilitic infection were denied. (Wassermann with the blood-serum negative.) During a bar-room brawl in

Panama he was struck on the head with a table leg and rendered unconscious for fifteen or sixteen hours. This was some time in 1908. He thinks there was nothing more than a scalp wound, requiring no treatment beyond a simple dressing. For about a year after, headaches were present almost continually, occipital in location and of a tingling sensation. There was likewise a reduction of tolerance for alcoholics, since then two glasses of whisky being sufficient to intoxicate him. He does not know whether there was any change in his mental make-up or faculties following this injury, as he paid no attention to this. He commenced to indulge in alcoholics at the age of eighteen or nineteen. He cannot give a detailed account of the extent, but, as a rule, he spent all his money not needed for living expenses for whisky. He would become intoxicated every time he went ashore, stating that there was nothing else to do and no place to which he could go. Practice of onanism was denied. He claimed to have begun normal sexual intercourse at about the usual age. Strenuously denied sexual perversions, in spite of the fact that he is now serving a ten years' sentence for sodomy. He denied the guilt of this offense; insisted that he was never arrested before in his life, and believed the present conviction to have been a trumped-up affair because they must have gotten sore on him, although he cannot figure out why. Following his conviction for the above offense he was sent to the State Penitentiary at Concord, N.H. For a short while after he got there he got along well; was kept continually at work in the chair factory. He did not like this work, as he was subjected to the inhalation of the dust and shavings, and feared he would develop tuberculosis from this, and asked to be transferred to some other place. This request was finally granted him, and he was put to work in the kitchen. He states he did not get along well there; very soon got into some sort of trouble and was put into a dark dungeon, where he thinks he remained for about twelve months, strapped to the bed. He never saw the daylight during this time. He does not know why these strict measures were taken with him, but it is a fact that he was tied down. He had no idea of the onset of the present trouble, but stated that he complained frequently to the doctor of headaches and vomiting. The headaches were occipital in nature and severe at times. He could not recall his transfer to this institution nor the events which transpired during the first two or three days after his arrival here.

The medical certificate which accompanied him here stated: "Patient has been convicted of sodomy and is at present serving sentence for same. First symptoms became manifest about February 6, 1912. Came under the care of prison physician at Concord, N.H., State Prison with severe headaches. Previous to above date it is said there were the following records at above prison in regard to this patient: April 15, 1911, and August 10, 1911, he had convulsions. These are not described in detail. The prison physician at the time noted that patient showed symptoms of organic brain disease. On February 26, 1912, he became violent, and has had to be restrained since then. For some time previous to that he had acted peculiarly. The symptoms immediately preceding his transfer to this institution are as follows: Has to be restrained to prevent violence to himself and others. Frequently suspicious when food and drink are offered him. At times noisy when he desires food and it is not given to him at once. Probable cause unknown. There is a vague history of head injury aboard ship in the tropics. Homicidal tendencies were present when the disease first became manifest."

Patient was admitted to this institution June 15, 1912, at 10.30 A.M. On admission he was carried in by two employees. His legs were shackled and he had wristlets on his hands. He was apparently unable to stand unassisted, and, when support was removed, fell to the floor. Pupils were widely dilated; internal strabismus of the right eye was present. Facial musculature was distorted, and he mumbled to himself in a low, indifferent tone of voice, over and over again, "Give me something to eat. I can't do it. Give me something to eat," etc., in a rapid monotone. He appeared to be in a deep stupor. He did not seem to realize his whereabouts, and attention could not be gained. He was totally inaccessible. When put to bed he became quite restless, rolled out on the floor, and was unable to assist himself back into bed. Musculature of legs was in a constant mild clonus, and the right foot was kept in position of talipes equinovarus. Pins pushed deeply into the skin all over the body caused no reaction. When food was brought to him he leaped upon it and finished the meal with extreme rapidity, stuffed his mouth full, never taking sufficient time for mastication or swallowing, and food was frequently expelled forcibly, probably from irritation of the air-passages. Questions addressed to him remained unheeded, but he kept up a constant mumbling in a low monotone, as described above. He was totally unable to stand on his feet unsupported, but when lying down his legs were moved about quite freely in an indifferent manner. When alone in the room he remained quietly in bed, head and face covered up with a blanket, but as soon as the room was entered he became restless, grabbing to those about him and holding on tenaciously. During his first night in the institution he slept well and was clean in habits. The following morning he was still inaccessible. He ate his breakfast quite voraciously, mumbling to himself all the time, "Give me something to eat" or "Give me something to drink." When water was brought to him he would endeavor to gulp the entire contents of the vessel at one effort.

During the day of June 16, the day following his admission, he was frequently seen sitting on the side of the bed with quite a pleasant facial expression, rubbing his arms and legs. When his room was entered, however, he at once began mumbling to himself similar phrases as those given above, became quite restless, grabbing at those about him and not paying any attention to questions put to him. The following day, June 17, he showed marked improvement; was very much quieter in behavior when approached; walked back and forth in his room

quite unassisted and in quite a steady manner; was seen looking out of
the window into the yard for about fifteen or twenty minutes. Upon
being approached by any one his gait seemed to become definitely less
steady, and diffused twitchings of the thigh and leg were noted. The
strabismus which was present on the day of admission had entirely
disappeared; pupils slightly dilated. In the forenoon of the 17th he
asked for his clothes and to be allowed to go out in the courtyard
for a walk. A few questions addressed to him were answered coherently
and relevantly. He said, in answer to direct questions, that his name
was J. E. M.; that he did not know his age; that he came off some
ship. Said the name of the ship was **Washington**; that he did not know
how long he was on that ship, but thought it was a good long time.
Asked where he was now, he said he was in the brig. "Where?" "Don't
know." Asked if he were crazy, he said, "No, sir." When he came here?
"A year ago." Asked what was the matter with him. "Nothing, sir. They
kept me tied up too much." Asked when his bowels moved last, he said,
"About a week ago."

On June 19 he gave a coherent and connected account of his past life.
He talked freely and coÃ¶perated in every way with the interviewer.
Requests were obeyed promptly and intelligently. Physical examination
on that date showed him to be a well-built, well-developed white male.
Face slightly asymmetrical. Skin was soft and smooth, free from
eruption, and covered with numerous elaborate tattoo marks. Linear
depressed scar in the occipital region. Muscle tone was good. Muscular
power was good in upper extremities. On first being tested in the
lower extremities said he could not resist very much passive
movements; upon suggestion, however, the muscular power of the lower
extremities became much stronger and equal to that of the upper
extremities. Grip was strong and equal on both sides. Station and gait
were unimpaired when a steady and erect attitude and firm gait were
suggested to the patient; left alone, he was inclined to be slightly
unsteady on his feet. With eyes closed and feet together, there was

considerable swaying present; said he felt like falling over. Voluntary movements were performed well. He described accurately a circle, a square, and triangle in the air with either hand. Movements were steady and accurate. CoÃ¶rdination was slightly impaired in f-f and f-n tests; the termination of the act was accompanied by a slight tremor. The musculature of thighs showed a more or less constant clonic twitching. When attention was called to this he was able to control it to a certain extent. Upon assuming a sitting posture the twitchings ceased. He said it was due to weak ankles. There was no tremor of protruded tongue or lips when showing teeth; fine tremor of the extended fingers and forearm when extended; no tremor of facial musculature. There was no paralysis, but there seemed to be a slight weakening of the lower extremities. No atrophies or hypertrophies noted. The triceps and radial reflexes were definitely exaggerated. Upon tapping, the quadriceps tendon caused a brisk marked contraction of thigh muscles, followed by mild clonus. Tapping of one knee tended to set musculature of opposite knee in mild clonus of short duration. Knee kicks were definitely exaggerated. Tendo Achillis exaggerated. No ankle clonus. Muscular irritability to mechanical stimulation increased. Superficial reflexes were normal, except plantar defense reaction was slight. Cutaneous sensibility was unimpaired: heat and cold readily distinguished. Light touches of pin pricks were felt and localized all over the body. Sense of position normal. No astereognosis in either hand. No excessive sweating. Eyes clear; irides brown; pupils round and regular, moderately dilated, reacted readily to all tests; eye movements well performed in all directions; no nystagmus nor strabismus. Vision--20/30 in each eye, improved by glasses. Skin of vitreous clear; slight weakness of external recti; cornea clear; field of vision normal for white; both fundi normal except for slight hyperÃ¦mia. Smell, taste, audition, and speech unimpaired.

Mentally the patient was clear. He comprehended readily what was said to him, and his replies were prompt and relevant. He was disoriented for time. He stated that he knew the nature of this place; that he was told it the day before by a patient. Claimed to have total or almost total amnesia for several months past during the year he was confined in the dungeon of the Concord Penitentiary. He had no idea of the trip from there down to this hospital. He did not remember his arrival, nor how he acted the first two days here. Stated that on June 17 he first began to notice things about him and to realize faintly where he was. Delusions or hallucinations could not be elicited as having existed at that time. He spoke of having been bothered at the penitentiary; of having been chloroformed; that they put stuff in his food, tried hard to get him out of the way, and because they could not do it sent him down here. Said the doctor poured ether down his neck. He does not know the doctor's name, but he knew it was ether, he smelt it, and that is the reason he could not use his legs on arrival. He had no idea why he should have been treated thus, but thought perhaps they had it in for him. Auditory hallucinations could not be elicited. When asked if he ever saw anything, he said it was pitch dark in the dungeon and no one could see anything. Said the food tasted bad all the time, and sometimes made him vomit. On one occasion he noticed some powder in the beans. No electricity, no shocks, no outside influence was used on him. He did not know how long he was tied down in the dungeon, as half the time he did not know anything at all. Said they put needles in him, and pointed to some marks on his arm as a result of hypodermics. Facial expression denoted perfect satisfaction; said he felt fine and did not worry about anything, as he is not of the worrying kind. Said he had been treated well here. Insight was imperfect. When asked directly if he had been insane, he replied "No." When the various symptoms which he manifested on admission were described to him he was inclined to agree that if he did show these symptoms he must have been out of his head. Remote memory was not impaired, so far as could be determined. There was an ill-defined amnesia extending over several months past, and up to June 17, when he claimed to have first realized his whereabouts. Attention was unimpaired. He reacted well to the intellectual tests, with the exception of the arithmetical problems, which he did poorly. Replies to ethical questions showed a rather low grade of morality, perhaps due somewhat to ignorance more than to anything else. In his conduct on the ward he was absolutely normal following June 17. He spent his time reading and in conversation with the other patients. He was perfectly satisfied in his surroundings, frank in his conversation with those about him, and gradually gained more and more insight into his condition. He still persisted, however, in his statements that ether was poured down his back. Said he remembered this distinctly as having taken place while confined in the dungeon. He was then, however, inclined to think that probably they did not have it in for him, and probably they did what they thought was best. In conversation with him today, on June 19, four days after admission, he showed perfectly normal behavior in every respect. Was frank in his statements, spoke of the amnesia mentioned above, and no delusions or hallucinatory experiences or physical symptoms present on admission could be detected.

When finally confronted with the picture sent from the War Department for his identification he showed some degree of emotional reaction, stated that the picture was his, but persistently denied ever having been a recruit in the army. On the whole, he took the matter rather lightly and good-naturedly.

The history of this attack illustrates a typical case of hysterical psychosis. The marked stupor and confusion, the numerous and varied neurological symptoms, the sensory disturbances, especially the profound anǼsthesia to pin pricks, the amnesia and rapid recovery after change of environment, all point to this diagnosis. It is a form of reaction frequently seen in prisoners, and has been designated, for want of a better term, as prison psychosis. At any rate, there can be no doubt as to the genuineness of the symptoms presented by the patient.

If we keep in mind that such a type of psychotic reaction is the result of the mutual interaction between an unstable, highly vulnerable psyche and an unfavorable environmental situation--in this instance prison environment--we understand the more readily the later history of this case.

On July 16, 1912, he was discharged recovered and turned over to the naval authorities to be returned to prison. Soon after his return to prison he was noted to be melancholy, uncommunicative, was not interested in condition of self or surroundings, had unsystematized delusions of persecution. Physically he was noted to be anÃ¦mic, showed general tremors when undergoing examination, reflexes were exaggerated, positive Romberg was present. The physician who accompanied patient to the Government Hospital for the Insane on his second admission stated that on the trip from Portsmouth Prison M. tried to assault a waiter in a restaurant in Boston, accusing the latter of following him. To the physician he said, while on the train, "Take your d---- eyes off me, or I'll brain you."

He was readmitted to the Government Hospital for the Insane on February 6, 1913. Physical examination on this admission was negative, except for some impairment of vision, for which he was given eye-glasses. Mentally he was found to be disoriented for time, though perfectly clear mentally, as was shown later in the examination; he said he did not know the name of the institution, though a minute later he gave correctly the name of the building in which he was located. He spoke in a very vindictive manner of the naval officials, who he said were persecuting him in various ways, and who he reckoned were then working to send him to some other d---- prison. On February 7, the day after admission, he wrote the following letter to the Secretary of the Navy:

HOWARD HALL, January 29, 1913.

MR. SECRETARY OF THE NAVY: ***Rev. Sir***.--Will you kindly have some
investigating, as I cannot have my life endangered. It is continually
in my food, and times I have found the compounded powders in the air
of my room choking me. Please let me know if you will do so, and I
shall close.

   Respectfully yours,
     J. E. M., H. H. 5, Station L.

No hallucinations could be elicited, and his delusional ideas were
confined to the naval officials. These, he said, were persecuting him;
they sentenced him unjustly in the first place, and threatened to get
even with them. He answered the intelligence tests fairly well, but the
examining physician noted that frequently he gave expression of
consciously giving erroneous replies to questions put to him.
Emotionally he was at first somewhat depressed, but later this
disappeared. In his conduct he was inclined to be very troublesome,
easily irritated, and fault-finding.

This disorder of conduct, however, became consistently more aggravated
whenever he was in the presence of the physician. While he gradually
became quite friendly with the attendants and willingly assisted with
the ward work, he became quite abusive whenever an attempt was made to
examine him by the physician. This became especially evident in
December, 1913, when the physician who had him in charge during his
first sojourn at the hospital again assumed charge of him. At that time
the patient had been on excellent behavior for a number of months, and
in his daily conduct showed no evidence of a psychosis. He continued,
however, to air his delusional ideas whenever the physician attempted to
examine him.

Everything went well upon the return of his former physician until December 22, 1913, when the latter attempted to examine him. The patient became very abusive and threatening in his attitude, began to air all sorts of bizarre persecutory ideas, and for about a month he continued in an excited and destructive state. At the expiration of this period he apologized to the physician for his conduct, said that he could not help going on a rampage once in a while, as it is all due to his mean disposition, and promised to conduct himself in an excellent manner if he were not returned to prison. This was early in January, 1914, since which time he has been a model patient in every respect. It is needless to say that he has not been given, since that time, any occasion for the development of another tantrum, and accordingly he remained free from psychotic manifestations.

He was a model patient after this, assisted willingly with the ward work, and on one occasion prevented the successful culmination of a daring plot on the part of several patients to escape from the institution.

Upon the recommendation of the hospital authorities and Dr. Sheehan, the naval officer stationed at this hospital, the remainder of this man's sentence was commuted, and he was accordingly discharged on June 29, 1914. For about six months prior to this his conduct was exemplary, and, though through a considerable part of this period he enjoyed freedom of the grounds, he never showed the slightest inclination to abuse these privileges.

The salutary effect of the commutation of this man's sentence is quite obvious. On the other hand, I am equally certain that had this particular individual been returned to prison we would have had him again before long as a very seriously ill patient.

This case is extremely interesting from many points of view. In the first place, it gives us some insight into that highly inflammable, hair-trigger, emotional type of individual who, when thrown into a stressful situation, is very likely to go to pieces mentally. It is a type which is always very difficult to manage under a prison régime, and which in my estimation requires some intermediary place between a hospital for the insane and a penal institution. It is likewise quite irrational in our judicial disposition of these cases to impose a definite sentence. If our prisons are to function as reformatory institutions, it is quite clear that in this particular case no one can possibly foretell how long a period it would take to bring about a reformation. It is as if a man suffering from pulmonary tuberculosis were told that he must go to a place set aside for such as he and stay there, say, five years, irrespective of whether he is well at the end of that time, or whether he might have recovered long before the expiration of that period.

In this particular instance we were led to recommend a commutation of the unexpired term of the sentence by the following considerations: First of all, I cannot consider sodomy a crime punishable by imprisonment, unless the act was performed on a subject who either is incapable of giving his consent or becomes a party to the act against his will, by force. Anomalies of the sexual function are not crimes, but diseases, and as such should come under the purview of the physician, and not the agents of the law. In the second place, this man served in the navy with an excellent record for about two years, and, so far as we know, is not inclined to habitual criminality, and therefore deserved at least another chance. But these considerations are somewhat beside the issue under discussion. The case, to my mind, illustrates very well how closely malingering of mental symptoms is related to actual mental disease, how both manifestations are expressions of the same underlying diseased soil, and how difficult, nay even impossible, it is to tell in a given case which of the symptoms are real and which shammed. On his first admission this man suffered from a grave mental disorder, from which, so far as anybody could determine, he made a complete recovery. Thrown back into the same stressful situation, he again finds himself unable to cope with it, becomes melancholy, suspicious, and mildly delusional. There is, however, considerable doubt in my mind as to the genuineness of these symptoms; unquestionably genuine is only the psychopathic make-up of this individual, which under stress permitted the development in one instance of a grave psychosis, in another of malingering.

Cases like the foregoing are by no means exceptions in criminal departments of hospitals for the insane. It is on account of this type of prison population that penal institutions furnish us with ten times as many insane as free communities.

Whatever convictions I possess concerning the subject of malingering were gained from a fairly extensive experience with insane delinquents at the Government Hospital for the Insane, and when I assert that I have yet to see a malingerer who, aside from being a malingerer, was likewise normal mentally, I do so with the full consciousness that my experience has been a more or less one-sided one. I mean to say that the material observed by me came to my notice within the confines of a hospital for the insane, and that my failure, therefore, to see the so-called pure malingerer is probably due to this circumstance. I shall not argue this point further, but merely state that it is true I have not had experience with the detected and convicted malingerer in the jail and court-room. I have had ample opportunity to study this same genus later as a patient in the hospital.

It would be an extremely interesting study to follow up the later careers of the so-called detected malingerers who are sent to prison and see how many of them later find their way to hospitals for the insane. A setting forth of these figures--and I doubt not for one second that the number is not at all inconsiderable--would not in the least have to be construed as a criticism of the diagnostic acumen of the original investigator. It would simply substantiate the truth of our contention that in the malingerer we see a type of individual who is far from normal, and in whom malingering as well as frank mental disease is not at all a rare phenomenon.

I have no doubt whatever that a considerable number of suspected malingerers are annually sent to penal institutions, there to be later recognized in their true light and transferred to hospitals for the insane; else it would be difficult to account for the fact that mental disease, according to many authors, is at least ten times as frequent among prisoners as it is among a free population. Certainly this cannot be attributed to environment alone, especially not to that of our modern, well-conducted prisons. The reason lies chiefly in the type of individual who populates our prisons. A number of them are either insane when sent to prison or potentially so, and when thrown into a more or less difficult situation, such as imprisonment, readily develop a mental disorder. We see this illustrated very well in the highly beneficial effect which transfer to a hospital for the insane has upon these individuals. I am convinced that one would not be wrong in agreeing with the opinions quoted below, that malingering, as such, is a morbid phenomenon and always the expression of an individual inferior mentally. It may be looked upon as a psychogenetic disorder, the mere possibility of the development of which is, according to Birnbaum[11] and others, an indication of a degenerative make-up, a defective mental organization. Siemens[12] says: "The demonstration of the existence of simulation is not at all proof that disease is simulated; it does not exclude the existence of mental disease." Pelman holds simulation in the mentally normal to be extremely rare, and he always finds himself at a loss to differentiate between that which is simulated and that which represents the actual traits of the individual. Melbruch[13] holds that simulation is observed solely in individuals more or less decidedly abnormal mentally, because in the great majority of cases, if there does not actually exist a frank mental disorder, these individuals lack in a marked degree psychic balance and are constantly on the verge of a psychosis. Penta, in a most thorough study of the subject of malingering, likewise comes to the conclusion that it is always a morbid phenomenon. It is a tool almost always resorted to by the weak and incompetent whenever confronted with an especially difficult or stressful situation. It is, therefore, almost exclusively seen in hysterics, neurotics and other types of psychopaths, in the frankly insane, and in grave delinquents.

With these remarks concerning malingering in the supposedly mentally normal, we may turn to a discussion of that large group of borderland cases which furnishes, outside of the frankly insane, the great majority of malingerers. I am tempted here to borrow Bornstein's classic description of the type of personality to which I am referring. According to him, these individuals come into the world with the stamp of a hereditary taint, with certain somatic anomalies (ears, palate, formation of skull, growth of hair, etc.), and already as children show those psychic characteristics which are decisive for their individuality. They are, above all, characterized by a marked hypersensitiveness and by a lack of harmonious relationship between the various psychic functions. This disharmony finds its expression chiefly in the predominance of the emotional element over the intellectual and in the entire subordination of the latter to the former. Their feelings, furthermore, express themselves in an abnormal manner, both as regards their intensity and duration. The emotional reaction is either excessively strong or, on the other hand, disproportionately weak compared with the stimulus, and in spite of the extravagance of the expression it quickly passes over or remains with an excessive obduracy for a disproportionately long time. Notwithstanding the apparent intensity of the outbreak in the former and its tediousness in the latter case, these emotional upsets almost always lack real depth. They are usually very superficial, insufficiently grounded, rather dependent upon accident; transitions from one extreme to the other make up the daily experiences of these individuals--from intense love to burning hatred, from deepest reverence to an irreconcilable disgust, from unshakable loyalty to brutal treachery. They lack energy and initiative, are undecided, vacillating, and inclined to self-reproach. The domination of the emotional sphere and the frequent incongruity and discord between the various forms of emotional expression frequently lead to the development of morbid doubts, morbid fears, a morbidly exaggerated egotism, and sensitiveness which leads them to scent everywhere personal injury and insult. Finally, they frequently show an overdevelopment of the sexual instincts and various deviations from normal sexual development. Many of them seem to lack totally in the power of reason, but act entirely upon impulse, upon the mere feeling that this or that proposition is true. Many others show a pronounced tendency to a metaphysic brooding and day-dreaming and to the transformation into fact of the dreamed air castles, without any regard to the iron logic of life which they cannot satisfy, with which they either will not or do not know how to reckon. Turning their backs upon the demands of life, centered in self, given up to the kaleidoscopic play of their emotions, which are of short duration, imperfect as to depth, varying in intensity, and depending upon any and every external influence, these individuals are very uncertain in their opinions, judgments, and motives for action. They go through life without any direction, without any guiding idea, without initiative, and without will, incapable of any kind of systematic labor, yet at times ready, under the influence of a temporary affect, to sacrifice everything in order to carry out what later on proves worthless and vain. Lacking in sure criteria and guides, they are slavishly dependent upon momentary external influences, and under unfavorable conditions of life suffer want and misery and give way to temptation, frequently falling into a life of vagabondage, drunkenness, and crime. In prison they often develop mental disorders, are looked upon as malingerers, and oscillate between prison and the insane asylum, only to begin the old game over again so soon as they again come in contact with life.

It is little wonder, then, that the psychiatrist in dealing with these unfortunates frequently finds himself at a loss to tell where health leaves off and disease begins. The psychoses which these individuals develop are in the great majority of instances purely psychogenetic in character, one of the many distinguishing features of which is a marked susceptibility of the symptoms to be influenced by external occurrences. This tendency of the symptoms to shape themselves in accordance with occurrences in the immediate environment frequently leads to the suspicion of malingering, because there seems to be altogether too much discretion displayed by these alleged insane.

I have elsewhere[14] reported a series of these cases and entered into a detailed discussion both of the personality and the nature of the psychoses from which these individuals suffered. Most of my cases had been both in prison and in hospitals for the insane on more than one occasion, every arrest and imprisonment having been apparently sufficient to bring out a fresh attack of mental disease.

The following case is fairly illustrative of this type:--

J. H., white male, age twenty-seven on admission, November 13, 1913. While serving a year's sentence at the Portsmouth Naval Prison for fraudulent enlistment the patient told the authorities there that on August 7, 1909, he had murdered a girl in Rochester, N.Y. He described the murder in great detail, stated that he met the girl in one of the Rochester cemeteries, attempted a sexual assault upon her, and when she resisted he choked her to death. He stated that he did not mean to kill his victim, but that he had inflicted the fatal injury before he was aware of it. It was remorse, he said, and the desire to expiate his crime which prompted his confession. He persisted in this confession until the naval authorities were persuaded to discharge him and turn him over to the civil authorities of Rochester, N.Y. Upon arriving there an alibi was easily established, freeing the patient of all suspicion of the murder, whereupon it took a good deal of investigation on the part of the authorities to establish the patient's real legal status. It was finally decided that he belonged to the naval authorities, and he was accordingly returned to prison and was given an additional sentence of a year for this fraud, which he began to serve on December 13, 1909. While awaiting this new sentence he assaulted a master-at-arms, who he claimed abused him, and for this offense he received an additional five years' sentence. He served this sentence until his first admission to this hospital on July 16, 1913, on the following medical certificate: First symptoms became manifest in 1910. The patient manifested fixed delusions of having murdered a girl on August 7, 1909. Present symptoms: Fixed delusions of a self-accusatory nature, delusions of persecution; accused a medical officer whom he had never seen before as being among those who were hounding him. Becomes excited, violent, profane, incoherent and obscene in speech, and attempted to assault the officer. He attempted suicide on February 15, 1910, while at Concord, N.H., State Prison.

During the patient's first sojourn at this hospital he conducted himself in an orderly manner, and, aside from the expression of mild persecutory ideas with reference to the prison personnel, he was free from psychotic manifestations. On only one occasion was he involved in some trouble while here, which was entirely his own fault. He was discharged on September 23, 1913, diagnosis "Not insane, psychopathic constitution," and returned to the U.S.S. *Southery* Prison Ship. Upon his return there it was noted that he was suffering from a double benign, tertiary, malarial infection, which it was maintained he had contracted in this hospital.

He was readmitted here on March 15, 1914, on a medical certificate which stated that the patient said he snuffed cocaine prior to admission to the navy; that the murder he believes he committed was due, according to his statement, to the refusal of the victim to permit sexual intercourse. The patient has at present the same fixed delusion of having committed this murder in 1909. He wants to expiate his crime to escape those who are continually hounding him. When irritated he flies into a rage, cries, tries to do himself injury, and talks incoherently. For no cause, while working in the yard, he struck a fellow prisoner and pursued him with a shovel. During maniacal attacks he can be restrained only with much difficulty, smashes furniture in his cell, and is slovenly in habits. Complains constantly of numbness and needle-like pains in vertex. As a probable cause, prison routine was given. It will thus be seen that the same fraud about the murder, which served at one time to bring him an additional sentence of a year, was considered at another time one of the symptoms which justified his return to this hospital. The patient's version of the reason for his return is as follows: Soon after his transfer to Portsmouth the guards began to annoy him, calling him crazy guy, hard guy, etc. He also got into trouble with the sergeant because the latter cursed him, began to express the same ideas about the murder, and thought this was the reason they sent him back.

The mental examination and physicians' notes made during his second admission showed no gross psychotic symptoms. The patient still maintained that he actually committed this crime in Rochester, and related it in great detail. He stated that when he was confined in Portsmouth Prison he became remorseful over this crime and decided to confess. His conduct during his second sojourn here was exemplary. He appeared at conference on April 20, 1914, and a diagnosis of psychopathic character was made. The opinion was expressed that it was extremely difficult to pick out the truth from the abnormal elements in the patient's story, and that there were a great many things in the general emotional reaction of the patient that fitted into the story.

It was believed that the patient had a sort of determination to get into difficulties for the sake of posing as a martyr and all that fits in with the grandiose element of his character. Being oppressed, he is taking it in a way that is very satisfying to his feelings of importance. Later during his sojourn here the patient became rather anxious to be returned to the penitentiary, stating that he had given up all the ideas which he had expressed on admission, and assured the physician that he was malingering on both occasions of his transfer to the hospital. He stated that his chief anxiety which led him to malinger was that he might be given additional sentences for his inability to get along in the penitentiary, and he thought the only way to avoid this would be to be pronounced insane. Patient was discharged from here to be returned to the penitentiary on July 9, 1914.

The patient was readmitted to this hospital on November 13, 1914, on a medical certificate which states: Diagnosis--Constitutional psychopathic state, not in line of duty, existed prior to enlistment. He was in the Government Hospital for the Insane in Washington for about four months this year. His condition is not improving. A sudden outburst occurred two days ago and he has been under close confinement since. He struck a recruit and after confinement in a cell destroyed a chair and had to be restrained. His retention in the prison in these barracks is not deemed desirable.

Nothing essentially new has developed in the case during this admission. The patient has from the first been quiet, well behaved, a willing worker in our industrial department, and free from signs of mental disorder. Of course, he again blamed the guards at the prison for the trouble which he became involved in and which necessitated his third admission to this hospital. A letter received from the naval medical officer stationed at the marine barracks, Norfolk, Va., the place of the patient's last confinement, was to the effect that while under observation there the patient made the impression of being a good worker, and normal in every way, except that he had a quick temper, and that the only difficulty they had noted was on the occasion when he assaulted the man at the prison, who appeared against him at the mast, and that after this scene he was put in the brig, where he threatened to kill any ---- ---- man who came near him. The medical officer was impressed with the fact that the patient was feigning insanity.

The patient's version of the circumstances which led to this last admission is as follows: He was reported to the commanding officer by a guard for some alleged minor infraction of discipline, of which he claims not to have been guilty. After the guard was through making his report the patient asked the commanding officer whether this alleged offense would prevent his release in July of this year, as he had been promised if he conducted himself well. The officer replied that it certainly would, upon hearing which he could not restrain himself, became quite overwhelmed with anger, and struck the guard who reported him. His behavior which necessitated his readmission took place following this episode. The patient dwells upon the fact that prior to this episode he behaved in an excellent manner under the prison régime for about four months, and that during his sojourn there he was practically a model prisoner, which was true.

He certainly has manifested no signs of mental disorder during his present admission, and still insists that he malingered all of the symptoms which led to his former two admissions because he feared more punishment at the hands of the naval authorities unless he was considered insane.

Anamnesis.--The patient comes from a family of farmers in mediocre circumstances. Grandparents are in Bohemia, and he knows nothing concerning them. Father died of Bright's disease; was alcoholic.

Otherwise family history negative.

Patient is uncertain about the time and place of birth, but believes
he is about thirty years of age at present. He entered school at seven
or eight, but proved to be a confirmed truant, and his father finally
had to take him out of school entirely. He was in the habit of running
away from home and school, to wander about the country, where he would
stop at different farm houses, claiming he was an orphan and without a
home, until his father would discover him and bring him back home.
After giving up school definitely he worked as a farm hand, earning
the ordinary wages paid for this labor. He changed places frequently,
was a spendthrift, and assisted his parents financially very little.
This mode of existence he led until 1904, when he forged his father's
name to a $25 check and received a five-year term of imprisonment,
part of which he spent in the Minnesota State Reformatory and part at
the State Penitentiary. In the fall of 1907 he was paroled, but broke
his parole by enlisting in the army, under the name of Kimlicka, at
Fort Snelling, Minn. About a month later the fraud was discovered
through his father. He was given a dishonorable discharge and sent
back to the penitentiary, where he remained about six months. At the
end of this time (December, 1907) he was granted another parole, and
went to work for a man named George Hall, on a farm in Minnesota. He
was there nearly two months, when he cut his foot while chopping wood.
He says that after this accident he was not able to do much work, and
his employer did not seem to like to have him hanging around, so he
went back to prison, which he says paroled prisoners were supposed to
do when they lost their jobs. As his time was up in two months, the
prison authorities made no effort to get him a new job, but kept him
there until his sentence expired. He left the penitentiary in March,
1908, and went home for a couple of weeks. He then went to Minneapolis
and enlisted in the navy under the name of James Hall, but did not
tell the recruiting officer about his prison or army experiences.
About four months after he enlisted he was caught with another sailor

in civilian's clothes in Newport, R.I. This was against the navy regulations. Patient says he did this because they did not allow him in dance halls, theaters, etc., in sailor's clothes. He used to keep his civilian's clothes in the Y. M. C. A. building in town, and would change there. He received a dishonorable discharge for this escapade. He says he had one court-martial before that, in July, 1908. He then went to Providence, R.I., and enlisted in the army under the name of Herman Hanson. In Fort Andrews, Boston Harbor, patient was caught in civilian's clothes again, and got into a brawl with a sergeant.

Patient says the sergeant was drunk and provoked the quarrel. As a result the patient was put in the guard-house, receiving a sentence of six months and dishonorable discharge. Two months of this sentence he served at Fort Andrews, and the rest at Governor's Island. After being discharged, he hung around New York City for a week, and then went to Rochester, N.Y. This was in May, 1909. Here he worked on a farm for Mrs. McCale, and the following month, June, 1909, he enlisted in the Marine Corps under the name of Vilt. He was sent to the Brooklyn Navy Yard, but after a week's sojourn there he got into trouble on account of not having his rifle cleaned. He feared that he would be reported for this and his previous frauds might be discovered, and he decided to desert. He returned to Rochester, worked for Frank Little and Roy Fritz. Soon after he enlisted in the army, this time under the name of James Hall, but was rejected on account of some nasal defect. This was at Columbus Barracks. After being rejected in the army he enlisted in the navy and was sent to Norfolk, Va. He was here likewise rejected on account of this defect, and while awaiting his discharge papers it was discovered that he had fraudulently enlisted. He was court-martialed and given a year. This was on November 20, 1909. His career following this has already been outlined.

If one takes into consideration the entire life history of this individual he will have little cause for surprise at the resort to malingering by this man when he found himself under an especially stressful situation. That he malingered every frank psychotic symptom which he manifested is beyond doubt a fact, even though he would not have admitted so much himself. But one would commit a serious error if on this account he would consider the man normal mentally. From childhood on this man has manifested traits of character which are absolutely psychopathic in nature. Among these may be especially emphasized the confirmed truancy and running away from home, the aimless, constantly-changing industrial career, the inability to pursue any line of endeavor towards a definite goal, the early criminalistic tendencies, the repeated commission of military offenses in spite of the frequent punishments, and, lastly, his total inability to adjust himself to the prison rÃ©gime, resulting in serious mental upsets which necessitated his admission to a hospital for the insane on three different occasions. It is perfectly natural that he should resort to malingering of mental disease in his last attempt at evading a stressful situation. Malingering is frequently the only means of escape for such as he, unable as they are to meet life's problems squarely in the face.

It is of no particular value to add more cases illustrative of the type of mental make-up which leads to malingering, especially since there exists a more or less complete unanimity of opinion on the subject among present-day psychiatrists.

CONCLUSIONS

The conclusions which may safely be drawn from the study of malingering as it is manifested in criminal departments of hospitals for the insane are as follows:--

1. The detection of malingering in a given case by no means excludes the presence of actual mental disease. The two phenomena are not only not mutually exclusive, but are frequently concomitant manifestations in the same individual.

2. Malingering is a form of mental reaction manifested for the purpose of evading a particularly stressful situation in life, and is resorted to chiefly, if not exclusively, by the mentally abnormal, such as psychopaths, hysterics, and the frankly insane.

3. Malingering and allied traits, viz., lying and deceit, are not always consciously motivated modes of behavior, but are not infrequently determined by motives operative in the subconscious mental life, and accordingly affect to a marked extent the individual's responsibility for such behavior.

4. The differentiation of the malingered symptoms from the genuine ones is, as a rule, extremely difficult, and great caution is to be exercised in pronouncing a given individual a malingerer.

NOTES

[1] BRILL, A. A.: "Artificial Dreams and Lying," *Journal of Abnormal Psychology*, vol. ix, No. 5.

[2] DELBRÃœCK, ANTON: "Die Pathologische LÃ¼ge," Enke, Stuttgart, 1891.

[3] FERRARI, L.: "Minorenni Delinquenti," Milano, 1895.

[4] PENTA, PASQUALE: "La Simulazione della Pazzia," Napoli, Francesco Perrella, 1905.

[5] WILMANNS: "Ueber Gefangnispsychosen," Halle, S. 1908.

[6] BONHOEFFER: "Degenerationspsychosen," Halle, S. 1907.

[7] KNECHT: Quoted by Penta.

[8] VINGTRINIER: "Des Alienes dans les Prisons," *Annales d'hygiene et de med.-legale*, 1852-53.

[9] JONES: Introduction to "Papers on Psycho-analysis."

[10] PELMAN: "Beitrag zur Lehre von der Simulation," Irrefreund, 1874, and *Arch. de Neurolog.*, 1890.

[11] BIRNBAUM, K.: "Zur Frage der psychogenen Krankheitsformen," Zeitsch. f. d. ges. Neur. u. Psych., 1910.

[12] SIEMENS: "Zur Frage der Simulation von SeelenstÃ¶rung," *Arch. f. Psych. und Nerv.*, xiv, 1883.

[13] MELBRUCH: Quoted by Penta.

[14] GLUECK, BERNARD: "Catamnestic Study of Juvenile Offender," *Journal of Am. Inst. Crim. Law and Crimin.*, viii, No. 2.

CHAPTER V
THE ANALYSIS OF A CASE OF KLEPTOMANIA

Introduction.--The past two years have been very profitable ones for the science of criminology, as they have brought to light two books on the subject which concretely reflect, on the one hand, the dying out of the old statistical method of studying the criminal, a method which will never tell the whole story, and on the other hand, the birth of a new kind of approach to the study of the criminal, namely--the characterological approach. The study of crime or antisocial human behavior from this newer standpoint at once becomes a study of character, and demands a scientific consideration of the motives and driving forces of human conduct, and since conduct is the resultant of mental life, mental factors at once become for us the most important phase of our study. Both of these books represent epoch-making culminations of years of hard labor and scientific devotion to criminology by two eminent students--Drs. Goring[1] and Healy.[2]

Dr. Goring's book, "The English Convict, a Statistical Study", appeared in 1913, and is the result of an intense statistical study of 4000 English male convicts, to which the author devoted about twelve years of his life. Dr. Healy's book, "The Individual Delinquent", which appeared in the early part of this year, reflects the results of thoroughgoing scientific studies of about 1000 repeated offenders, during the author's five years' experience as Director of the Juvenile Psychopathic Institute in connection with the Juvenile Court of Chicago. Numerous reviews of these two books have appeared in medical and criminologic literature, and we shall only touch very minutely upon the difference in the methods of approach to the subject of these two authors as they concern the subject under consideration in this paper. I can do this no better than by quoting from a critical review of Goring's book by Dr. White,[3] as it happily touches upon our very subject--namely, stealing. "Take the more limited concept of 'thief', for example. One man may steal under the influence of the prodromal stage of paresis who has been previously of high moral character. Another man may steal under the excitement of a hypomanic attack; another may steal as the result of moral delinquency; another as the result of high grade mental defect; another under the influence of alcoholic intoxication, and so forth, and so on, and how by any possibility a grouping of these men together can give us any light upon the general concept of 'thief' is beyond my power to comprehend."

When one remembers that the 4000 units with which this really marvelous statistical machinery has worked for twelve long years had nothing more in common than the fact that they were English male convicts--the force of White's argument becomes quite apparent. I need not state that this view of Goring's work is not intended to detract one iota from the full measure of credit which this author deserves. His work will stand forever as one of the monumental accomplishments of the twentieth century.

Our views concerning Healy's contribution to the science of criminology will be reflected in the course of this chapter, which will indicate, I trust, in a way, his mode of approach to the problem, though he may not agree with me concerning the details of my interpretation of the case I am about to report.

Definition.--Like many another I dislike the term "kleptomania" and would much prefer the term "pathological stealing" to denote the condition under consideration. Pathological stealing is not synonymous with excessive stealing as one would gather from the sensational use of the term in the lay press. Neither is Kraepelin's dictum that Kleptomania is a form of impulsive insanity, necessarily correct. It is obviously, however, a form of abnormally conditioned conduct. Healy's criterion of Pathological stealing is the fact that the misconduct is disproportionate to any discernible end in view. In spite of risk, the stealing is indulged in, as it were, for its own sake, and not because the objects in themselves are needed or intrinsically desired. This definition at once excludes all cases of stealing from cupidity, or from development of a habit. It furthermore excludes stealing arising from fetichism, pronounced feeblemindedness and mental disease, such as is for instance illustrated in the automatic stealing of the epileptic.

According to Healy, the vast majority of all instances of pathological stealing are those in which individuals, not determinably insane, give way to an abnormally conditioned impulse to steal.

The Psychoanalytic Study of Anti-Social Behavior.--In introducing the term "Psychoanalysis" into this chapter I am fully conscious of the task I have set before me, of writing clearly and convincingly in a work of this nature on that vast and highly important subject which one at once links with this term. To strip it of its highly technical considerations, psychoanalysis is primarily and essentially a study of motives, intended to bring about a better understanding of human conduct. We shall leave out from consideration the very intricate technique which this method of approach to the study of human behavior employs except to indicate the chief source upon which it relies for its information, namely, the individual's unconscious, that is, that part of the individual's personality which is outside of the realm of his moment-consciousness, and which is inaccessible either to himself or to the observer except through special methods of investigation. It would be highly desirable, indeed one would say almost imperative, to give a full discussion of the "unconscious" before a proper and sympathetic understanding of what is to follow can be made possible. This, however, is obviously out of the question in a limited chapter like this. Volumes have been written on the subject. I will only ask my readers to agree with me for the sake of gaining proper orientation with reference to the subject under discussion, in the conclusion which I quote from a masterly paper on the "unconscious" by White.[4] "We come thus to the important conclusion that mental life, the mind, is not equivalent and co-equal with consciousness. That, as a matter of fact, the motivating causes of conduct often lie outside of consciousness, and, as we shall see, that consciousness is not the greater but only the lesser expression of the psyche. Consciousness only includes that of which we are aware, while outside of this somewhat restricted region there lies a much wider area in which lie the deeper motives for conduct and which not only operate to control conduct, but also dictates what may and what may not become conscious." The foundation upon which the method evolved by the psychoanalytic school rests has been aptly summed up by Healy, namely, that for the explanation of all human behavior tendencies we must seek the mental and environmental experiences of early life. One of the chief aids in gaining that knowledge we have in the study of the dream and symbolic life of the individual. The reasons given for our necessarily limited discussion of the unconscious, are likewise true of the dream and symbolism. Both of these subjects would require for a proper elucidation considerably more space than this chapter affords.

Through the dream the unconscious betrays itself;--the dream represents the fulfillment of wishes and cravings which because of psychic and social censorship have become repressed into the unconscious. During sleep these barriers are in abeyance, and the unconscious psyche is given the opportunity for full play, albeit in a disguised and highly symbolic form. The proper interpretation of dreams presupposes a knowledge of the nature of symbolism in the life of man.

When we come now to a consideration of the facts brought to light through the psychoanalytic study of man we are confronted with a still greater difficulty of presentation. There is so much that is of vital importance in this new psychology that we hardly know where to begin. As I am addressing those who are primarily interested for the moment in criminology, I may do well to begin with the subject of psychic determinism. In contrast to the common sentiment of all people in favor of free will in mental processes, the facts elicited by psychoanalysis point to a strict determinism of every psychic process. Psychoanalytic investigations have shown that in mental phenomena there is nothing little, nothing arbitrary, nothing accidental. In his book on the Psychopathology of Everyday Life, Freud[5] has thrown very convincing light on this subject. Certain apparently insignificant mistakes, such as forgetting, errors of speech, writing and action, etc., are regularly motivated and determined by motives unknown to consciousness. The reason that the motives for such unintentional acts are hidden in the unconscious and can only be revealed by psychoanalysis is to be sought in the fact that these phenomena go back to motives of which consciousness will know nothing, hence were crowded into the unconscious, without, however, having been deprived of every possibility of expressing themselves. Thus we see that no mental phenomenon, and by the same token no part of human behavior, happens fortuitously, but has its specific motive, to a very large extent, in the unconscious.

The question may suggest itself here "why this extensive participation of the unconscious in mental life", which brings us to a discussion of the principles of resistance and repression.

In speaking of the "unconscious" I purposely left out from consideration the way in which the sum total of its content was separated from the conscious mental life of the individual, in order to bring it in alignment with the discussion of the principles of resistance and repression. The content of the unconscious, broadly speaking, is brought about through the activity of these two principles. If one endeavors to unearth by means of psychoanalysis the pathogenic unconscious mental impulses, or if one endeavors to bring to consciousness some instinctive biologic craving which may be responsible for the individual's conscious behavior, one regularly encounters a very strong resistance on the part of the patient, a force is regularly betrayed whose object it seems to be to prevent them from becoming conscious and to compel them to remain in the unconscious. This is Freud's conception of the principle of resistance and from its constant coming to the fore whenever an endeavor is made to penetrate into the unconscious, Freud deducts that the same forces which today oppose as resistance the becoming conscious of the unconscious purposely forgotten, must at one time have accomplished this forgetting and forced the offending pathogenic experience out of consciousness. This mechanism he terms repression. We spoke of an offending pathogenic experience, or in other words what has been termed a psychic trauma. But the same principle holds true of certain instincts which because of their peculiar nature become engaged in a kind of struggle for existence with the ethical, moral and esthetic attributes of the personality and are thrust out of the conscious mental structure as one might say by an act of the will.

We are especially concerned here with these inacceptable instincts, for the elucidation of which a brief review of Freud's theories on sexual instinct is essential.

Thoroughgoing and painstaking dissection of the human soul, such as has been practiced by Freud for nearly a quarter of a century and by many followers of his theories in the past decade, revealed to him a number of unmistakable facts from the developmental history of the individual which forced him to postulate his very radical and revolutionary theories of the sexual instinct in man. Recent behavior studies in the higher anthropoids have likewise revealed very interesting facts concerning the sexual instinct of these animals. Freud was led to make certain assertions from his painfully acquired experience, such as the unfailing sexual agency in the causation of neurotic manifestations, and that his experience of many years has as yet shown no exception to this rule, which quite naturally provoked a good deal of bitter and fanatic criticism not only from lay people but from experienced physicians. The cause for this lies in the nature of the thing itself, that much tabooed subject of sexuality. Unfortunately, as Hitschmann[6] says, physicians in their personal relations to the sexual life have not been given any preference over the rest of the children of men and many of them stand under the ban of that combination of prudery and lust which governs the attitude of most cultivated people in sexual matters. Especially unsavory appears to most people Freud's theory of infantile sexuality, a subject which has heretofore been looked upon chiefly from a moralistic standpoint, and was spoken of by others merely as odd or as a frightful example of precocious depravity. It is somewhat strange that of all the frightful depravities, if we wish to call it so--inherent in man, of the marked criminalistic components universally present in man which psychoanalytic studies have revealed--the sex depravity should have provoked the most fanatic attacks. Indeed to those who are accustomed to look at man with the psychoanalytic eye, Rochefoucauld's incisive statement does not at all sound strange. He said, "I have never seen the soul of a bad man; but I had a glimpse at the soul of a good man; I was shocked." I therefore crave the indulgence of those of you who are not familiar with psychoanalytic literature for what I am about to quote briefly from Freud's theories on the sexual instinct in man.

Freud lays special stress upon infantile sexuality as it is manifested in the suckling and in the child. The infant brings with it into the world the germ of sexuality, which is, however, extremely difficult of comprehension since at this stage the sexual feelings are not directed towards other persons but are gratified on the child's own body in a manner which Havelock Ellis has termed "autoerotic." This autoerotic gratification is gained through erogenous zones, that is, certain areas of the body which are peculiarly sensitized to sexual excitations. Among these erogenous zones may be mentioned the mouth, lips, tongue, anal region, the neck of the bladder as well as various skin areas and sense organs. Already in 1879, Lindner, a Hungarian pediatrist, devoted a penetrating study to the sucking or pleasure-sucking of the child. Freud emphasizes that the suckling enjoys sexual pleasure, in the taking of nourishment, which it ever after seeks to procure by sucking independent of taking food. To many it may occasion surprise to learn that sucking is exhibited independently of its relation to the hunger instinct. It is, however, plain that the mouth is at first concerned only with the gratifying of the hunger instinct; later the desire for a repetition of pleasurable experience gained in this way is separated from the need of taking nourishment, thereby transforming this mucous surface into an erogenous zone. It is likewise difficult to conceive by the inexperienced in psychoanalysis, that the child derives pleasurable sensations from the anal zone. Because of the important rÃ´le which anal eroticism plays in our case we might speak more fully of this form of autoeroticism. One not infrequently observes in little children that they refuse to empty the bowels when they are placed on the closet because they obtain pleasure from defecation, when the retained stool by its accumulation excites strong irritation of the mucosa. The importance which scatological rites and ceremonials, that is, certain peculiar niceties practiced in connection with the emptying of the bowels, play in the evolution of the race have been extensively discussed in literature. Havelock Ellis[7] says in this connection--"The most usual erotic symbolisms in childhood are those of the scatologic group, the significance of which has often been emphasized by Freud and his school. The channels of urination and defecation are so close to the sexual centers that the intimate connection between the two groups is easily understood. There is undoubtedly a connection between nocturnal enuresis and sexual activities, sometimes masturbation. Children not infrequently believe that the sexual acts of their elders have some connection with urination and defecation, and the mystery with which the excretory acts are surrounded, helps to support this theory. Up to puberty scatologic interests may be regarded as normal; at this age the child has still much in common with the primitive mind, which, as mythology and folklore show, attributes great importance to the excretory functions."

Many of these ceremonials one regularly discovers in the analyses of neurotics. We shall not dwell further here upon the erogenous zones activity in the suckling, but emphasizing again its importance along with the importance of autoeroticism in the sexuality of the suckling will pass to the next phase of the psycho-sexual evolution of man--the latent period.

The germs of sexual excitement in the new-born develop for a time, then undergo a progressive suppression in a period of partial or complete sexual latency. During this period, which is normally interrupted at about the third or fourth year, as result of organic evolutionary processes and the indispensable help of education, those mental forces are formed which appear later as inhibitions to the sexual instinct and narrow its course like dams; mental forces such as disgust, the feeling of shame, the esthetic and moral standards of ideas. During this "latent period" a part of these sexual energies is separated from the sexual aim and applied to cultural and social ends, a process which Freud has designated by the name sublimation as important for culture, history and the individual.

Sublimation or the socialization of the sexuality therefore is the transformation and utilization of certain components of the sexual instinct for aims no longer sexual in nature. At the end of the latency period the child's sexuality reappears, frequently but not necessarily induced prematurely by seduction. In addition to the autoerotic gratifications spoken of above, the child is now capable of the choice of a love-object accompanied by erotic feelings. Because of the dependency of the child this first choice of a love-object is directed towards parents and nurses either of his own or of the opposite sex. "Incest complex"--Now too the child under the influence of occasional seduction may become polymorphous-perverse, that is, may become subject to any form of sexual perversion. He likewise shows a preference in the selection of his love-object for his own sex, homo-sexuality.

At puberty two significant changes take place in the psycho-sexuality of the individual. First the primacy of the genital zone asserts itself, and second, the heretofore autoerotic character of the sexual activity is lost and the instinct finds its object. In order that the former change may be successfully brought about, there is necessitated an amalgamation of all instinctive tendencies which proceed from the erogenous zones and a subordination of all the erogenous zones to the primacy of the genital zone. All this is facilitated by the development of the genital organs and the elaboration of the seminal secretion. To these conditions there is also added at puberty that "pleasure of gratification" of sexuality which ends the normal sexual act, the end pleasure. The second function, the choice of a love-object, is influenced by the infantile inclination of the child towards its parents and nurses which is revived at puberty and similarly directed by the incest barriers against these persons which have been erected in the meantime. If on account of pathological heredity and accidental experiences, this amalgamation of the excitations springing from various sources and its application to the sexual object does not occur, then there result the pathological deviations of the sexual instinct, determined in part by earlier processes, such as a preservation of a definite part of the original polymorphous-perverse tendency. The perversions are thus developed from seeds which are present in the undifferentiated tendencies of the child and constitute in adults a condition of arrested development.

Thus we see that the sexual impulse does not suddenly emerge as a new phenomenon at the age of puberty, but that the form assumed at this period is gradually evolved from rudimentary elements present even in the earliest years of life. Sexuality is not absent in the child, it is merely different, being unorganized and imperfectly adapted to its later functions. All this primordial mass of pleasurable activities enumerated above, undergoes profound modifications as the result of growth and education. One part only becomes selected and differentiated so as to form the adult sexual impulse in the narrower sense. A greater part is found to be incompatible with social observance, and is repressed, buried, forgotten. The repressed impulses, however, do not die; it is much harder to kill old desires than is sometimes thought, they continue throughout life to strive toward gratification. This they cannot do directly, and are thus driven to find indirect, symbolic modes of expression. The energy is transformed into these secondary, more permissible forms of activity, and furnishes a great part of the strivings of mankind that lead to social and cultural interests and development in general--sublimation. (Jones.)

I don't know whether I have succeeded in putting clearly enough the Freudian views of sexuality, limited as I have to be in my expositions of his theories. I do wish, however, to leave the impression which one must gain from two sentiments frequently expressed by various authors, namely, "Man sexualizes the universe," and "Man is what his sex is."

Sexuality and Criminality.--A method of psychological analysis which aside from its originally restricted field has already thrown so much light upon various cultural aspects of life, such as art, poetry, religion, folklore, and mythology, cannot fail to furnish some very helpful discoveries for the problem of criminology. As far as pathological stealing is concerned a number of very suggestive studies have already appeared, a review of which Albrecht has prepared for the Journal of the American Institute of Criminal Law and Criminology. The fact that rich, or at least well-to-do, women are sometimes guilty of theft in the big Department stores has always received a certain amount of attention. Studies of this phenomenon have been made by Duboisson, Contemps, Lasegue and Letulle. In each case examined the woman declared that some unknown power had suddenly compelled her to touch some object, and put it in her pocket.

Stekel,[8] a Viennese psychotherapeutist, claims to have repeatedly proved to himself by psychoanalysis that the root of all these cases of kleptomania is ungratified sexual instinct. These women fight against temptation. They are engaged in a constant struggle with their desires. They would like to do what is forbidden, touch something that doesn't belong to them. We cannot give here the analyses reported in the literature, though I assure you that they carry convincing proof of the tremendous rÃ´le sexuality plays directly or indirectly in the causation of pathological stealing. This is not confined only to thieving connected with fetichism, numerous cases of which have been reported in the literature. But even less radical Freudians than Stekel admit the importance of sexuality in pathological stealing. Thus Healy, who is eminently fit to speak authoritatively on the subject of recidivism, and who is unusually conservative in his statements, has the following to say:--

"The interpretation of the causes of this impulse to steal is of great interest. We have shown in our chapter on mental conflicts how it may be a sort of relief phenomenon for repressed elements in mental life. The repression is found often to center about sex affairs." Again, "The correlation of the stealing impulse to the menstrual or premenstrual period in woman, leads us to much the same conclusion. Gudden, who seems to have made the most careful studies of the connection between the two phenomena, maintains that practically all cases of shoplifters whom he has examined were, at the time of their offense, in or near their period of menstruation." Healy does not go beyond this. He is as yet not ready to agree that some sex difficulty is the only conflict back of kleptomania.

With these introductory remarks we will proceed to the discussion of our case. X----, a colored boy aged 23, was admitted to the Government Hospital for the Insane on January 16, 1915, from the District Jail, where he was awaiting trial on two indictments for larceny.

Anamnesis obtained from the patient, his relatives and official sources is to the effect that the patient comes from an unusually refined colored family, his father being a rather prominent colored minister in this city. The patient is one of eight children, all of whom with the exception of the patient have led a normal and fairly successful life. He was born in Washington, D.C., April 17, 1892. Birth and early childhood up to four years of age were normal. At that time he was rather seriously bitten by a large St. Bernard dog, following which he was ill for about two months. He was rather restive under this enforced confinement and one day in attempting to escape from the house he fell from a second story window. His relatives attribute all his difficulties to these two accidents, for it was soon after that his stealing tendencies became manifest. The patient himself can place only approximately the onset of his stealing propensities, stating that he was quite young and that his first theft consisted in stealing ten cents from his father. It was in connection with this theft that he first experienced the sensations to be described later. His school career was irregular owing to the interruptions necessitated by his repeated sojourns at the Reformatory. He entered school at the age of 7 and at 11 was sent to the Reform School for the first time. This step was taken by his father because the patient for some years previously had been frequently placed under arrest on charges of larceny. He showed, according to the statements of his relatives, a decided preference for horses and vehicles of all sorts, which he would utilize for joy riding, although he not infrequently stole objects of which he could make absolutely no use. One time, for instance, he stole a dozen bricks from a neighbor. The Chief Probation Officer of the District of Columbia, who was an official of the Reformatory during the patient's sojourn there, states in a letter to the hospital the following: "While there he (X) gave very little trouble, except in the way of stealing. He would steal any and every thing he could lay hold of. It mattered not whether the article was of any use to him or not. After stealing an article or articles he would make very little effort to hide it, and when taken to task and charged with having stolen an article he would acknowledge it but would say that he did not know what made him take the article, only that something told him to take it and when this thought came to him he did not have the power to resist it, but felt that he was compelled to take it. At the Training School we looked upon him as a rather peculiar subject. We really never considered him insane except that his desire to steal might be classed in that line."

It is somewhat difficult to get a coherent and full account of the patient's delinquencies. His record at the National Training School is as follows: "Rec. on September 4, 1906, sentenced by the D.C. Juvenile Court charged with larceny, escaped August 30, 1907. Returned from elopement September 5, 1907, special parole to father October 23, 1909. Recommitted by D.C. Juvenile Court February 3, 1910, charge larceny. May 2, 1911, escaped from Freedman's Hospital while left there for treatment after operation. Returned on May 25, 1911, from Baltimore, Md. July 13, 1912, escaped." During his various sojourns there he was noted to be wilful and unprincipled. Every time he gained his freedom his father attempted to keep him at school, thus he attended night school and Law Department of Howard University for short periods. His father likewise put forth many genuine efforts to reform the boy, plead with him and begged him, supplied him with considerable spending money, but his efforts were as fruitless as the various punishments he underwent. The boy would behave well for a while, but sooner or later he would be arrested for stealing. Patient states that he stole many times when he successfully evaded the police, that he frequently took unusual chances in his escapades, preferred to steal in the daytime and it was this that led him to believe that God had chosen this particular mode of life for him, and that as a result of this conviction he practices the habit of giving one-fourth of his earnings to charity. He had learned from his father that somewhere the Bible teaches to give one-fifth of the earnings to charity, but owing to the manner in which he acquired his possessions he felt that he ought to give more to charity, a rather characteristic mode of rationalization for a man of his type.

Aside from the arrests recorded above he has been arrested in the cities of Baltimore, Philadelphia, and New York, always for stealing, and spent about 19 months in the Pennsylvania Industrial Reform School.

His latest arrest and subsequent admission to the Government Hospital for the Insane was the result of an attempt at housebreaking on August 1, 1914. He states that he entered this house with the full intention of robbing it, that he found considerable jewelry and some $30 in money which he collected on a dresser, when he suddenly began to think of his mother, and the anxiety he would cause her should he be caught in the act, whereupon he left everything on the dresser and left the house. He was detected leaving the house, which brought about his arrest. Patient states that such acts on his part were not unusual, that he not infrequently left a robbery incomplete upon thinking of his mother.

On admission to this hospital the patient made a normal impression. He gave a coherent and clear account of his past life, was apparently quite frank and truthful and endeavored to coÃ¶perate with the examiner to the best of his ability. He was clearly oriented, free from frank delusions and hallucinations, but said in explanation of his stealing habits that it is the influence of God that makes him steal, because he has been so successful at it, and because he has always given one-fourth of his income from stealing to charity. (He rationalizes very efficiently in this manner.) He likewise stated that frequently in the night before he commits an offense he dreams of a man leading him and instructing him what to do. He used to think that it was a representative of God whom he saw in the dream, but since he has had the talk with Dr. H., who told him that it was only the devil who tempts him to do these things, he has changed his mind about it. Special intelligence tests revealed no defect, and his stock of information was commensurate with his educational advantages. He was well informed on current events and readily adapted himself to his new surroundings.

Physical examination showed him to be a fairly well developed colored male, slight acneiform eruption over back, slight asymmetry of head, ears close set to head, lobules attached, palate high arched. There was likewise present a slight depression in right supra-clavicular region, lung over this area slightly impaired. Heart sounds slightly roughened, urine and Wassermann with blood serum negative.

During his sojourn here his conduct has been exemplary. He worked steadily in Howard Hall workroom and occupied his leisure time in reading and playing musical instruments, two of which he knows how to manipulate fairly well. It is significant that as far as known the patient has not evidenced any tendency to steal since here, although during the first few days of his sojourn here he experienced the sensations which usually accompany his stealing escapades. A carefully kept record of his dreams, in which matter the patient apparently coÃ¶perated to the best of his ability, likewise failed to reveal any of the pre-stealing dreams mentioned above.

Analysis.--The suggestive points in the patient's history are the repeated commission of a similar offense, namely, stealing, notwithstanding the frequent punishment received, the stealing when he actually had no necessity for it, being at times when he stole well supplied with money, the stealing of objects for which he had no use and which he could not convert into money, as stated in the Reform School Records, the patient's belief in his destiny as a thief and the methods he employed in atoning for his conduct, such as giving one-fourth to charity, and lastly the peculiar physical and mental sensations which accompanied the act of stealing. The inquiry was conducted along these lines. In the first interview the patient could throw very little light on his difficulties. He stated that he had tried repeatedly to quit stealing, that he realized he was causing his parents a great deal of anxiety on account of his habits, and bringing a good deal of trouble on himself, that he genuinely regretted his past acts and that he believed he could possibly abstain in the future from stealing. Later interviews revealed, as has already been stated, that his first theft was committed upon his father, when he stole ten cents, and it was upon this occasion that he first experienced the peculiar bodily and mental sensations. He describes these in his own words as follows, "I begin to feel giddy and restless and feel as if I have to do something. This feeling becomes gradually more marked until I feel compelled to enter a house and steal. While stealing I become quite excited, involuntarily, begin to pant, perspire and breathe rapidly as if I had run a race; this increases in intensity and then I feel as if I have to go to the closet and empty my bowels. After it's all over I feel exhausted and relieved." The feeling of exhaustion and relief was in a later interview spontaneously described by him as being like that one experiences after coitus. In the early days of his career he used to go to the closet in response to the anal sensations, but he never had to actually evacuate his bowels so that of late he does not do this any more. At first he had those sensations only when stealing from his father, later also when stealing from his mother, and finally he would experience them whenever he stole. It is of interest to note here his attitude towards his father. In the early stages of the analysis he staunchly maintained that he loved his father very much, that he honored him and felt very sorry for all the troubles he was causing him, but further inquiry revealed positively the fact that he showed a decided preference for his mother, that the latter always took his part when he was punished by his father, that he felt extremely angry at his father on a number of occasions in the past because the latter punished him often, but it was only after the analysis and proper insight on the part of the patient into the following dream that he admitted that he had sometimes wished his father dead. He dreamed on February 4th that his father had died, that he could see his father in a coffin, and his mother, sister and brothers weeping. "I awoke before I could finish the dream." The first attempts with the patient at analyzing this dream produced quite an upset, a good deal of emotionalism and tears, especially when it was suggested to him that the dream might express a wish. In an interview on February 15th he said that he no longer thought that the above suggestion was such an impossibility, that perhaps there was a good deal of truth in it, although he is certain that consciously he had never entertained such ideas in reference to his father. There was no affective manifestation in connection with this statement.

Another dream which he had the night before the preceding dream is, to my mind an extremely important one, reflecting as it does the patient's real conflicts. He dreamed on February 3rd that two of his brothers came over to visit him. They brought a young girl over that he used to keep company with, and told him that if he would marry they could get him out. He replied that he would never marry any girl, and one of his brothers said, "Then you will never get out of this place." They then quarreled, the brother insisting that he just had to marry, but he still refused. The girl plead with him to marry her, saying that she would do a good deal for him, but he still refused. In parting one of his brothers said to him, "Then go to your ruin, we will never do anything for you again." The patient then awoke perspiring and mad as if he had actually been quarreling. Thus the dream reads "Marry and you'll get out of here, otherwise go to your ruin, we will never do anything for you." In other words, "Lead a heterosexual life and your troubles will be over, continue as you are now, you'll go to ruin." This argument of the unconscious taken together with the group of sensations which patient always experienced when stealing, and which he spontaneously likens to the sensations of a sexual act, and furthermore the quite evident anal erotic fixation, already throw a good deal of light upon the patient's difficulties.

He further dreamed one night that his mother got him a situation with a widowed man. His duties were to take care of and keep in good order the man's three horses. One of these horses was a vicious one, the other two were mild. If one were to think of the three horses as of a phallic symbol the significance of this dream at once becomes apparent. The patient associated the vicious horse which always tried to bite him with his father. Here, too, it was the mother which comes to his aid.

A number of other dreams recorded by the patient manifest simple wish fulfillment and are of no especial interest.

In his habits the patient was always of a jolly, sociable disposition, enjoyed fun very much and for many years back he had a keen desire to become a detective. In fact if he had any ambition in life at all it was this. On many occasions in the past he played detective; he would track people on many occasions for hours at a time. What is of marked significance is the fact that on a number of occasions when he did this he experienced similar bodily sensations as he did when stealing. The detective sensations were never as intense as those accompanying stealing and never reached the climax. It was only yesterday that the patient told me spontaneously in the course of an interview that he supposed he never reached the climax in his detective experiences because he has never arrested anyone. Thus we see that along with his antisocial sublimation of his anal eroticism, the patient attempted a more useful sublimation. Unfortunately the one depended simply upon his exertions and bravado, while the other required for its fulfillment society's recognition of his desire and some ability for detective work. I am firmly convinced that these two activities of the patient, namely, stealing and detection of crime, are the results of his endeavor at sublimating a totally inacceptable homosexual career. On one occasion, and he claims that it is the only one in his life, a fellow prisoner in the Reformatory attempted a sexual assault upon him. He retaliated by striking the fellow on the head with a chair, for which he was severely punished. While we may rely quite fully upon the information furnished by the patient and upon that obtained from other sources for the purpose of building up our theory of the case, it will not be amiss to take into consideration those points in the patient's conduct while under observation which further substantiate this theory.

We have it from a reformatory official that while at that institution the patient frequently stole articles which were of no value whatever to him, that he did not attempt to conceal his thefts, and that when upbraided for his conduct, he stated that he could not help it, etc. At that institution he evidently entirely relied upon his stealing sublimation for his sexual gratification. It may be that as yet he had not become conscious of the possibilities of the detective play.

In this hospital he had desires for stealing on two occasions, soon after his admission, but resisted the temptation. Following the manifestation of our active interest in his case, he became more and more confident in his ability to withstand these temptations, and as far as could be judged manifested a genuine desire to reform. Of course the biologic sex difficulty is still present, its demands are probably just as insistent as ever, and having rejected, for the present at least, the possibility of expression through the stealing channel, he resorts to the only other channel he knows of, detective play. In line with this he handed me one morning (March 30, 1915) a note which stated that some information had come into his possession which he thought would be of very great value to me, and requested a private interview. After cautioning me as to the method of procedure he assured me that he did this piece of detective work solely because he felt very grateful for our effort to help him out of his troubles. We must note the meticulous manner in which he carried out the entire procedure. For some time past he had been in the habit of handing me each morning a uniformly folded sheet of paper containing the dreams of the previous night. On that morning he had two of these folded sheets in his vest pocket but handed me only the above mentioned note, because he says he feared that I would read only the one containing the dream and miss the other. During the interview which followed as result of the above note, he handed over to me a bunch of petitions written by a famous litigant in the criminal department, which were to have been delivered by the patient to his relatives with the object of getting them to their final destination. Aside from the fact that the author of these petitions is by no means a simpleton, or very credulous, it must have taken a good deal of ingenuity and skill on the part of the patient to gain this fellow's confidence, knowing as I do that the latter has a special grudge against the patient because they are the only two in the Howard Hall Department who enjoy some special privileges in common, such as attending chapel and amusements, etc.

This compulsion of attending chapel, as he puts it, with a negro, has been the litigant's chief grievance during the past two months, and he has accordingly expressed himself in some very choice language when speaking of the patient. Nevertheless the patient has succeeded in gaining his full confidence, and the interest and pleasure which the patient manifested in detailing to me his mode of procedure in accomplishing this is really very striking. It was during this interview that he stated, "I suppose the reason I never reached the climax when playing detective is because I have never arrested anyone. This is the work I would like to do, Doctor, I hope some day I'll be able to get a job with some detective agency."

I regret to have to omit many interesting details from the analysis of this case. To me the analysis of this case has been a revelation. For a number of years past I have been intensely interested in the problem of recidivism, and although I have had many opportunities to study the recidivist, and have seen a number of very interesting cases, the histories of a few of whom I have reported several years ago, I have always felt that I had never touched the real specific cause of a life of recidivism in a given individual. Why a man, an apparently intelligent man, and many of them are far from suffering from a purely intellectual defect, should choose a career of crime and in spite of repeated penalties should keep on recurring to it, has always been an unsolved mystery to me. I have been especially perplexed about those cases which repeatedly committed the same crime, and although in some instances an apparently plausible explanation was found in an existing psychosis, or strong psychopathic make-up, these explanations were in many instances unsatisfactory.

Let us see what the repeated commission of theft means to the individual whose history we have just reported. We have seen that his own explanation of that series of physical and mental phenomena which always accompanied the act of stealing were not only very much akin to the physical and mental state which accompanies the act of sexual congress, but were actually recognized as such by the man himself. In other words the motive and instinctive prompting which led this man to the act of stealing were the same which lead normal men to the act of sexual congress. It would be inconceivable without further explanation why this colored boy should repeatedly resort to stealing as a means of sexual gratification in spite of the trials and tribulations which this carried with it, when he had all the opportunities to gratify this desire in a natural heterosexual manner, as others of his race have no difficulty at all in doing.

The answer lies in the type of sexual gratification which his stealing supplied. We have mentioned the anal sensations, the feeling as though there was something in the rectum of which he had to rid himself, and which for years led him to run to the toilet soon after the commission of a theft. To one versed in the psychology and manifestations of the sex instinct this can only mean one thing, namely, that we are dealing here with a homosexual whose erotic receptors were concentrated in the anal region, with an anal-erotic.

The possibility of a full, happy, satisfied existence for this individual lies in the gratification of this biologic, instinctive, and perverse sex-craving. It is the intense revulsion, the protest of his whole personality against such mode of sex-expression which brought about the habitual stealing in this individual. So soon as he discovered that the emotional accompaniment of the act of stealing served to gratify this biologic sex-craving he clung to it with the tenacity which characterized his life of recidivism. In other words, the process of sublimation of which we spoke took an asocial turn in this individual, with the resultant pathological stealing.

It would lead us far beyond the scope of this chapter to discuss the problem of the genesis of homo-sexuality, and we shall not attempt it.

The impression which I desire to make is that in this case of pathological stealing we are dealing with a form of asocial behavior which has its roots in a mighty instinctive, biologic craving, which demands gratification at any cost.

Furthermore, because of the nature of this etiologic factor the chances for reformation are very poor, which prognosis has already been justified by the subsequent career of this patient. He is at present again under arrest for grand larceny and housebreaking.

It would be premature to draw any general conclusions from this study, or to promulgate any general principles of treatment. All that the chapter is intended for is to stimulate further interest in criminologists for research along these lines.

NOTES

[1] GORING. C.: "The English Convict." His Majesty's Stationery Office, London, 1913. pp. 440.

[2] HEALY, W.: "The Individual Delinquent." Little, Brown, & Company, Boston, 1915.

[3] WHITE, W.: "The English Convict." A review in *Journal of Am. Ins. Crim. Law and Criminology*, vol. v.

[4] WHITE, W.: "The Unconscious." *The Psychoanalytic Review*, vol. II, No. 1.

[5] FREUD, W.: "Psychopathology of Everyday Life." English Translation by BRILL. The Macmillan Co., 1914.

[6] HITSCHMANN, E.: "Freud's Theories of the Neuroses." English translation by C. R. PAYNE. Nervous and Mental Dis. Monograph Series, No. 17, 1913.

[7] ELLIS, H.: "Sexual Problems." Modern Treatment of Nervous and Mental Diseases. Edited by White and Jelliffe, Lea and Febiger. Philadelphia and New York, 1913.

[8] STEKEL, W.: "The Sexual Root of Kleptomania." *Zeitschrift f. Sexualwissenschaft.* George H. Wigand, Leipzig. English Abstract by ALBRECHT, in *Journ. Am. Inst. Crim. Law and Criminology*, vol. 2, p. 239.

The Codes Of Hammurabi And Moses
W. W. Davies

QTY

The discovery of the Hammurabi Code is one of the greatest achievements of archaeology, and is of paramount interest, not only to the student of the Bible, but also to all those interested in ancient history...

Religion   **ISBN:** *1-59462-338-4*   **Pages:132**
MSRP $12.95

The Theory of Moral Sentiments
Adam Smith

QTY

This work from 1749. contains original theories of conscience amd moral judgment and it is the foundation for systemof morals.

Philosophy **ISBN:** *1-59462-777-0*   **Pages:536**
MSRP $19.95

Jessica's First Prayer
Hesba Stretton

QTY

In a screened and secluded corner of one of the many railway-bridges which span the streets of London there could be seen a few years ago, from five o'clock every morning until half past eight, a tidily set-out coffee-stall, consisting of a trestle and board, upon which stood two large tin cans, with a small fire of charcoal burning under each so as to keep the coffee boiling during the early hours of the morning when the work-people were thronging into the city on their way to their daily toil...

Childrens   **ISBN:** *1-59462-373-2*   **Pages:84**
MSRP $9.95

My Life and Work
Henry Ford

QTY

Henry Ford revolutionized the world with his implementation of mass production for the Model T automobile. Gain valuable business insight into his life and work with his own auto-biography... "We have only started on our development of our country we have not as yet, with all our talk of wonderful progress, done more than scratch the surface. The progress has been wonderful enough but..."

Biographies/ **ISBN:** *1-59462-198-5*   **Pages:300**
MSRP $21.95

The Art of Cross-Examination
Francis Wellman

QTY

I presume it is the experience of every author, after his first book is published upon an important subject, to be almost overwhelmed with a wealth of ideas and illustrations which could readily have been included in his book, and which to his own mind, at least, seem to make a second edition inevitable. Such certainly was the case with me; and when the first edition had reached its sixth impression in five months, I rejoiced to learn that it seemed to my publishers that the book had met with a sufficiently favorable reception to justify a second and considerably enlarged edition. ..

Reference   **ISBN:** *1-59462-647-2*

Pages:412

MSRP $19.95

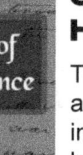

On the Duty of Civil Disobedience
Henry David Thoreau

QTY

Thoreau wrote his famous essay, On the Duty of Civil Disobedience, as a protest against an unjust but popular war and the immoral but popular institution of slave-owning. He did more than write—he declined to pay his taxes, and was hauled off to gaol in consequence. Who can say how much this refusal of his hastened the end of the war and of slavery ?

Law   **ISBN:** *1-59462-747-9*

Pages:48

MSRP $7.45

Dream Psychology Psychoanalysis for Beginners
Sigmund Freud

QTY

Sigmund Freud, born Sigismund Schlomo Freud (May 6, 1856 - September 23, 1939), was a Jewish-Austrian neurologist and psychiatrist who co-founded the psychoanalytic school of psychology. Freud is best known for his theories of the unconscious mind, especially involving the mechanism of repression; his redefinition of sexual desire as mobile and directed towards a wide variety of objects; and his therapeutic techniques, especially his understanding of transference in the therapeutic relationship and the presumed value of dreams as sources of insight into unconscious desires.

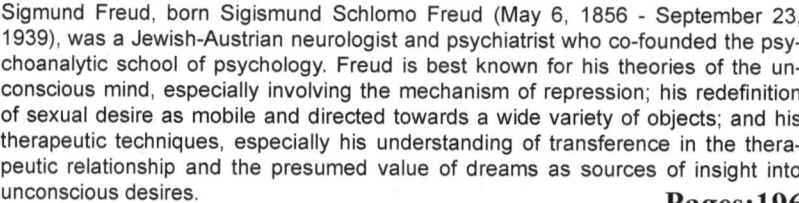

Psychology   **ISBN:** *1-59462-905-6*

Pages:196

MSRP $15.45

The Miracle of Right Thought
Orison Swett Marden

QTY

Believe with all of your heart that you will do what you were made to do. When the mind has once formed the habit of holding cheerful, happy, prosperous pictures, it will not be easy to form the opposite habit. It does not matter how improbable or how far away this realization may see, or how dark the prospects may be, if we visualize them as best we can, as vividly as possible, hold tenaciously to them and vigorously struggle to attain them, they will gradually become actualized, realized in the life. But a desire, a longing without endeavor, a yearning abandoned or held indifferently will vanish without realization.

Pages:360

Self Help   **ISBN:** *1-59462-644-8*

MSRP $25.45

www.bookjungle.com *email: sales@bookjungle.com fax: 630-214-0564 mail: Book Jungle PO Box 2226 Champaign, IL 61825*

QTY

The Rosicrucian Cosmo-Conception Mystic Christianity *by Max Heindel*   ISBN: *1-59462-188-8* **$38.95**
The Rosicrucian Cosmo-conception is not dogmatic, neither does it appeal to any other authority than the reason of the student. It is: not controversial, but is: sent forth in the, hope that it may help to clear...   New Age/Religion Pages 646

Abandonment To Divine Providence *by Jean-Pierre de Caussade*   ISBN: *1-59462-228-0* **$25.95**
"The Rev. Jean Pierre de Caussade was one of the most remarkable spiritual writers of the Society of Jesus in France in the 18th Century. His death took place at Toulouse in 1751. His works have gone through many editions and have been republished...   Inspirational/Religion Pages 400

Mental Chemistry *by Charles Haanel*   ISBN: *1-59462-192-6* **$23.95**
Mental Chemistry allows the change of material conditions by combining and appropriately utilizing the power of the mind. Much like applied chemistry creates something new and unique out of careful combinations of chemicals the mastery of mental chemistry...   New Age Pages 354

The Letters of Robert Browning and Elizabeth Barret Barrett 1845-1846 vol II   ISBN: *1-59462-193-4* **$35.95**
by Robert Browning and Elizabeth Barrett   Biographies Pages 596

Gleanings In Genesis (volume I) *by Arthur W. Pink*   ISBN: *1-59462-130-6* **$27.45**
Appropriately has Genesis been termed "the seed plot of the Bible" for in it we have, in germ form, almost all of the great doctrines which are afterwards fully developed in the books of Scripture which follow...   Religion/Inspirational Pages 420

The Master Key *by L. W. de Laurence*   ISBN: *1-59462-001-6* **$30.95**
In no branch of human knowledge has there been a more lively increase of the spirit of research during the past few years than in the study of Psychology, Concentration and Mental Discipline. The requests for authentic lessons in Thought Control, Mental Discipline and...   New Age/Business Pages 422

The Lesser Key Of Solomon Goetia *by L. W. de Laurence*   ISBN: *1-59462-092-X* **$9.95**
This translation of the first book of the "Lernegton" which is now for the first time made accessible to students of Talismanic Magic was done, after careful collation and edition, from numerous Ancient Manuscripts in Hebrew, Latin, and French...   New Age/Occult Pages 92

Rubaiyat Of Omar Khayyam *by Edward Fitzgerald*   ISBN:*1-59462-332-5* **$13.95**
Edward Fitzgerald, whom the world has already learned, in spite of his own efforts to remain within the shadow of anonymity, to look upon as one of the rarest poets of the century, was born at Bredfield, in Suffolk, on the 31st of March, 1809. He was the third son of John Purcell...   Music Pages 172

Ancient Law *by Henry Maine*   ISBN: *1-59462-128-4* **$29.95**
The chief object of the following pages is to indicate some of the earliest ideas of mankind, as they are reflected in Ancient Law, and to point out the relation of those ideas to modern thought.   Religiom/History Pages 452

Far-Away Stories *by William J. Locke*   ISBN: *1-59462-129-2* **$19.45**
"Good wine needs no bush, but a collection of mixed vintages does. And this book is just such a collection. Some of the stories I do not want to remain buried for ever in the museum files of dead magazine-numbers an author's not unpardonable vanity..."   Fiction Pages 272

Life of David Crockett *by David Crockett*   ISBN: *1-59462-250-7* **$27.45**
"Colonel David Crockett was one of the most remarkable men of the times in which he lived. Born in humble life, but gifted with a strong will, an indomitable courage, and unremitting perseverance...   Biographies/New Age Pages 424

Lip-Reading *by Edward Nitchie*   ISBN: *1-59462-206-X* **$25.95**
Edward B. Nitchie, founder of the New York School for the Hard of Hearing, now the Nitchie School of Lip-Reading, Inc, wrote "LIP-READING Principles and Practice". The development and perfecting of this meritorious work on lip-reading was an undertaking...   How-to Pages 400

A Handbook of Suggestive Therapeutics, Applied Hypnotism, Psychic Science   ISBN: *1-59462-214-0* **$24.95**
by Henry Munro   Health/New Age/Health/Self-help Pages 376

A Doll's House: and Two Other Plays *by Henrik Ibsen*   ISBN: *1-59462-112-8* **$19.95**
Henrik Ibsen created this classic when in revolutionary 1848 Rome. Introducing some striking concepts in playwriting for the realist genre, this play has been studied the world over.   Fiction/Classics/Plays 308

The Light of Asia *by sir Edwin Arnold*   ISBN: *1-59462-204-3* **$13.95**
In this poetic masterpiece, Edwin Arnold describes the life and teachings of Buddha. The man who was to become known as Buddha to the world was born as Prince Gautama of India but he rejected the worldly riches and abandoned the reigns of power when...   Religion/History/Biographies Pages 170

The Complete Works of Guy de Maupassant *by Guy de Maupassant*   ISBN: *1-59462-157-8* **$16.95**
"For days and days, nights and nights, I had dreamed of that first kiss which was to consecrate our engagement, and I knew not on what spot I should put my lips..."   Fiction/Classics Pages 240

The Art of Cross-Examination *by Francis L. Wellman*   ISBN: *1-59462-309-0* **$26.95**
Written by a renowned trial lawyer, Wellman imparts his experience and uses case studies to explain how to use psychology to extract desired information through questioning.   How-to/Science/Reference Pages 408

Answered or Unanswered? *by Louisa Vaughan*   ISBN: *1-59462-248-5* **$10.95**
Miracles of Faith in China   Religion Pages 112

The Edinburgh Lectures on Mental Science (1909) *by Thomas*   ISBN: *1-59462-008-3* **$11.95**
This book contains the substance of a course of lectures recently given by the writer in the Queen Street Hail, Edinburgh. Its purpose is to indicate the Natural Principles governing the relation between Mental Action and Material Conditions...   New Age/Psychology Pages 148

Ayesha *by H. Rider Haggard*   ISBN: *1-59462-301-5* **$24.95**
Verily and indeed it is the unexpected that happens! Probably if there was one person upon the earth from whom the Editor of this, and of a certain previous history, did not expect to hear again...   Classics Pages 380

Ayala's Angel *by Anthony Trollope*   ISBN: *1-59462-352-X* **$29.95**
The two girls were both pretty, but Lucy who was twenty-one who supposed to be simple and comparatively unattractive, whereas Ayala was credited, as her Bombwhat romantic name might show, with poetic charm and a taste for romance. Ayala when her father died was nineteen...   Fiction Pages 484

The American Commonwealth *by James Bryce*   ISBN: *1-59462-286-8* **$34.45**
An interpretation of American democratic political theory. It examines political mechanics and society from the perspective of Scotsman James Bryce   Politics Pages 572

Stories of the Pilgrims *by Margaret P. Pumphrey*   ISBN: *1-59462-116-0* **$17.95**
This book explores pilgrims religious oppression in England as well as their escape to Holland and eventual crossing to America on the Mayflower, and their early days in New England...   History Pages 268

www.bookjungle.com *email: sales@bookjungle.com fax: 630-214-0564 mail: Book Jungle PO Box 2226 Champaign, IL 61825*

QTY

The Fasting Cure *by Sinclair Upton*   ISBN: *1-59462-222-1*   **$13.95**
In the Cosmopolitan Magazine for May, 1910, and in the Contemporary Review (London) for April, 1910, I published an article dealing with my experiences in fasting. I have written a great many magazine articles, but never one which attracted so much attention... New Age/Self Help/Health Pages 164

Hebrew Astrology *by Sepharial*   ISBN: *1-59462-308-2*   **$13.45**
In these days of advanced thinking it is a matter of common observation that we have left many of the old landmarks behind and that we are now pressing forward to greater heights and to a wider horizon than that which represented the mind-content of our progenitors... Astrology Pages 144

Thought Vibration or The Law of Attraction in the Thought World   ISBN: *1-59462-127-6*   **$12.95**

by William Walker Atkinson   Psychology/Religion Pages 144

Optimism *by Helen Keller*   ISBN: *1-59462-108-X*   **$15.95**
Helen Keller was blind, deaf, and mute since 19 months old, yet famously learned how to overcome these handicaps, communicate with the world, and spread her lectures promoting optimism. An inspiring read for everyone... Biographies/Inspirational Pages 84

Sara Crewe *by Frances Burnett*   ISBN: *1-59462-360-0*   **$9.45**
In the first place, Miss Minchin lived in London. Her home was a large, dull, tall one, in a large, dull square, where all the houses were alike, and all the sparrows were alike, and where all the door-knockers made the same heavy sound... Childrens/Classic Pages 88

The Autobiography of Benjamin Franklin *by Benjamin Franklin*   ISBN: *1-59462-135-7*   **$24.95**
The Autobiography of Benjamin Franklin has probably been more extensively read than any other American historical work, and no other book of its kind has had such ups and downs of fortune. Franklin lived for many years in England, where he was agent... Biographies/History Pages 332

Name	
Email	
Telephone	
Address	
City, State ZIP	

☐ **Credit Card**   ☐ **Check / Money Order**

Credit Card Number	
Expiration Date	
Signature	

Please Mail to: Book Jungle
PO Box 2226
Champaign, IL 61825
or Fax to: 630-214-0564

ORDERING INFORMATION

web*: www.bookjungle.com*
email*: sales@bookjungle.com*
fax*: 630-214-0564*
mail*: Book Jungle PO Box 2226 Champaign, IL 61825*
or PayPal *to sales@bookjungle.com*

Please contact us for bulk discounts

DIRECT-ORDER TERMS

**20% Discount if You Order
Two or More Books**
Free Domestic Shipping!
Accepted: Master Card, Visa,
Discover, American Express